Contents

The Deserted Village

Barry Swan

Valley Press

Dedicated to the Christian Brothers
without whose instruction
this book could never have been written

First published in 1997
by Valley Press
236 Tokyngton Ave, Wembley,
Middlesex HA9 6HJ

Typeset in Sabon by LaserScript Ltd,
Mitcham, Surrey
Cover design by Reema Graphics Solutions Ltd,
Wembley, Middlesex
Printed and bound in Ireland by Colour Books Ltd, Dublin

ISBN 0 9530768 0 6

Chapter One

Michael David Argod, Rathgar resident, was an only child. He was born of the union between a prominent minister of the Church of Ireland, the Reverend David Argod, a doctor of Divinity; and the former Elizabeth Hetherington of the well-known County Monaghan family. Michael's ancestors on his father's side were of a long line of church ministers, one of whom, his great grandfather, had been the first archbishop of New South Wales, and it was believed by many that Michael would continue in the same tradition.

His mother, a tall crow-like woman of intelligence and industry, thought otherwise. From when he was an infant she encouraged her son to show independence of mind allied to strength of character. Her husband on the other hand busied himself with impressing on Michael the value of conservative ideals and traditions. Eventually, the lad became a respected and reputed scholar, though remaining secular, and both father and mother were quite pleased with him.

Michael's grandfather on his father's side, Sir Herbert Argod, who had just celebrated his ninety fifth birthday, was a third cousin on his father's side to the First Duke of Southminster who, when he lived, was a member of the House of Lords and a famous collector of art and museum pieces. That duke's grandson, the present Third Duke of Southminster, having succeeded his late father, was twenty ninth in line to the British throne and this in turn placed Michael's grandfather ninety second in the line of succession. The fact that recent members of the Argod family had not been honoured with any titles put Michael somewhat further behind in the list of heirs but, everything taken into consideration, it was a fact that Michael Argod, Irishman, Professor of Literature and Anthropology, thirty years of age, married though childless as yet, was one hundred and twentieth in direct line of succession to the Crown of England.

Dan O'Toole was born and reared on a small farm in the mountain land of County Wicklow. From the standpoint of modern civilization it was an abandoned and neglected country, accessible only though a marshy, reed-infested mountain pass named in English the Gap of the Wild Hares. In the solitary and isolated townland, Bailedecoinin (Place of the Rabbit), there lived approximately one hundred people. Their small homesteads were scattered over a narrow valley and along the flanks of the hillside. In fact nobody was aware how many people were there, for the census takers had never come. In the further parts of the mountains there lived nameless and strange hermitical shepherds and madmen whom nobody in the townland would claim to be related to. At random points in time, chosen with a logic comprehensible only to their own minds, these white-haired, ragged hermits would make an appearance in the public house, muddy street or church, talking rapidly, mysteriously and unceasingly.

Through the Gap of the Wild Hares there came occasionally an old, battered van which ferried rudimentary food, medicinal and hardware supplies and sometimes a priest, if he could make it. The majority of the inhabitants had never gone out through this pass and there was a belief of longstanding that he who did venture through the gateway would never be seen again. There was one man in Bailedecoinin who claimed that he had been to the outer world, but nobody believed him as he was considered eccentric.

The only occasion a policeman was ever seen in Bailedecoinin, as far as the oldest inhabitant could remember, was when old Mr. O'Toole sent a message by the van that his son had gone to Naas to visit the dentist and had not come back again. Dan had just turned twenty one. The night before they had a great ceili, a festival of song and dancing in celebration of the lad's coming of age and the whole townland attended. The fiddles and accordion and dog-hide drum and pipes were brought into play and the old fellows sat in the corner beside the roaring fire and tapped their feet and remembered times past. O'Byrne's public house was the scene of every occasion for celebration, and indeed for mourning too. A reason why Dan's birthday was held to be a major cause of rejoicing was that he was the first young man for many years to celebrate his coming to manhood while still living in the townland. Dan's friends and school-companions, each and everyone, had gone away; or were asleep beneath the cold, wet earth, some minute consolation being found in their being at least at home amongst their loved ones.

As the accordion and fiddles of the band struck up the reels and jigs and the folks danced in the best time as they were capable of, it being many years since they last had a hooley, and the drum of Tigheen Breathnach gave out an irregular and loud beat, he rapidly losing his memory over the past twelve months, and the whole place rejoicing and swinging in happy-go-lucky fashion, nobody would think that such a thing as tragedy or sorrow ever existed.

Dan spent a good part of the time on a stool, drinking uisce beatha and talking to everybody. His father and mother (they had been very old when he was born)spent most of their time at his side and were very proud in their hearts. Everyone was trying to get Dan to dance, telling him all the girls were mad fighting over him. Even the oldest of the folks, men and women who had not left their houses (or perhaps even their beds) for the whole year, took to the floor for at least the symbolic dance. Dan, his eyes becoming blurred, acknowledged the salutations and good wishes as well as the jokes with appreciative words and happy chortles. He had never danced in his life, instead preferring to sit in a corner and drink or talk. Sometimes he might oblige and render in a deep, low voice a mournful Gaelic song. Or occasionally, in long-drawn monotones he would tell a story from the repertoire of some old Seanachi of Bailedecoinin. Tonight something special would be expected of him. When the time came a hush descended over the room and everybody turned and looked at him. Dan laid his glass to one side and slowly rose to a standing position. Little did anybody in the room realize that what was now to take place was also a farewell, a last stand in the midst of home and kin.

It was said by some as they went home that night that Dan had gained for himself the rightful honour as Bailedecoinin's new Seanachi, for he had recited the ancient tale of Duirmuid and Graine well into the small hours, holding everybody's attention even as the rain lashed down outside and the mountain wind came screeching to the windows and door.

A long time later when he had finished, he went and put an arm on the frail and bony shoulders of his two old ones and the neighbours grinned and shouted happily. And then to everybody's surprise and delight Dan, his face red and seemingly nervous, asked Mrs. Comerford if he could have the privilege of her company in a dance and she laughingly answered that the privilege and pleasure would be all her's. Loud clapping and cheering arose in the room and Pat McGee, the band leader, ordered a jig.

The O'Toole farm was twenty acres in extent, a small portion on level land for the crops, pigs and hens, and the greatest portion on steep hillside, where the sheep and goats grazed the thin, weedy grass. There was common land too higher up, where in summer the flocks would be taken to make good use of the seasonal growth. It was on the furze-littered hillside, spotted yellow in summer but bleak grey for the rest of the year, that old Mr. O'Toole now spent most of his time. He was a sight to wrench the heart. The times that he now spoke to people were few and far between; instead his conversation was with the stars and the sky, the flowers and birds and with his own self. He spoke of people gone away, of animals long dead and of all who were his companions in the early days. He spoke of those who had died of tuberculosis, referred to as the Bas Dubh or Black Death in Bailedecoinin. Events and personalities became confused in his mind so that finally even the memory of his son, Dan, whom he believed to be dead and in Paradise, was still barely with him. Dan's individuality gradually disintegrated in the old man's mind, so that eventually the son and father became almost the same person, in the fields and places of childhood. Just, at certain moments when all was calm, he might hear the voice of the boy carrying in the breeze between the flowers and the rustling leaves.

But even these short moments of grace were becoming rarer and rarer. He was no longer capable of looking after his few sheep and pigs. The animals seemed to realize this, behaving always respectfully in the presence of the tottering man and going into their pens at the correct time without any directing or need to be shouted at. The fowl took care of themselves, going into the small barn whenever they felt hungry and climbing up on the heap of oats to peck till satisfied. Sunrise to sunset was spent in the field, wandering abstractly about, and lately he had taken to staying there in the nightly hours, especially on brooding, stormy nights, when he would sit on a large boulder and talk loudly.

Dan's mother had been a fine old countrywoman in her prime, remembering the best of the Gaelic songs and stories. These were passed down from generation to generation – her family as well as the O'Byrnes, O'Tooles and all the others in Bailedecoinin had lived there since the first Celtic invasions. The O'Byrnes and the O'Tooles were always marrying one another and her own wedding to Thomas O'Toole was, it is said, arranged before either of them had been born.

Needless to say the disappearance of Dan broke her entirely. At first there was still some hope that he might return and she spent the days in prayer. Then they had a funeral service for him and after the wake she retreated into herself never to talk again. The furthest, darkest corner in the house was her abode, never leaving it and keeping only hard bread and milk at her side for nourishment. Not even a prayer would she speak now.

When Springtime came to the land and the rabbits and hares and lambs were playing in the fields and everything fresh and young was in predominance, a cloud of sorrow hung over the valley. Winter never left Bailedecoinin now, for the young were dead and gone. How could old and withered hearts be made happy again when nothing had been left to them? Their lives had seen Spring and Winter only, for the best and most hopeful never came to maturity and fruition. Instead promise and potential were displayed, to be extinguished.

It was not Dan alone who was missed – and he was a great loss with his talk and his hand at haymaking-time – all the young folk who were no more were mourned. The O'Byrne boys and girls, the strapping Dunphys, the O'Hanlons and Dwyers would never be seen again. Everyone in Bailedecoinin now were either very old or very young. The numerous small children who went to the school and played games at the well could not compensate for the loss. The last straw, the final crushing blow which conclusively broke the spirit of Bailedecoinin so that even the little children were afraid to laugh or talk out loud, came just one year after Dan left. The first marriage in twenty years took place, that of Timothy O'Byrne to Mary O'Hanlon. The celebrations lasted three days and three nights and all sorrows were forgotten; even the clergyman who had been called in from outside to perform the ceremony was drunk.

One week later the new Mrs O'Byrne fell ill and died. The tragedy came as sudden as a policeman's knock. It was decided that her wake, which lasted a month, would be the last public event to be held in the townland. From then to this day there has neither been a dance, game or wake in Bailedecoinin. The dead are buried quickly and the folks stay in their houses, coming together only for Mass on the rare occasions that it is held, and even then not stopping to speak to one another.

Chapter Two

Dan O'Toole and Michael Argod were the best of friends. It was unusual that two people from such disparate backgrounds should ever meet, let alone become bosom buddies.

Argod was at the top of his world, successful and respected by one and all. Dan O'Toole on the other hand was unemployed and becoming more unfit with the passing of each day. While Michael was distinguishing himself at Trinity College, breaking all the records for study time spent in the library, receiving private audiences with the college president and porter and being sent all-expenses-paid to the hallowed confines of Cambridge, Dan O'Toole, while not languishing in the all-expenses-paid get-well Health Clinic, was trying to eke out a living with nothing but his own weak will and the pittance doled out by National Assistance.

Argod lived in a plush, detached villa in swanky Rathgar. O'Toole dwelt in a small, forlorn room in the bleakest part of Rathmines; and small though the room was, he had a further trial in having to share it with another person who was a rather trying character.

Michael had been a puritan, it never occurring to him to take a drink or cigarette and being entirely upright in all his doings. His day was strictly ordered according to certain rules and traditions. For instance, he would begin every morning with intense physical exercises and never in his life did he miss one of these. He kept them up even when he was sick in bed with pneumonia, dragging himself out on to the floor and ending in such a state that he always had to be helped into bed again. He maintained that they hastened his recovery and that they were also a vital factor in all his successes to date. Other rules of his were to eat regular meals of a vegetarian nature, though occasionally fish and duck were allowed, teeth to be washed four times daily and to be in bed by ten o'clock at the latest.

His wife Hillary encouraged him to keep to his schedules. She had great hopes for the future of her husband, and she put his career before everything else in the world. They had met at the ancient if decadent university in the heart of Dublin and their common interest in many fields had brought them closer together. These interests included drama, classical music, the reading of good books and walking tours in the Dublin mountains. They were hoping to have a son one day and both were agreed that he would not become a clergyman.

What hope had Dan for the future?

He had an education that was lacking (for their school in Bailedecoinin never saw a regular teacher, so any good neighbour who had the time or the initiative was welcome to come in and take over. As a consequence of this succeeding generations of children were subjected to the privilege of being taught by all the madmen of the townland who were attracted to the schoolroom and whose monopoly of the education system was never questioned as they were believed to be marked by holiness).

His health was always failing and weakness alone was all that remained of his will-power.

Indeed in certain ways Dan seemed to be a plagued fellow. When he went into the Home to recover from a very bad case of TB., notoriety soon attached itself to his name. For one thing, he would consume great quantities of food. The fact that it was free was held to be the sole reason for his vast appetite and resentment was increased by the fact that the wretch, by cashing in on the hospital's policy of not refusing food to any dying person who asked, was diminishing the supplies available to other people.

Even though it was forbidden to have alcohol in the place, he was frequently drunk on heaven knows what; although it was supposed that a wild-looking individual who used to visit him had brought the beverage. (In fact this was the same Nick Heeney of whom more will be heard later).

Dan was not the type of person who would attract sympathy easily. He was awkward and country-looking. Whatever he wore always appeared shabby on him and his skin was a queerish yellow colour. His brown hair was dirty and long and his eyes had a distant look. He was considered a bogman, a country yokel.

The word went out that he was a waster and a moron. Because he had been brought into hospital in a state of starvation, only semi-conscious and on his last legs; and because he then proceeded to fill himself up on the life-saving meals, he was considered a trickster and half a savage.

It was when he was at the Home (St. Michael's for the Very Sick, situated high up in the airy Dublin hills), that he was introduced to books and, very soon, he was never without one open in front of him. This gave rise to another rumour, that he was a chancer, for they swore that if he always had a book by his side, he never actually read them but, instead, lay back staring at the walls or ceiling in silence.

Whatever may be the truth of the matter, there is no doubt that the affair of the books caused a change in him and, afterwards, he was to become a familiar and reprehensible figure in the city public libraries and sometimes he would turn up at classes in the university where, quietly, he'd sit at the back and listen intently.

★ ★ ★

Eventually released in a reclaimed state of health, Dan went back to his old way of life, drifting about Dublin city. He was another Ulysses, a wandering Wicklow man and destined if for anything tramphood, it seemed. To many people who saw him he appeared as one of life's victims.

One morning he decided to visit the university. Before he entered the great building he spent some moments in silent contemplation of its stark immensity. Standing some distance away, his mind attempted to comprehend the massive stone structure, shining in its silvery eminence. That such monuments could be built at all was a testament to the mysterious powers of man. Humans had made aeroplanes and rockets and discovered electricity and many other accomplishments had revealed themselves to Dan, but none of them could equal the effort and achievement that had gone into Dublin's buildings!

He proceeded inside and wandered around the different corridors. A voice, the likes of which he had never heard before, came to him from out of one of the lecture halls. He stopped to listen. Vehement, well-educated arguments were being made inside and his ears began to tingle. He was listening to a mighty orator. The voice sounded like the sea on a wide shore, consuming all that came in its way like searing, white-hot fire. Words were thrown and juggled in the air; there was an artistic dance of speech. He was listening to Julius Caesar addressing the Roman population; the Pope giving his message Urbi et Orbi; it was Lenin harassing a crowd of poor Moscow workers; it was Eamonn De Valera at his best such was the mastery, the daring, the professionalism.

After a while of listening to this Dan became excited. He was almost hypnotized and he stood there oblivious to the flurry of people going by him in the corridor. He had never heard anybody speak like that before! This master of the spoken word was full of passion; it was as if his life depended on his performance. There had been a great philosopher once who had to give a speech before an emperor and an audience of aged politicians in order to save his life. It was like that in there now; the man was talking for what he was worth! Dan laboured in breath with every nuance, inflexion and phrase. Each word rooted him to where he stood so that he was unable to move.

It would be wrong to say that the speaker holding the floor there was simply a captivating man of the gab-one more or less trained in the art of public debate of whom there are plenty in the world. It was a question of insight and of great intuition. This man was not only a master of his chosen topic – he was a visionary.

Dan opened the door and peered in. He saw that the speaker was a strict-looking character with a very tidy appearance but a somewhat ruffled face. He had brown-blonde hair and sharp, critical eyes. The hall was packed tightly with people and the lecture came to a momentary halt as they looked at Dan. There was giggling and laughing in the room as he made his way forward to sit on some steps at the front, which gave him a close view of the man.

A hot feeling of anger and embarrassment ran through the lecturer as he gazed at the intruder.

"Take off your hat. This is a lecture theatre," he said in a high-pitched voice; it was full of anger and outrage.

Dan in a surprised mood took off his hat. (He had always worn this hat since it was given to him by the Dublin Salvation Army at Rathmines, in the days when the sky was his roof and a park bench his bed. He seldom took it off, not even during his hours of repose). The lecture recommenced. When it was over and the lecturer departed, Dan interrupted a group of students nearby who, their books sprouting out of them everywhere, had become somewhat deeply involved in an academic discussion on the topic just debated by the now – absent lecturer. He held his hat tightly under his arm and, unsure as to whether they would understand him, said:

"That man gone out there – I've never heard the likes of him. Could you tell me who he is?"

Unfortunately, despite his diffidence and his modesty, many people had the habit of taking exception to O'Toole, especially it seemed when he was at his most vulnerable in relation to others, such as when seeking help or information. Perhaps this was because of his manner of speech, which some found objectionable, as his grammar and his interior Wicklow accent were incomprehensible to outsiders. This was a sad case surely, but certainly not rare in our great convoluted, metropolitan masses where human beings are often secondary to concrete. At the back of the vast hall two young men had left their seats and were seeking an outlet to the door. One of them, a big opulent fellow, was saying under his breath, "It's him all right. I couldn't believe my eyes at first. He is not all there at all at all."

This was the man who lived in the same room as Dan. His name was Timothy Roche and he spoke with a Cork accent.

"What is he like?," asked his companion, who was rather nondescript-looking and also spoke in a Cork accent.

A quick glance over his shoulder told Roche that O'Toole was preoccupied.

"I get a great laugh out of him sometimes," he said quietly. They moved out of the room, unseen by Dan.

By this time each member of the student group had given Dan a thorough visual examination, but he received no reply to his question and they turned their backs on him.

A tall, loping, red-haired gent was more kind to him and gave him the answer to his query. The speaker had been Michael Argod, 'A brilliant professor and visionary', who was 'half an Englishman'.

According to this fellow Argod was famous as a detached, abstract and innovative thinker who would give no inkling of what he really believed about anything. He apparently hid his personality behind a complete, total and solid shield of professionalism. Many held him to be the best teacher at the university, in all Ireland, if not in the whole world. There were some people who did not like Mr. Argod, said the gent, but none who did not respect him.

Later in the morning, as Dan walked over the flagstones in the grounds of the college and paced by the colourful flower-beds in the gardens, he was lost in a day-dream. It was early summer and the buds were everywhere. Astonishing people, young and ancient, foreigners, people of different colours, Africans, Americans all surrounded him. His mind bubbled with wonderful thoughts and peaceful consolations. Eventually a tiredness afflicted him and, finding a bench, he put his head down and was almost immediately asleep. People were careful not to disturb him and he had the whole seat to himself. After a time his sleep became somewhat fitful.

The evening cleared itself of its residing, dingy clouds and a fresh, cool breeze arrived to embalm the homegoing multitudes. A red glow appeared on the skyline where the sun had gone down, and the whole evening was filled with an unexpected flavour of calm and peace. People were more pleasant and everywhere courtesy was seen to abound. Dan's thoughts had become puzzled from his sleep and a question nagged his quiet face. His slow, preoccupied walk took him southwards. A concurrence of the two main events of the day – where he had been and where he was about to go – formed in him the question that he had been asking himself. He wondered how familiar Mr. Argod had become. It was as if he had known him all his life. That noble face in the lecture hall, which he had never seen before, he knew. The voice which issued forth that morning, that sounded as if it came from a sphere elevated and distant, he had heard before. Those visionary eyes that he looked into, he had looked into before. Or was it the case that there was someone who was the very image of Mr. Argod? Coming up to the door of Bell's bar, with the darkness beginning to spread its wings over the city, he took a last look at the departing day.

Inside, recovering from a week already spent if nothing else (it was a Friday evening), and relaxing in the manner they knew best, were the friends and acquaintances of Dan.

Even his room-mate, Timothy, was there, only he stayed apart from the rest of the company with his pal at the back of the room and it was seldom that he and Dan ever greeted one another in public. Fred Dunne, a Special Branch policeman 'in his spare time' as he put it, Patrick O'Reilly the artist, Nick Heeney from Galway, all greeted him. Absent only at the present moment was Mr. Trevor Archibald.

* * *

At this same moment, tea-time over the city, certain diverse ladies were setting about in their homes preparing the table places and waiting for the kettle to boil and in some cases, awaiting also the return of their husbands. Two of these ladies are of interest because they were the wives one each respectively of Fred Dunne and Trevor Archibald, and the third, Jane Wood, because she had become a friend of Dan O'Toole when she visited him in the Sanatorium, as part of the St. Vincent de Paul Society (for the Poor) activities.

Mary Dunne, Fred's wife, was born in County Kilkenny and attended the local Infants' school without incident in the Sacred Heart convent before going on to the Primary section. She completed her three years in the Sister of Mercy Secondary school, obtaining an Intermediate Certificate. This at the time represented a considerable achievement, times being harder and education more prized and appreciated than it is today. A qualification in Domestic Science, gained in Night school while employed as an assistant manageress at a small hotel in Kilkenny city, was a further achievement. Her father was a small farmer who also owned a shop, in which her mother spent much of her time. The combined income, though not large, was sufficient to keep the family (which included her sister, a nun, who had long since departed for a new future in Africa) in moderate comfort. Their politics were Fianna Fail but were non-participatory, being active only in the polling booth. They were a modest family. Mary met Fred in the days when he was still an ordinary member of the Garda Siochana; a smart, trim young man who used to direct traffic at the busy intersection in front of the church on Sundays where she first saw him. They liked each other when they met at the Saturday night dance, and were sufficiently interested to go upstairs for a lemonade and Guinness and to make a date. She found Fred to be a straight-forward enough fellow, who was not too demanding and who shared many attributes with her. He too came from a small farming background in nearby County Carlow and both of them had similar, non-advanced educational experiences and attainments. There was also a common interest in small talk, leaving indulgent discussion of the larger issues of existence to those people who were more abstract and who had little else to concern themselves with.

Their courtship lasted for eight years and when he was transferred to Kildare she followed him up to the short-grass county, obtaining work in The Horse's Saddle, a medium-sized hotel catering for the peculiar racing crowd of that region. Once, she was given a tip of twenty pounds by a race-goer, no doubt a lucky punter. The decision to marry was based on their having saved a certain sum of money. Then, a few months after their honeymoon in the Ring of Kerry, Fred was, to their great surprise, taken into the Special Branch and they moved to live in Dublin, a place which neither of them had any previous liking for or experience of. After that, Fred never seemed to have much to do and most of his time was spent standing outside public buildings. Life since their marriage never had the romance of their courtship years. It was a sad thing for both of them too that no children came along. The company in Bell's was the chief means of distraction in Fred's life and they often heard him remark that marriage was a mistake and going as far as getting engaged was enough. Mary's main activities were the preparation of meals for herself and her man (when he was in), and the knitting of garments, some of which were for poor children living down the street.

She was resigned this evening to the fact that Fred was not coming home for tea. Nevertheless, she continued preparing the table, as if there still existed a remote possibility that he might walk in at any moment.

Some distance away Hillary, wife of Trevor Archibald, was also preparing tea. She was having difficulty adjusting to her husband's new schedule which, in comparison with the old days, had become highly erratic in recent times. But other more happy thoughts were on her mind this evening as she quietly set about her tasks – she knew she was pregnant, for the first time, and this joyous news her husband had no knowledge of whatsoever. She had suspected weeks before that it was a possibility but had kept everything a secret until she was certain, so as to be able to surprise him.

This particular individual, whom she believed was working late on research for a book somewhere in the National Library, was right then about to enter Bell's bar.

The third lady, Jane Wood, lived with her mother and they were the only surviving members of the Wood family of Kerry. A third cousin was thought to be alive and living in Australia but if the truth be known the Woods were neither a prolific nor a long-living family and Jane's mother's survival to near the age of sixty would have been considered quite unusual by her relatives, if they had been around to observe it. The cause of this lack of a grip on life and existence may have been the rudimentary poverty of their ancestors, as well as no doubt to some inherited characteristics.

Jane, who worked in the Department of Posts and Telegraphs, was dark-haired and like all Kerry girls could be alluring. This was so especially if she took care with her clothes and made an effort with her appearance, but unfortunately like most Kerry girls she did not bother with her appearance and was indeed quite a tomboy. Despite this there were some men at the Department who were interested in her. She had a steadfast manner which was uncommon in women of her age and she was untroubled in expression. There was no doubt that, given half a chance, these men would have proposed an evening out, if not marriage, to her and any one of them might have been considered a good model of a husband. It is hard to know what she saw in Dan

O'Toole or what particular quality there was in him that caused her to be attracted to him. Since his release from the hospital she had met him on a number of occasions when walking the street or in the Green. To her disappointment he never asked her out or showed any interest in her counselings.

Across Rathmines Road a bus pulled up in the night. The street lamps shone like searchlights in a dark world, illuminating the pavements and walls. People embarked and disembarked. The bus's heavy motor and the noise of other vehicles made a din. Some were returning to their homes in the terraces, others were visiting friends or going to the pictures. As the bus pulled away an erect man stood on the spot. For a while he was rooted there. All the other passengers had gone as this man looked around him, surveying intently the scene. Cars passed in front, going in both directions. A little further up the way, above, the large town clock struck the hour. He watched and waited as the shadows of night creatures, sometimes in view and sometimes hidden, made ghostly appearances. A black cat passed down.

At last the man moved. He pulled up his high collar and made tentatively to cross the street. He wore a black coat with a black scarf around his neck. His finely combed hair was black also, with a face intent behind clever eyes. A black beard further distinguished his appearance and he walked stiffly. As soon as the street crossing had been negotiated, his walk became brisk with his arms held straight by his sides. He rounded a corner into a narrow, quieter road. He now hunched over a little and his hands were clasped behind his back. There was an intent frown on his face as if he was thinking very hard. Above the slanting rooftops a thin edge of the pale moon was racing by dark, billowing clouds. Glancing at this gave him the feeling that the sky was moving along in sympathy with him. The sound of the traffic now became dimmer and soon the walls about developed the stillness of a tomb. A sharp turn brought him into an alleyway whose surface was of the old-fashioned cobbled style. This was bounded by a high wall, behind which were grotty if quaint workyards and empty grounds. Faint lights made out two small houses ahead of him and at the end, where the alley turned into an even narrower street, was a more brightly lit house. It stood like a welcoming reward at the end of a maze and it was in fact his destination.

In Bell's bar Fred Dunne had become bored. He looked at Dan, who crouched in a corner and seemed to have passed out of this world entirely; there was not much chance of getting any chat out of him. Mr. Nicholas Heeney on the other hand was one of those people who never talked. He just sat there staring into his pint. That left the honourable Patrick O'Reilly all clad out tonight (look at him!) in red trousers and fluffy multicoloured shirt with flowers painted on it, being true to his calling as an artist. And like a true artist he was lost in a daze, partly due to his drinking and also because he was most likely having a vision of some thing or scene he was going to paint. His dazed eyes were misty and joyous. They were all in the back end of the pub which had a wooden floor and a low ceiling. It was not a big place.

At the other end were the alternate customers, local people, none of them young and some of them as near to the next life as it's possible to get in this one. They always stayed apart from where Fred and the others were as if there existed some invisible'apartheid' wall. The talk of these Dublin people was always subdued when Fred and company were present, and it was always conducted in groans and whispers of a dialect which was complex and impossible for outsiders to understand. Any contact or communication between the two groups in Bell's was carried out by means of grimaces and sign-language. Everybody preferred it that way, picking no bones over it. The man of the house was Andy Bell. He was small and bald. His only offspring was large and red-haired, who occasionally came in to help and to display a massive coat of red fur on his wide chest. The son's name was Mike. Andy, a widower, lived solely for his pub which would one day pass on to Mike. There was no doubt of Andy's great pride in his pub. Although it was quiet and probably the least-known one in Dublin due to its hard-to-find location, he felt happy with the personal nature of its services and gratified with the loyalty shown by his customers, who came every night.

Dunne looked like a beady-eyed crow in the midst of the rest of the company. His time in the Branch allied to the influence of life in the capital had changed the country youth into a somewhat secretive city man. He couldn't have looked more unlike the healthy and perhaps idealistic young garda of his not-long-past youth. Quite suddenly much of the physical strength seems to have left him. Day by day the frame became narrower and the energy that was in him scarcer until it was sufficient just for the tasks of sleeping, eating and drinking. Bell's was a second home.

Trevor arrived at the door, said goodbye to the night-sky and went in. Fred was so glad to see him that he shouted a loud greeting. Each that looked on T. Archibald there; Fred Dunne, Roche and friend, Heeney, the two O's, Bell and the elderly men, saw something quite different. In each heart a different emotion tugged. Andy Bell the custodian, said:

"Good evening Mr. Archibald. How are you?"

An eerie atmosphere, light and vague, had settled on the place, due to silence.

"I'm on top of the world," said the fast-moving Archibald as he made for a seat.

He gave each man he saw a brief nod of hello as he passed. They returned it, silent, holding back, until he went out of their territory.

A drink was brought to him. He took off his coat and scarf, revealing a dark, expensive suit. Fred aided him in finding a convenient resting place for his garments. The latter (as also the others who were acquainted with Archibald) had some awe for the man and his ways. They tended to do things in deference to him. The greatest mystery was that nobody knew anything about him, about his work or about his homelife. A mystery man he was called, who would come out of the dark and then disappear back into it after quick 'goodnights' and an impersonal wave of a hand. That he was an extremely educated man there was no doubt and his well-cut suit and apparel testified to a material prosperity.

"Where's the fiddler?", asked Trevor of Fred below his breath.

"He hasn't come in yet," said Fred.

There was a fiddler who appeared once a week to entertain them at Bell's. He was a shy, leprechaun-type man and he would never look anyone in the eye at any time. His talent was large and sometimes he pulled out the uileann pipe and did a tune on that. Occasionally Heeney sang and once or twice Dan was seen to arouse himself from the depths of introspection to give a note or two in Gaelic. It was a characteristic of Heeney and O'Toole that both would sing in the 'vernacular'; it was also believed that the two of them when alone conversed solely in the Irish tongue. In the matter of musical entertainment however, Andy was always sure to see that neither Heeney nor anybody else tried to steal the spotlight from the fiddler, who was always accorded full honours.

Another reason Heeney was not allowed to sing very often was that his somewhat broken voice appealed to few there. The advantage of these musical occasions, as appreciated by Mr. Bell himself, was that they brought a rare note of unity, a feeling of comradeship (however false) among everyone in the pub when they occurred. Every individual, each sect there, without exception, were as one in the house of the 'landlord'. Bell was as intent on the well-being and as solicitous over the cares of his flock as any good parish priest. He disliked very much to see discord or disunity among his patrons and the fiddler, sitting on his stool, the object of each eye and ear, served as a healer, at least partly, of life's pain and vicissitudes.

Patrick O'Reilly observed Trevor's expensive suit. He thought that Archibald looked almost like royalty sitting there, with his head held high up. A red-tinged brown aura he had, with a king's crown, imbued into Bell's white wall like a coin. Patrick imagined painting him in a great court, the king of Ireland with pints of porter for his servants and all colours dark and green in a massive hall. He was interested in Trevor's countenance because it pleased him and because there was something puzzling about it. He could not understand what that puzzle was.

O'Reilly had many paintings, works that he stored away in his room in the northside. He lived in poverty, devoting his life to excelling in the craft of his art. An allowance from his poor parents in Cavan supported him, thereby further impoverishing them, all in the cause of the important artistic work he was doing up in Dublin. However his demands were few and far between. His weakness was that he was a shy individual who usually feared to approach people. He had never sold a single painting and he had never tried to. He listened in awe to Trevor's talk, the man's terrible talk.

Archibald spoke loudly and with what they all considered a posh accent. This talk of his made them all the more taken aback with the character. They considered him high-filuting. On the other hand Trevor sometimes caused surprise by the vehemence of his feelings on various topics and by the curses he often pronounced. He was a rare mixture and they thought that they might be in the company of a genius. The signs were there – a tense expression and elevated brow. Generally speaking Archibald talked as if he knew the answers to all the mysteries of the world. From what could be understood of his talk, it was apparent that Trevor considered that the affairs of life are conducted in blinkers. There was a lot that he might do to put things in their proper perspective, and save the world, but he really doubted whether it was all worthwhile. In other words he was not so much a rebel as someone who could see more clearly than most the flaws in creation and this special 'second sight' (which also may have testified to a trace of Celtic blood in Archibald, although everything else about him belied such a racial origin) gave him a privileged detachment from life as most know it. He also, in every discourse, always managed to get in a few harsh words about his wife.

There was a loud urgency in his voice this evening which made everyone in Bell's stop their conversation and listen. Fred Dunne looked questioningly, Dan opened his eyes, O'Reilly's mouth dropped and Nick Heeney slowly lifted his face from his drink.

He had all the necessary regalia for dealing with his wife. A rope, a whip, a blade. He would that very night make her plead for her life. He would have no hesitation in going all the way. He spoke at length on the efficacy of physical punishment. Somehow this outburst led him to talk about freedom of speech and the lack of it everywhere in the country. Enslavement of the finer instincts of the human spirit was the game and when you had your man by crikey – you held him down.

Patrick O'Reilly interrupted, in a voice barely audible and trembling;

"With you, I believe, Mr. Archibald, that we are all called upon to assert ourselves in the ways best suited to our talents.

Just as, say, a very bloody revolution is man's self-assertion and is something that is fundamentally good, I try to change the world in my paintings – but that is on a minor scale of course. Would that I had a portion of the talents of the Greats! Anyway, I would hope that they are paintings first and anything else afterwards. All the same, I do try to make my paintings shout, as it were."

Trevor gave a lofty, somewhat patronizing glance at Patrick; "That's right, O'Reilly. Don't listen to the critics – they are jealous of you and they wouldn't know a genuine work of art from their grandmother."

"Talking about the wife-," said Fred quietly in Trevor's ear as if he were divulging a secret of state, "mine is very congenial and as sweet as a lamb. To tell you the truth, so small is the trouble I have with her that I don't have to give her a moment's thought from one end of the day to the other."

Fred clicked his teeth and drank heavily of a jar of porter. In his possession, hidden from general view by the black porter, lay a golden goblet of whiskey. In the light of Bell's Fred's face was a bit grey and his eyes seemed to become smaller and blacker. His clothes appeared rather drab.

"Those people whose women are slaves are right," went on Archibald.

"You're a hard man, Trevor," said Fred.

"That is just one of a number of foreign customs we should introduce into this country," he continued.

Nobody made any attempt to answer him.

"Or perhaps. . .," he said in a cynical tone and with a broad sweep of his hand at his drinking companions both near and far; "someone here might want her? Especially if she was going cheap. . .".

He turned to Dunne and said,

"But I don't expect any of these gentlemen are interested in women."

Pretty soon the group was being accosted by one of those red-faced drunks who always make it their business to know what everybody else is doing or saying and simultaneously forcing their own talk on good, bad and indifferent. Sharp eyed and funnel eared, they are the bane of every potential scoundrel, clown and poet in the land.

"Hello – I hope I am not interrupting ye. I am sitting over there. Like yerselves I am minding my own business."

They all turned to look at his empty stool in the distance.

"But do ye know what a woman is. . .?"

When the man had started speaking his voice had been calm and steady, but now it was accelerating into a screech or whine and the poor fellow was in a frenzy, his face beetroot-red, arms waving and unsteady on his feet. He continued to address no one in particular, grimacing at the wall and his voice becoming more high-pitched still:

"It's a trashing a blackguard like you needs. My father and mother – she was a woman – could use bad language along with the rest of them, but they'd give the lashing of their lives to anyone who spoke against womanly virtue. You may be sure that many were the beltings I got when I stepped out of line."

He suddenly stopped, stuck for words, looking embarrassed and strangely self-conscious. Archibald's reaction surprised everyone in the pub. He banged the table with his fist. Their glasses trembled and Nick Heeney frowned.

"How dare you interrupt a gentleman relaxing in the company of his friends," said Trevor loudly.

Andy Bell was worried. Nothing like this had happened in his pub for ages and he had a dreadful vision as he stood there of the altercation enlarging to engulf the entire house in a shindig of immense proportions. There were plenty of them there to take sides. Andy just did not know what to do, being a gentle man, and he would have felt a good deal better if

Mick were in. The man was taken aback by Archibald's aggressive gaze. He muttered in a more subdued tone:

"I was just doing my duty."

There followed a long silence as the two participants in this drama tried to fathom the quality of each other's soul. The interrupter smiled at last and waved his wide-open hand:

"Ye're a man I see knows what's what. No harm done. It be a poor world if we let women have their way. They all need to be kept in their place, you know, these women."

He shuffled back to his corner.

The fiddler came in late, too late to play but not too late for a drink, even though it was now three hours past the legal closing time. It was doubtful if any of the Garda Siochana were aware of this late revelry (with the exception of Dunne of course) for the existence of this back-street pub was not well-known to them. Andy's customers could stay there all night if they wished and there were occasions when the company remained from dusk to dawn, departing into the sobering early wind well-satisfied. Andy was seen arguing bitterly with the fiddler, who was defending his lateness with much expression. He had been to a wake. No doubt Andy blamed his late arrival for the near-riot as an evening of music is seldom disrupted by rancorous talk.

T. Roche and pal, hunched together, hid their heads in their drinks and talked. Soon they moved silently outside the saloon, like ghosts in transit from tombstone to tombstone, buoyed up by their drinks and not certain of making it home. In the sleeping dead city only the clatter from within Bell's would tell any roving spirits there remained life on earth. However the sight of Roche and the other, slinking through the various alleys, would forewarn the lost ethereal entities that the unearthly hours did not belong to them alone. The sound of their boots fled in the night.

Dan, his brown-freckled face shadowed by his hat, looked dimly at Trevor Archibald. There was another puzzle in his head; it was that Archibald reminded him of somebody. Now there was something he had been thinking about earlier; what was it? Archibald it seemed reminded him of a person he had seen or met recently. Was it that Archibald reminded him of Archibald? That did not make sense, but it was all the sense he could make of the matter. At last there emerged outside the drinking party. The dark sky above formed a dome over their presence. The twinkling stars in the black, oily heavens were in rings over their heads, each individual, it seemed, with their own appointed stars. Every man there, in that sleeping world, was like a lone player in a great cosmic drama.

"Nick has given me good news," said Dan when everybody was listening, "he says he'll have poteen next week."

Dunne gave a grunt of pleasure.

"It's like ages since we last had some," he said.

Nick Heeney was still inside the pub, always being the last to come out. Andy brought him to the door and Dunne's arm helped him on the street, a token of gratitude perhaps for what he was shortly to provide them with, as well as a hand of encouragement in the heart-rending struggle of everyday existence.

O'Reilly felt pleased too, for Heeney's poteen enabled him to find his poetic muse without much expense and very quickly.

As was his wont Trevor made off quite fast, alone – a mystery man there all right.

Everyone said 'goodnight' to Andy. The pub light was reflected on this face and that as each got his bearings. Fred parted from them, to hopefully catch a taxi on the Rathmines Road.

"It's a quiet night and the sky is clear. It won't rain," said Dan O'Toole.

The piece of moon that had been out earlier had,strangely enough, moved its position quite a distance to the south and they all stood transfixed for a few moments in the great calm and mystery of the night.

"Aye," agreed Patrick; "it's grand. You can almost hear the stars moving."

"When it's starry like this I do think the spirits and devils do be about too," said Dan.

"You can hear nothing now; only the stars up there is all there is. Sure the city is a cemetery," said Patrick.

"It's a strange feeling I do get from the sky," said Dan.

"When I was a kid," said O'Reilly, "I saw a white ghost floating across the sky. I was staring for hours. Then it vanished. I have never seen it again. Perhaps I will paint the experience one day."

"I don't know what to think when I look up there. It makes me feel a bit funny," said Dan.

"It was there before us and will be there after we're gone," said Patrick.

"What is that?", asked O'Toole.

"The sky," Patrick answered.

* * *

Trevor's car pulled quickly off the Rathgar Road. It was not known to anyone but himself where he kept it hidden; it was his habit to arrive in the Rathmines area by bus and to return home by car. On the way up from Rathmines he had undergone some intense emotional changes. A huge black cat (it was more a panther than a cat), with its tail high in the air, had run in front of him causing him to swerve and almost crash. Previously to this, his mind had been in a state of equanimity; now it became disturbed and he cursed all things and especially the wife at home. He drove aggressively into the neat drive that was his home. On approaching the front door a feeling of trepidation took hold of him as he realised that he would have to offer another convincing account of how he had spent the night labouring away at his all-important work. It was four o'clock and the latest he had come home yet. He wondered what would happen if she smelt the drink from his breath, but he had a feeling that Hillary would not recognise the smell of alcohol. In the dark his hand fumbled with the key and he could not find the lock on the door. He imagined giving her a clout instead of having to answer her questions. He continued to fumble and it was she who opened the door to his wondering face.

"It's you at last," she said.

"Hello Hillary. . . I'm sorry I'm late. . .".

She interrupted him. Her strong hand held him in suspension.

"Listen Michael dear, don't say a word. I have some great and wonderful news for you. Close the door and come in."

They drifted down the old street side by side, not a word spoken and taking over the centre of the thoroughfare. From afar they appeared like men intent on their destiny, looming larger up front and smaller from behind. The few remaining hours of rest would be spent in Dan's bed. At dawn Pat and Nick would set off for their own abodes.

Dan, alone of all of them there in that crowded and airless bed, lay awake as the first shafts of dawnlight appeared on the pale window. The rays were springing up over England beyond, he thought. And further on lay Russia, asleep too, he supposed. Russia in her green and wide dress lay spreadeagled out asleep, a mighty giant. Only the muffled snores of her rivers and the breath of her cold winds disturbed the earth. Right then she woke and turned, looking into the eye of the rising sun. Her high mountains move and slowly she arises, her bent back struggling to master the early day. Smoke-fires appear all over, getting the breakfast ready.

John Bull was probably getting ready too. The old fellow would sure enough go about it in his own fashion. The first heat-rays cause a loud cough, tingling the ancient features and annoying him a bit. He kicked his feet and put down his head. The dawn appears as an unwelcome stranger. There is the early mist to cloud the runny eyes. A bark from an early dog is the herald of renewed life. Its running feet trod over his cold flesh. John Bull snorts and runs through the open gate, stampeding everything in sight.

Dan was unable to drop off into a deep sleep. He felt that there was a big challenge in the new day ahead of him. The revelations of Mr. Argod would be solicited and digested. Another world would open up to him. Perpetually puzzled by the world a great mystery surrounded everything in his life. In his mind there was an emptiness, a never-ending tunnel down which he wandered. When he was lost in this Limbo, his bearing would collapse and his eyes took on a withdrawn look. People kept away from him. In the volumes of books in the libraries he had discovered bits and pieces of information, but he had never been able to arrange them into a picture of anything. He knew that there must exist, somewhere, the answer to his questings.

A wave of light was aimlessly in the room. The tattered wallpaper must have been very old. Its design of roses had long since lost its gloss of red colour. Still it was a comfortable enough room in that the rain stayed mostly outside. The canal ran by the front and there were some glum trees through which the sun glinted on regular occasions. A strange tune went through Dan's ear and wafted musically in his mind. A relaxation came to his features and his mouth opened.

The wandering wave of light had become fixed and there were more now to join it. A fine day, please God. Tim Roche, in his own bed, writhed and turned in an uneasy sleep while Dan fell into a deep slumber.

Chapter Three

Patrick O'Reilly, hand clasped to his heart, stood musing at strokes of paint he had put on a canvas which stood on a stand in the middle of the room. His pale, thin face had a pensive look and his black hair, combed firmly back, was exceedingly oily. His red trousers gave his lower person a ragged appearance, being ill-fitting and daubed with paint. He did not seem at ease in his clothes. The canvas on which he worked was very expensive, being of the highest quality, for it was only the very best of material that Patrick would consider for his work. His obtaining of this canvas however was much less praiseworthy, having been stolen from the Kildare Street National College of Art.

It was early in the afternoon and, happily and busily employed on his new work, he was surprised when a knock came to the door. In a somewhat distracted frame of mind he opened it and was immediately filled with consternation. A girl, whom he had never seen before, stood there. He stared at her in great surprise. He felt sudden and inexplicable guilt – as if she had come to accuse him of something.

Speaking in a soft, firm voice the young woman announced that she was from the Saint Vincent de Paul Society, a society which does much good work amongst the poor and downcast, and she wondered if she might have a word with him. There was no need for him to worry about anything she might say, for she was there on her own initiative and not on that of the Church or police or anybody else.

With a stammer Patrick invited her in. He was a nervous individual – now his speech impediment came back worse than ever and he felt terrible. His hands trembled as he guided her to the only chair in the room, an ancient, deep-red armchair – its back was so high it looked like an emperor's throne. She spoke again in a voice which sounded like crystal-clear water to his ears, so cool was its self-control:

"My name is Jane Wood and I am a friend of an acquaintance of yours. Has Dan O'Toole mentioned me at all?"

Patrick was too confused to be also surprised at the startling revelation of a lady in Dan's life. All he could say was no, he had never heard Dan mention anybody of that name.

"Oh," said Jane, surprised.

She surveyed her surroundings critically. The place was extremely untidy with no order to it. Littered everywhere were paintings, taking up most of the room. There were brushes in old jars, pots and pans. Most things were splattered with paint, his trade mark. The only evidence that someone lived there was a small bed in the corner, stuck away like an embarrassment. There was in the room a most unappealing and strong odour.

He doesn't look a very happy person, she thought. He was in fact very like a great many other cases she had come across in the past. She was here now over the matter of Dan, but she must remember to bring up O'Reilly's case at the next society meeting.

"All this must keep you very busy," she said.

"You don't think it's a waste of time?", he asked her anxiously.

She replied in a matter-of-fact voice:

"I suppose there is nothing wrong with it. This kind of thing is very good if it occupies an idle mind and keeps a person out of trouble. It is all quite harmless, I'd imagine."

"It is my life," said Patrick abjectly.

He had a feeling of worthlessness and dishonesty. A grim expression overcame him. What was he painting for at all? Nobody paid any attention to his work. It was not that he sought acclaim – even criticism would be welcome. But the very existence of his diligently produced art was ignored by the world. He was an idealist and there was forever in his soul a dream which lay in a world of happy music where art reigned supreme and days were spent in peace and communion with like-minded fellow artists. It was when he looked at his actual surroundings, at the lack of interest in art shown by his friends, that he really became disheartened. Then he would consider emigrating to North Africa or perhaps Australia. That is how he foresaw his likely end, in bitter exile, a blossom in the desert. Yet he would continue to paint. He would paint as long as there was breath in his body. He was addicted to paint and colours; people to him were staring faces in real-life portraits; the world was a living mass of colour; at times it became a monstrous sea, a gigantic, wave-tossed ocean which threatened to swallow him up. He painted with a mania – the madness of one trying to flee a nasty fate.

"But you shouldn't take it too seriously," said Jane, observing his sad countenance.

"It will be the killing of me," he said mysteriously.

The reason for her coming, she said, was to have a few confidential words with him about Dan. She was very concerned about O'Toole. He had listened to her advice at the hospice and he had promised that his way-of-life would change once he was out again. She had met him quite a few times in the street and never failed to smell the drink from his breath. She didn't even think he recognised her on these occasions – his 'conversation' was very obscure. There was no sign of the submission or good sense he had shown while at the hospital.

"It is my wish to have a good talk with him in the hope that it will do some good."

Patrick tried to concentrate on what she was saying. Her presence caused him great tension and he stared rather wildly at her. He always found it difficult to look anybody in the eye but this was worse. A constriction came to his throat, his heart raced and he clutched his neck with trembling hands in an effort to remain calm. When he had managed to gather his thoughts he said: "I can invite you to a hooley we'll be having at Nick Heeney's place next Friday night. You will be more than welcome."

Jane hesitated, especially at the mention of the name Nick Heeney. She pondered secret doubts before accepting.

"Well, thank you very much, it's very kind of you. I can only think that some good will come out of my being there, although I must say I am not a party-goer."

Patrick was pleased at being able to help her. He relaxed a little now. She agreed to have a look at some of his works and he proceeded to show her around with great enthusiasm.

"This one is my favourite," he said pointing at a painting.

They both viewed it. It showed a dark scene, a view of the complexity of life against a background of innocent beauty. It had taken him a year; a picture of children playing under the shadow of a giant tree against a background of picturesque flowers behind which were dark, mysterious images in a park. He stood beside her and the wild look had returned to his eyes. His breathing was irregular and perspiration rose to his face. The attack on Jane came with such unexpectedness that she gave up any resistance.

Afterwards, having kissed her all over her face, which was dishevelled and wet, Patrick had been very contrite and embarrassed. Great emotions were whirling around in his head and he found it difficult to talk or concentrate. Then he was filled with a fear that she would go and report him to the authorities, in particular the Gardai. He would be accused of debauchery and at the very least he would be charged with indecent behaviour. Judges took a very serious view of this particular human failing, considering it a graver offence than arson, armed robbery or even murder itself.

"Oh, why was I ever born?", he moaned.

To his great surprise not to mention relief, Jane had not seemed too upset. He watched her tidy up herself; she was quite calm and there was neither bitterness or condemnation on her face. She forced a smile as she looked at him, disregarding the offence that had certainly been caused. She felt chiefly pity.

"I am ssssorry," he said.

"We can't help these things sometimes", she replied, "and the best we can do is forget that it ever happened. We should always realise that there is an animal side to our nature and if we are not careful it will catch us unawares."

She was already trying to put the incident out of her mind.

He showed her every courtesy to the door. Their goodbyes were civil and she also obtained Heeney's address. He stood there watching as she walked up the basement steps to the street. A great lump came to his throat as he watched her depart hurriedly.

⋆ ⋆ ⋆

Michael and Hillary Argod, the two of them dressed in britches and boots, walked hand in hand up the track on the side of the hill. In their other hands were a walking stick held for show by Michael and an umbrella by Hillary for protection against the elements, which she never trusted. While his wife was immersed in talk Michael was trying to concentrate on other things, such as the scenery. It was a fine saturday afternoon and Hillary was happy as she pulled the more contemplative Michael along. He had to warn her not to exert herself too much, she being in her condition. She replied that he was like an old mother-hen, fretting over nothing. He had certainly been on edge since hearing the news and had not slept a wink. He stumbled over a stone and gave out a loud curse.

"Michael, I wish you wouldn't use those expressions. You have become too fond of common language lately. The next thing is you'll be forgetting yourself in front of the relatives."

He quietly murmured remorse.

"Lord – it will be December," he suddenly blurted out.

"Yes, it is possible that he will be born on Christmas Day. Wouldn't that be a great honour?"

"Yes, it would be a great honour," said a surly Michael.

"We shall call him George. It's an aristocratic name. The Royal Family are fond of it."

"Yes, dear."

"You really don't sound all that happy. Are you not glad over this wonderful news? Any natural man would have joy in his heart."

"Do you think I am an unnatural man?," asked Michael angrily.

"Don't raise your voice. We are supposed to be civilized and not common class. Let's sit down over there and eat the food."

Beyond was a view of Dublin city. This was their favourite spot in the whole hills. Michael took the rucksack from his back while his wife found a comfortable place for them in the grass. Down below was a scene like that of the Promised Land, where slow floating clouds, incense bedecking a green vision, were poised smugly over the land beneath. The city seemed far away, in another world, resting uneasily on the innocent earth – was it the City of God or of the Devil? A thrush sang in a bush and they turned to see it. However her nest, camouflaged in leaves in a fork, was quite safe from discovery by such city-folk as the Argods.

The early summer wind was scented with the bloom of new flowers and shrubs and beneath were the hopping insects. High above a few birds dared to go higher and deep below some insects tried to burrow deeper. Nature was alive with the Spring. Her intonations and reverberations on the bosom of the earth were known to every other creature but not to the Argods, whose chief appreciations were just the warmth of summer and the cold of winter.

He handed his wife a sandwich as she talked away about their forthcoming child who, she said, would be reared in exactly the right way. She sat on the brow of the hillock and did not feel at ease; her hands were tense and she withdrew her sensibilities to an interior spot. She was an intensely private type of person and even here she felt there were eyes peering at them. There was a feeling of new pride in her. Whereas in the past she had always felt a certain inferiority in relation to her husband, her producing a child and heir outweighed in importance both Michael's brain power and his proposed book.

"Our son you know Michael will have aristocratic blood in him. He will possess a portion of royal blood and it will set him apart from all other people in Ireland. He will be very proud of his ancestry just as you are now, Michael. One day a heritage of nobility will once again be valued for what it is in this country. We have been denied our rightful place in society. When you have produced your important work there is a chance of a knighthood, especially if we move up north. That would make things much easier for George. In the Restoration in the Ireland of the future why shouldn't our George be the new King of Ireland? It is a dream, I suppose, but not an impossible dream."

If by mischance it happened to be a girl, she continued, there would be a much smaller problem as she would fulfill her role as a proper lady, learn to play the piano, go to ballet lessons and become a fine aristocrat's wife. A Protestant, or Free-thinking lapsed Catholic of ample means and high position would be acceptable as a husband.

The peaty sun flicked out at them and its swimming shadow alternatively darkened and brightened their ground in a change of colours. All around them the wind and cloud and air raced together across the majestic sky. A little stream ran backwards across noisy pebbles; they could hear its tinkle but did not know where it was. Michael mumbled acquiescence as his wandering eye surveyed the distant scene. Slowly there dawned on him the full realisation of his impending fatherhood. He had an upsurge of an unusual, strangely primitive pride. He smiled as Hillary watched him. Then suddenly a frown came over his face:

"By heaven Hillary he will not be a lord, nor a sir, prince, king or any noble. I would be more proud of him as a labourer in the fields than as any alien, tyrannical monarch."

Hillary was astounded at his words, not knowing what to make of them. She thought now that perhaps he was working too hard at the university; the strain was affecting his whole behaviour.

She spoke to him in a quiet voice:

"His high birth will place him above others. That is a fact of life. We have a responsibility to our ancestors and also to posterity which we cannot escape. It is a grave burden."

They sipped their milk and ate in silence for a while. When their talk resumed it was refrained and they tied in their words with the ritual of the meal.

After a while Michael began doing his physical exercises. He stretched his arms out in front of him like Tarzan in the jungle. He bent to touch his toes and perspiration appeared on his forehead. As he proceeded with press-ups his gasps startled Hillary. He collapsed in a heap, a ghastly pale colour on his face.

"Heck, Hillary, it's getting harder all the time. I think I'll have to take things a bit easier."

Hillary was of the unspoken opinion that it was more rather than less exercise which he was in need of.

"Do you want to be fat?," she asked.

"There are many famous fat people in history. What about Winston Churchill?"

"I wouldn't compare you to Winston Churchill; he was a commoner."

The glow of the setting sun was visible behind the clouds and there was a natural sadness in the air over the day's demise.

"I think I'll have to carry on back down to my work for a few hours after we get home," said Michael apologetically.

"I will encourage you in your career, Michael. Try not to be too late though, I thought you were never going to get home last night."

Delving through reams of work was the furthest thing from his mind right now. If the truth be known it was a fact that over the last year he had become somewhat lazy. This trait was not too obvious yet, either to himself or to others; it is a devious vice which can strike the best individuals in the most subtle of ways – without their recognising it for what it is. At the very moment Hillary was praising him for his diligence he was picturing himself relaxing with his cronies and breaking away from the strictures of daily life, wife and home. As his wife talked he did not even hear her words. He was thinking about someone for whom he had a secret admiration, Fred Dunne, and what Fred had said concerning his own life; that he was satisfied to just let it drift by and not let it bother him. Fred was a real cynic all right. He appeared to have solved the problem of his marriage too. Maybe Fred was a bit of a failure though. That would be a way of looking at it. How would he like it if his own son turned out like Dunne? Would he wish that?

And there was a hidden side to Dunne. How often it was the case that progress was brought about by a few, a minority of zealots, small groups of eccentric outcasts who single-handedly turned the world upside down. Now Fred's job would be to lock these people up. Sometimes it was hard to see Dunne as a strict upholder of the law, an uncompromising bringer-to-justice of the most desperate cases. Who could say? Often there was a big difference between the public man and the private man and he wondered which they were seeing in Bell's.

"Don't forget we are going to the opera in Rathgar Town Hall tomorrow night," said Hillary.

"It's the first I've heard of it. When was all this arranged?"

"It was discussed weeks ago. We are going with the Blaizes."

"Oh. Which opera is it?"

"Rathgar is getting together with Upper Rathmines to put on Bluebeard. It's their biggest effort yet."

He made a derogatory remark about the Rathgar Amateur Musical Society which shocked Hillary. Michael Argod, keen lover of music and the arts, was not simply trying to upset his wife. His recent rude behaviour was a by-product of his overall dissatisfaction. There was the certain knowledge that he wouldn't enjoy himself at the opera, though he had always done so in the past; and he did not know why this was the case.

Rathgar on a late evening in early summer looks very sedate as the sobriety of the houses contrasts solemnly with the blossoms and blooms in the hedges. The streets are quiet. Michael and Hillary relaxed as they drove in. Their wolfhound ran over and was stroked on its head by Michael. Hillary made some remark about the flower beds. Her husband looked around at the garden and saw that everything was very nice.

★ ★ ★

It is more than likely that the majority of people can but guess at the immense emotions which must wrack an artist as he considers the destruction of his art. It is the agony of a creator who contemplates the extinction not just of hopes and dreams but of his own vision. Patrick O'Reilly had trod around the room a thousand times after the departure of Jane. Tears of sorrow drenched his face, followed by tears of uncontrollable laughter. He was going to destroy his paintings and perhaps follow their destruction with his own under the wheels of a passing bus, or at the bottom of the River Liffey. He had wasted his life on false hopes and impossible fancies. The turmoil inside had made him almost distracted and his tears were now the last dry and bitter dregs of his illusions coming like blood from a stone. He felt that life and existence were inconsequential, empty and worthless.

It was Trevor Archibald who interrupted him, just as he was setting light to the paintings piled up for a bonfire in the middle of the room. He had been banging on the door for some time before Patrick had become aware of it. Trevor was shocked by the sight in the room. He quickly set about putting out the fire, swatting it with his coat, displaying great expertise in the art of professional fire-fighting. When it was made safe he grabbed Patrick, pinioning him where he stood.

"O'Reilly, are you crazy? What are you doing? The whole house was going on fire."

"I was just going to burn some old sketches and things, that's all," said an abashed Patrick.

Trevor glowered down at him.

"It looks like you were getting rid of the whole works. This is terrible man."

"I'm finished with painting. I'm not going to go on fooling myself. It's all useless. It's no use."

"Useless? What are you talking about man? Can you not see the greatness of your work? Are you gone off your head altogether? You will be the most famous person in Ireland one day."

O'Reilly sat down on the floor. He put his hands to his face.

"Your proposed destruction of those paintings is a matter of concern to the world at large. You gave birth to them but they are not your's to destroy. They don't belong to you anymore, nor to me nor to any one individual; they belong to the whole world. Think of that. You would deprive every race, generations yet unborn of what your hand has produced. And all just to satisfy a momentary feeling of frustration – frustration that every artist has to undergo. One brief, irrational act and everything is gone up the spout. How will you look back on the waste when you are an old man? How will your descendants look back on it? Think of them."

Archibald studied Patrick to see what effect his words were having on the unpredictable artist. Whatever doubts he might have concerning the state of O'Reilly's mind he had no doubts about the worth of his painting. In Archibald's opinion the lad had a definite ability with the brush. And, while if it were anybody else who had come into the room (certainly his pub pals if not every single other Irish person) he would most likely have been allowed to continue the work of destruction, if not even helped in it, it was a lucky stroke that it was Archibald who had come in. Here was a man who was abhorred at the sight of the waste of anything of possible value.

Patrick seemed affected, for his body shook and there was a fresh outflow of tears.

"Does this mean that I should go on painting?", he asked.

"Of course it does. In fact you will be a better painter now. You have been through the flames of self-doubt. You have stood on the brink. It has been a rare test for you, not given to every person."

It took some more effort and talk from Trevor before Pat's dark mood lifted and he smiled again.

"What brings you here, Trevor? I am somewhat taken aback by your visit, your gracious presence in my seedy den. It is a pleasant surprise."

"There is something I want you to do for me. I also wanted to see how the other half live in the northside! I have heard a lot about the dinginess of this area."

"Well I am honoured. Are you a Blackrock man, or Clonsilla or Rathgar? But that is none of my business. I can't offer you a drink but you are welcome to my every other hospitality."

"You know what I was thinking about as I crossed the Liffey? I was thinking that I would like you to do my portrait. It is not that I am a vain man, God forbid; it just struck me as an interesting thing to do. You could earn a few bob into the bargain."

Trevor was very relaxed now and he stretched out his long legs from the big chair on which he sat. He looked around with curiosity and took in the unusual surroundings. He thought that Patrick's room was very like Patrick himself. It was just the set-up he had imagined him in. Patrick for his part was thinking about Trevor's request. He was delighted to agree. He would have been willing to do it for free; indeed he would even have paid for the privilege. In his opinion Archibald had classical features and the challenge was one that any artist would have been glad to accept.

"I will make a few preliminary sketches and see what the result is," he said happily.

It did not take him very long to make a number of quick drawings, surveying Trevor from different angles. Archibald said that he was impressed by the professionalism of his approach. Patrick replied that his features were a worthy challenge and that he would do his utmost to produce a picture which would show forth the 'hidden character behind the real man'. This was something, he explained, that is the aim of all art and was the secret of success of those works that were art's crowning glory.

"I am impressed," said Trevor.

"Do you know something?"

"What?"

"I suppose it's my imagination but it seems to me that there's a remarkable resemblance between you and those faces that appear on the coins and notes of England. Isn't that a very strange thing?"

"No, it is not," laughed Trevor, "for it has been said that I have royal blood in me."

A puzzled Patrick continued with his sketching. The subject of the previous night came up and Trevor said that he could not remember having an argument with anyone, but if Patrick said that it had happened it must have happened.

"Dan O'Toole did not look too good last night, "said Archibald.

"He is missing the poteen," said Patrick.

"Well then, he should be able to recover soon. But I imagine it's not more poteen that the lad needs to pull himself together. He needs . . . guidance."

"Is that not true of us all?," replied O'Reilly.

Later in the evening the two helped themselves to a bottle of spirit that miraculously appeared out of the blue. Patrick told him about the visit of Miss Wood earlier in the day and Archibald wondered. When he learnt that the same lady would be attending at Heeney's the look of intensity on Archibald's face increased.

* * *

When Dan woke up everyone else was gone from the room. So he lay back staring at the ceiling for the next two hours, thinking about things. Outside was the patter of soft raindrops which meant he had missed what fine weather there was that day. When it was well on into the afternoon he pulled himself to the edge of the bed where he scratched the hairs of his legs for a while.

"I'll do it now," he suddenly said aloud.

"It'll have to be a brand new suit, nothing less."

He found his hat (in the corner for it had been removed from his head and flung there by Roche before the irate Corkman had left the room) and went out the front door of the grey, terraced house. His manner of walking could be described more as a series of spurts than a fast walk. He wobbled slightly as he went along. Round about harmless children were playing in the funland paths of Ontario Terrace and staid couples walked by the banks of the canal. He kept his eyes on the ground as he walked for he was always finding things. It is good policy to walk with your eyes down, for any number of reasons but particularly if, like

Dan, one was predisposed to picking up pens and other useful items. The collection of pens that he had meant that he would never have to buy one when the time came to use them. And if he really was a student at the university now then that time had come. Money he found too; once a pound had turned up amongst scraps of paper, twigs, cigarette ends and decaying foliage at the end of Hatch Street.

At the corner of St Stephen's Green he saw Fred Dunne standing outside a tall building. Dan walked over and greeted him. Fred looked bored and glum and his smile was wan as Dan came up to him.

"Where are you going Dan?," he asked.

"I'm going to get a new suit. It's about time I had a good one. Do you have a gun on you there, Fred?"

"I have indeed. I have been moved over to Administration this week, as you can see," he said, looking up at the huge building.

"Do you think *they* will ever attack?", asked Dan.

"If they did you wouldn't see me hanging around. I'd be gone in a flash!"

O'Toole laughed heartily.

"Come on down to O'Connell Street with me, Fred. You're wasting your time here. We'll have a pint, come on."

"I agree that your suggestion is a good one. In fact it is the most sensible thing I have heard all day. Unfortunately it's also a fact that I haven't a penny on me, not a red cent. So there's not much use me going anywhere at the moment. You got home all right last night?"

"Yea. Begob Trevor was in a rare mood."

"That man," said Fred with a sigh, "is a wonder. I often wonder too where he's from. Did you ever catch anything about his past?"

"He's a hard man to get to talk to. I think he looks down on me."

Considering the mystery of Dan's own past it was no wonder he could not provide enlightenment on Trevor. It was six of one and half a dozen of the other," Fred thought.

"I guess I'll shove off as it's a bit late and the shops will be closing any minute. Good luck," said Dan.

"I hope you have luck yourself with the suit. Have you come into a little cash?"

"I've no money at all, Fred. I'll have to get it on the instalment."

"More power to your elbow."

"Good luck again, then."

"Good luck."

"On the instalment my arse," said Fred quietly.

Dan strode through the busy throngs on Grafton Street. He kept getting in the way of everybody, bumping into grouchy old women, knocking aside fragile children and angering old men. The gay music coming from certain shops gave the vicinity a holiday flavour and Dan tried to get in the mood. By the time he got to the draper's Mr Finch the manager was ready to shut up. After a long, hard day there is no surprise that he was a very tired man; he was one of those people who work their heart and soul out for their employer, usually in return for pittance. Despite many hardships these people still thank Providence for her goodness. The likes of Mr Finch are not necessarily patient types at heart but keep their nerves on a fine leash, always presenting a friendly and helpful front. Nearly always anyway.

Dan had walked in just as he was about to close the doors. Worse was to come for the ragged customer was insisting on trying out every suit in the shop. The task of getting him into these suits was so wearisome that it began to seem to Mr Finch that the decrepit young man had come simply to try his patience or make a fool of him. In the end he threw Dan out on to the street. A small stool followed and, hit on the head,

Dan fell to the pavement, to the astonishment of many people. He could hear Mr Finch shouting. Two nuns, on home-leave from the African Missions, stood by and watched the scene.

"Go back to where you come from. Your kind have no right to be in our city," screamed a red-faced Mr Finch.

He kicked Dan who managed to pull himself along the pavement out of boot's range at least.

"In Africa they treat each other better than they do here," one of the nuns commented.

Fred Dunne saw him coming along again and it was clear that he had been in a scrape.

"Where's your hat?"

Dan felt his head.

"It must have fallen off me head. This man nearly killed me. He went mad, Fred and I had to run for me life."

"Was he the man you were trying to buy a suit from?"

"Yes, Fred. He was."

"I see."

"A blooming wretch!", said Dan.

"Perhaps so. I think you need a drink to recover. A drink and a chat. Let's go for one, or two. Andy will be willing to postpone payment when he hears what happened. He's a good-natured so-and-so. You will see, Dan, there are some people left in the world with a touch of decency in them. Good old Andy! C'mon, we'll only get wet on the outside standing around here."

And sure enough, moments later as they made their way southwards the sky opened up. Without his hat Dan was overcome by glumness. Fred tried to console him with glorious descriptions of waiting jugs of porter in Bell's. To his great surprise Dan began to speak in Gaelic. Dunne could not understand a single word of it and he asked him to translate what he had been saying.

"A hat," said Dan, "would be as welcome back as is St Bridget's Day, or festive June when they make the hay."

Fred told him that his sayings were rare and they both laughed.

Andy Bell was indeed sympathetic when he saw O'Toole; he put an arm on his shoulder and led him to a seat. He said that they both would have ample refreshments for the evening; it can be stated that nowhere in Ireland is there a publican to match Andy for generosity.

"That stout, well-padded fellow who lives with you; he looks well-off; he's a Corkman, isn't he? Are you good friends?", Fred was saying to Dan later.

"I wouldn't be sorry if I never saw him again."

"Do you think that he could get you a suit, Dan? Is there any chance of that?"

"He wouldn't let me have the crap of an old worn rag that he'd be throwing away. He'd rob a dog of a bone. Nothing is sacred to him. I found my best pens in his box. Now that you mention it, his clothes take up the whole place. He must have hundreds of suits."

"Listen Dan. What is to stop you taking one when he isn't looking? If he has that many he'll never miss one."

"Begob that is an idea! He'd be none the wiser. I have to go to the university on Monday morning. It's an important business and it wouldn't do to appear in dirty old rags. I'm going to be nicely dressed in the future, Fred."

As he made his way home later Dan was in a happy if dizzy state. When at last he arrived inside his room he remembered to take a look at Timothy's spare clothing. He stared at the row of suits in the wardrobe; they were of varied kinds and it took him a long time to decide which one would be the best. He settled on a neat, navy blue suit. It was brand new; he felt very pleased. A fresh feeling of confidence and well-being was in him and he had a trouble-free sleep that night.

Chapter Four

Early Monday morning, round about eight o'clock, at Tuam in east county Galway, Nick Heeney himself climbed on the Athlone bus with a suitcase crammed full under his arm. What do you think was in it, unbeknownst to the driver, conductor, the gardai of Tuam or any other person around except the bold Heeney himself? A dozen bottles of poteen safely packed in. His grim face showed no emotion as he sat securely down in the back seat. He paid no attention to the other travellers as they clambered about. He fixed his gaze outside on the quiet street and held the luggage in a tight grip by his side, the devil a bit of worry about him.

However as the vehicle slowly pulled out of the prosperous Galway town he did look out the back window, half-expecting and half-not-expecting to see the gardai in hot pursuit. A good six months was spent in readying the spirit now in his possession. It was well-distilled, the best in the west. One bottle alone could last a household for a month of continuous drinking. The lot would have been worth a good deal on the export market. And indeed has it ever been debated as to why poteen is illegal, while other deadly concoctions of respectable and powerful companies are freely sold and encouraged by one and all? Poteen's medicinal effects are beyond dispute. It has been reported how foreign races indulge in the most intoxicating of potions to the approval of their governments and the betterment of their religion and art. Suffice to ponder whether plain antagonism towards the common man is at the root of the whole thing. Is it just a case of old-fashioned oppression of the west of Ireland peasant; also a question of jealous rivalry by respectable breweries and distilleries keen to maintain their market? As for Nick, he did not have the opportunity for such deliberations as his time was taken up with the providing, transporting and distribution of the drink. Not to mention last and least the indulging of it.

He was to change at Athlone into the train for Dublin but, firstly, he was to have a severe altercation along the way with the bus conductor that nearly ended in disaster, not to mention discovery. The poor officious creature of a conductor took it into his head that Nick's suitcase did not belong where it was and should be positioned elsewhere. Maybe he did not like the look of Heeney, who was a brawny and tough lad, and decided to use his office for a little self-assertion and bullying. There was no seeing as to how the luggage was doing any harm where it was. Whatever the reason, he said that Nick must part with it and Nick shook his head and stared out the window at the hedges speeding by. This annoyed your man the more and he gave what he called a last warning. By this time the whole bus was looking at them and Nick felt the blood rise in him. A tug of war developed over the suitcase and sworn mutterings issued forth from both combatants. It was not a pretty sight to see two grown men acting so and the language they were coming out with (there were children on the bus), but greater forgiveness can be granted to Heeney, considering the contents of the case. The end of it was nearly Heeney smashing the whole proceedings over the head of the unwary conductor, only the driver stopped and pulled into the side of the road. It being a characteristic of the true Gaelic race to act first and think later Nick would gladly have gone to jail just to get satisfaction from the old cod. In any case it did not come to that, thank God. Faith didn't they drop Nick and his luggage there on the roadside and speed off and come right back again minutes later when the sky opened up and take him back on board, all forgiven. Maybe they had all partaken of poteen the night before, or were subject to fits of remorse common to Christians and brought on by the peace-making words of the old priest sitting at the front of the bus. He was welcomed back like a long-lost son and the conductor was the most friendly of all, much to Nick's suspicion. Great care was taken of the drenched gentleman and the happy company set off again for Athlone. Somebody started a song and at the end of it all even the sour Heeney was smiling.

He moved around on the train later in search of a stout but he did not part for an instant with the poteen. As he drank quietly at the window, looking out at the fleeting pastures, seeing blurs for cows, his rugged arms were resting on the case. For the bit of it he might have been only another unfortunate emigrant on his way to England for a future in the drains and ditches of that land, a sight extremely common on these routes and not a remote chance of his catching the attention of anyone. He had another stout to help along the previous one and he was joined by a very drunk man, who sat down beside him and started to go on. This man appeared to be upset by the deeds or misdeeds of some monster called 'the government'. It was the government this, the government that and the government the other. Everything in this life (and the next one too, for that matter) was the fault of the government. Since the time the first government was set up nothing had gone right in the world. Thousands were leaving the land and they were doing nothing about it. Millions more were leaving the country to give to the foreigner, in Australia, America and England the benefit of their talents, never to return, and where was the government? The weather last August had spoiled the harvest where he came from and not a word of warning, advice or comfort had been tendered by that bunch. And, what was more, the weather this year was not looking any better either and there was that mob sitting on their backsides up in Dublin. Putting in a new government did not help in the least, as one was as bad as the next and the hardships of life continued the same, or got worse.

"There is one thing they do like to do anyways," he said, "they like to keep us in our place with their laws. They are past-masters with the laws business. Sure there is hardly anything you can do nowadays without going to jail for it. You can't even go to the lavatory at the side of the road today! It's worse than the bloody Penal Laws and they were the work of the foreigner."

After this there was a long, sad story from him on the course of his life which, he wished, would soon end. His parents and grandparents had died from hunger and he with his many brothers and sisters were out working in the potato fields before they had even reached the use of reason. He could not read or write and when he had left his village he discovered that he could not speak the language of the country either. This caused him to consider suicide but a good priest had warned him that if he did life would not be any better for him in the next world either. So it was off to

England with him, to drudgery and digging (he would have liked to have been an artist of some kind) which did his health no good and now he had not even a penny to his name. They had nearly reached Dublin before his tale of woe was out and at the end of it he said with not a little triumph:

"The government is the cause of it, it's their fault."

True as that may be, it is a sobering fact that if everybody thought along those lines there would be no governments and then a licence would be given to all kinds of anarchy. Nevertheless such considerations did not trouble our bucko who seemed to have everybody on his side in that rail carriage as he ranted on. Nobody disagreed with him and nobody interrupted him either, least of all Nick Heeney who had to listen to all the talk.

"And I'm only too glad to be going into exile again in the land of the heathen, for nobody could care less for me here and I know they're only too happy to see me go."

Naturally at this stage the fellow had reached a high point of anger and was looking to see if anybody would dispute with him. Nobody did.

There were so many people speaking out against the government it was a wonder there was one at all. It would be an interesting matter if a national referendum were carried out on whether there should be a government in the first place. If the question was put to all those people in that rail carriage, or in the whole train, what would be the result?

Because they arrived at the station before they had expected to goes to prove the truth of the saying that a good chat halves the journey; it does not even have to be a 'good' chat for the old fellow had been very annoying. As early as four o'clock Nick was back in his room and hiding the bottles under the bed. He concealed them thoroughly, wrapping them in old newspaper he had obtained specially for the purpose and then putting the cache in a cardboard box. He kept a wary eye and ear out for the landlady,Mrs. Lee, who he believed watched his every move. He was constantly trying to catch her out in her snoops, setting little concealed traps in the room and making sudden swoops on the keyholes and doors of the house. However it was a fact though he didn't know it that the lady was terrified of him and did her living best always to keep out of his way.

After pulling a thick sandwich (it was a whole loaf and the ham was the size of a man's arm) from a paper bag and swallowing it in two fast bites, Nick wrapped himself up in a blanket and went into a much-needed sleep.

★ ★ ★

A downpour long and windy had raced across Ireland that Monday. When Nick was leaving Galway a rainstorm was descending in rapid and thunderous fashion on the Arans and bays and it was just two leaps behind him all the way to Dublin. The huge, dark swirls of cloud whose delinquent behaviour must have astounded the detached and innocent stars darted down to inflict water and damage on the earthlings of Dublin city. It first struck the outskirts of the metropolis at the stroke of seven – and the nation's weather-forecaster had underestimated its power all the way, so people were surprised at the deluge of water. As the waterfall pelted the streets and laneways, water creating on water a symphony of sound, some diverse folk imagined it was a case of Noah having come back again. People and all forms of mobile life vanished from the streets so that there was an atmosphere about similar to that which will prevail at the end of the world. There was thunder and lightning and here and there an individual fell to prayer in the hope that the danger would pass. That second other-world of the heavens, perhaps envious of the surface-earth's monopoly of things and events, had fallen into a fury and was taking vengeance on its underling. The sky, as if it was saying all patience is gone and for your brazen earthiness and independence, was venting its spoilt rage on the placid face of the earth. Andy Bell's men tucked in for the night, glad for the noise outside. Dogs and cats, goats, everything on the loose sought shelter and the Liffey rose a foot in a minute. By eight o'clock enough electricity poles had been brought down to ensure that entire sections of the mighty city were in darkness. In Heeney's room the window was wide open, in welcome of the incoming tide and wind.

Nick awoke and yawned so loudly that even the thunder had to take a back seat. He tumbled to the floor making such a thud that the wooden boards bent and the house shook. Then he stumbled in the dark knocking over a stool, the bang being sure to frighten the life out of Mrs Lee down below. He dragged himself to the washbasin and threw water on his face. He paused a while in silent contemplation, resting his arms on the sink, immobile and brooding. (It was Fred Dunne who once said that Nick had a bit of the criminal character about him – that was when Nick wasn't listening!). He took a glass and went and pulled out one of the bottles. He unscrewed the top and the vapours rushed out like red-hot gasses and filled his nostrils. As he stood stiffly in the middle of the room there was a bright light in his eyes and he set his teeth. Holding one end of the bottle firmly, the smoking top was led on its slow journey down to the glass. He filled the measure of one large whiskey and recapped the bottle tightly. He stared at the glass, his eyes becoming used to the darkness. He felt his throat and decided to accompany the drink with some cool, clear water. This was fetched in a cup and at last he was ready. He sipped it – it was good and hot. A bit hotter than the usual and he quickly followed it with some water. It was doing a wonder of good down in his stomach, causing tremors inside of him. It was the quickest-working stuff he had ever come across, for within the space of a few seconds it was having its powerful effect. Then a strange thing happened.

Nick Heeney was very fond of music and in the evenings, when the glow of contentment was in him and he was alone in the solitude of his room, he would like to turn up the radio when a ceili came on, and the hearty notes and the roll of the drums would rise to fill the house and go out the window in a cascade of sound. At these times he was more than just a fairly-contented man. There was no radio now, due to the storm; nevertheless he heard the music, magnified in its intensity and its exhilarating effect. After just one sip of this new beverage he was singing aloud in tune with this phantom music. A tremendous change came over him and he sang and hummed and tapped his feet. He tried to keep in time with the sound, shaking his head and banging on the table and wall nearby.

Another sip – while the going was good – and he had emptied the glass. He dashed to the sink for more water, his mouth open and tongue protruding. The water helped, but he could not make it back to the chair, the sound of his private 'Fleadh Ceoil' having become a confusing roar. There was a worse moment at the window (it was a peculiarity of Nick that he had a fear of heights and he always tried not to look out of windows), and he fell backwards to the floor. When he had managed to drag himself to the bed a mighty wave of energy brought him low, carrying him into a state of utter forgetfulness. There was no doubt that it was a powerful brew.

Three people appeared out on the streets that stormy night. Alone of all the population they braved the elements. While wizened old sailors stuck to their fire-places and water-fowl and sea-birds even did not show, these individuals were out on their particular or peculiar tasks with no thought whatever for the weather.

Trevor Archibald, instead of going home to his dear and expectant wife; instead of reading up more research for his non-existent book; instead even of going to Bell's, was that evening rambling through the streets of town deep in thought and considerably agitated with vexation. Life had become confused for him. An educated man like himself should not have such trouble with life. There was this prospect for instance of having a child; it was a source of discontent to him. No doubt a stable home, a conscientious mother, modern comforts, strict principles (well-away from the clergy) and a father to be proud of in the shape of Michael Argod, were all there. The little child would be brainwashed in the deep waters of Bach, Brahms and Mozart, the best in classical culture, before he would be able to talk. He would be introduced to a variety of experiences such as mountain-walking, horse-back riding and maybe even water-skiing on the Blessington lakes, before the age of four. He would the taught to sing properly and ballet dance. He would be granted the greatest intellectual freedom, coupled with tolerant parental oversight. His hidden aptitudes and attitudes would be sought out. As probably will happen there will be rebellions and these will be understood if not encouraged. Should the barnstorming youth walk out of the house in protest, never to return, he will be proud as a father.

"Blah blah," said Trevor suddenly, "it is all rot."

He walked on in the direction of O'Connell Street, trying to refocus his thoughts. He ignored the pelting rain as his eyes sought the pavement; he struggled within himself and with his vexations which had been increased by the events of that morning. Despite this considerable turmoil inside he remained quite calm on the surface, so that he looked a little bit like an intelligent cleric out for a stroll.

"Utter balderdash," he was repeating to himself.

"She would have him to be King of Ireland! I have never heard anything so ridiculous. Of what use is an empty throne? For that is what he would receive, the son of Michael Argod. Who would admire him then, sitting on the gratuitous gift of a bare throne? That woman does not speak any sense."

These and other thoughts preyed on Trevor, causing the blood to rise in his head.

"He would more likely be the *subject* of Ireland in that case, the subject of mockery and jokes; that is what his well-meaning parents would have made of him. . . ."

He had by now reached the General Post Office, where he stopped and took shelter from the downpour. Its tall roof was as high, as massive as the sky and he stood still under its arches whose great columns, hiding him from view, were like ancient sentinels supporting the universe.

"How many of our kings today are born with the silver spoon in their mouth? Real royalty, their ancestors, had to start out as paupers, but we forget that! More than likely they were simply bright-eyed upstarts, usually illegitimate, many of them being mere fluff in the wind before they marched on to establish great kingdoms and pacify unruly tribes. Isn't that what kingship is about? The world has gone wild with its elections. What do they solve? Look at these countries with their presidents, or even kings or queens *by appointment or accident of birth!* What is in the making of a king? One thing he never was and that is a working man of the soil. It is to the peasant's field and the mines for the majority of mankind. A palace would never have been the destination for instance of any of those people in Bell's bar. Yet these folk probably represent the completed evolution and highest achievement of the masses! That is the way it has been ordained by the immutable laws of nature!"

He suddenly found himself back at that time of bursting and burning when the great building was alight. He watched the flaming timbers and heard the cries of the men. In the streets were great numbers of people waiting expectantly for someone to speak. He addressed them in a loud and impressive voice, surprising even himself with his own oratory. He warned them about continuing to expect satisfactory leaders, waving his arms and leaning forward in emphasis of his words. The approval of the crowd was expressed in roars of applause.

Then Trevor left the Post Office and went on in the rain to O'Connell Bridge. He had an increasing sense of urgency and elation which caused him to come out of himself with a mania of fervour. He leaned over the bridge, staring into the depths below.

In another part of town Jane Wood was stranded in a church where she had gone to pray. Since it was continuing to rain heavily she did not see any point in going out just yet; in fact she was quite content here and had no great urge to go home. She was dressed in almost completely black clothes and as she knelt and bent her head the only light in the church came from the flickering candles which wavered like uneasy ghosts.

Why, she wondered, was life so unfair? Why was there so much misery in the world? Sorrow and destitution were to be found everywhere, every seemingly innocent invitation was a trap. She offered up a prayer of intercession for Patrick O'Reilly, that he might be turned from the course of folly he was set upon. Her most heartfelt – and longest – prayers were for Dan O'Toole. When she had first set eyes on him in that ward she had immediately realised that he was a person in great need. He was a case nobody else in the world would try to help – condemnation and avoidance would be his fate. She had there and then vowed herself to the task of helping him, no matter what the cost. It was with some trepidation that she now faced the prospect of turning up at Heeney's place on the Friday; she asked fervently that she would be helped when the time came. The falling rain and the sounds of the storm were a cruel accompaniment to her heart's sorrow. She would not have cared if an almighty deluge had swept away herself, the whole town and church.

Eventually she made her way home through a real-life 'Vale of Tears', almost welcoming the drenching which soaked her through ; rainwater vied with her tears for predominance as she groped her way through the streets. When she got inside her front door her mother fussed over her and told her she would catch her death. She was rubbed down and dried, given boiling hot tea and soup and the upshot of it was she recovered her good humour, smiled at old mum and began to chat away somewhat impetuously. The elderly lady indeed listened to her only daughter. She was very tolerant of the girl's ways and was not surprised to hear of the nocturnal wanderings through the streets and churches. However, certain things worried her. Her daughter's continued spinsterdom and apparent lack of interest in suitable men was one. It had been years since Lar Kenny, a very presentable young man who worked in the same office as Jane, called on her and took her out for the evening; and she had often encouraged her daughter to have him back again. But it seemed that Jane had shown no further interest in any romance after that.

Deciding that Nick should be back by now with the poteen Dan O'Toole left his room and walked out into the street with barely a thought for the unruly conditions around him. This indifference to the elements was innate in him, reflecting perhaps the stamina formed in its denizens by the wild Wicklow countryside. He wore his old, battered raincoat and the only reason for sadness was the absence of his hat; he resigned his upper levels to getting a good drenching. An hour later he arrived at Heeney's door where his loud banging brought out the alarmed Mrs Lee.

"Good heavens – that anybody should be out on a night like this," were her anxious words as she stood aside to let in the man she knew only as Mr Heeney's friend.

"It is surely a lovely, wet, windy night," said O'Toole happily.

When Nick did not answer to the knocking on his door Dan opened it, wondering what could have happened to his friend. He stared around him and eventually he was able to make out Heeney's shape on the bed. The room was very cold and there was a great wetness about the place. He saw the poteen and settled down to sip some of it.

He felt an extremity of gratitude towards Nick; after a taste he felt even more grateful for it was marvellous, much stronger than any previous batch. Its effect on Dan was not the same as it had been on Nick; it did not cause a sudden confusion but, instead, a great calmness of mind. His spirit became clear and he felt grand. He was very relaxed as he sat there watching Nick asleep.

When Heeney slowly showed some signs of life, Dan began to regale him with the story of events that morning at the university.

* * *

As Nick Heeney was travelling from the west that day, Dan O'Toole was at the university where once again he had attended Mr Argod's lecture. O'Toole felt smart in his new suit and he had taken great care before he set out to polish his shoes (as he had seen Roche do) and brush his unkempt hair. He looked cleaner and smarter than he had ever done in his whole life.

From the humble quietude of everyone in the theatre at the entrance of the philosopher it was obvious that Mr Argod was respected, if not loved, by one and all. Dan sat up close so as to be able to hear every word.

Argod spoke with fire in his voice and Dan was taken aback by the fierce intensity of his gaze. He delved into a vast arsenal of facts about mankind. He theorized on topics such as the likely future of what he called 'homo sapiens', and on the possibilities of immortality. His teaching had a profound effect on everybody listening. Many of these were the probable or potential leaders of society and it could be questioned as to the wisdom of allowing a situation where a person could have such great power over so many easily-influenced young people. He gave impromptu recitations of passages from literature. He went on about people who were great prophets, who had been neglected and forgotten by most people but whose time would soon come. Names that they never knew even existed resounded in their ears. There was, he said, a possibility that the secret of everlasting life, the extension of existence into an indefinite future for every man and woman, was going to be discovered and 'perhaps not a hundred miles from here'. This was called the 'elixir' of life. It had been sought in every age and searched for throughout the world by men greater than themselves. Who were they to be sceptical of visionaries who had built civilizations up from nothing and laid claim to half the world? The span of man's existence had been considerably lengthened, for instance, in the valleys of Soviet Georgia and also in the Andes in South America. What was the common feature in the life of the folk there? What was it that enabled them to extend life for one, two or three hundred years? It had been discovered that there were distinctive aspects to their diets. Local, particularised ingredients were put into their food and beverages. Impressive too was the clean air and the healthy, sheltering mountains around them. How ridiculous was the Russian claim that the longevity of their subjects was due to Leninism, for these old people were elderly, white-haired sages before Lenin was even born.

"One day I would like to visit such a place," he said with great emotion.

They were all impressed with this revelation. Nobody in that hall had ever considered before this morning the possibility that there were places where life went on in a manner quite different to that of their own, and where people might live and die, not en masse and systematically but according to their own rules and habits. Listening to Mr Argod they realised that the world was certainly not exactly what they had been led to believe it was. The prophet of Failure or Pessimism, he said, was the only kind of prophet he did not like. He told them about the personal vices of famous men in history. Their opinions were affected by their prejudices and fantasies, he said. Human history had often been in the hands of people who should never have been allowed to hold posts of even minor importance. But that, he said, is how the world is run.

Dan listened and wondered.

Suddenly he was back to years before, when he had been wandering around Naas and had found himself standing alone on the Dublin Road, his tooth aching. Then too, a dim recollection had come to him, of his old mother sitting quietly one evening beside the dying fire. As he sat there drinking a portion of goat's milk she had suddenly spoken to him in Gaelic, these surprising words:

"Seek the elixir of life."

He leaned back now, greatly preoccupied in his mind. The person next to him stared intently at him – there was a mysterious and far-away expression on Dan's face.

Was this elixir of life the object of his searchings ever since he left home? Was it true now, as Argod said, that it was not to be found in books, or in the city, but elsewhere? And what of his friends, Dunne, O'Reilly and the others – were they all on the wrong track? Who were the false prophets? Dan, standing out in Roche's previously unworn suit, gave a loud sigh of perplexity, again distracting everyone around him.

Timothy Roche, sitting at the back of the lecture theatre, was amazed to see his room-fellow at the lecture again. He was even more surprised to see what O'Toole was wearing. His first reaction was one of outrage and he wanted to go down to him there and then. His Cork better-sense told him otherwise. He turned to his companion and said in a quiet voice:

"What is one old suit to me anyway? He hasn't done me the least bit of harm at all, though you may be sure he thinks he has. I will get my own back. Us Roches were never ones to take a slight sitting down; he will see that. I'll bide my time and strike when the iron's hot. You see life is a complicated business and you need to keep your wits about you. The wise man knows when to gather in the harvest. That is my philosophy, and I learnt it well long before I ever came to this place."

His voice became a conspiratory whisper:

"O'Toole stealing my suit, dastardly though the act is, is really a stroke of luck. I have something over him now; I have a power that I will use soon. He and his cronies are on to something, I know it. Whatever it is they have up their sleeves I'll find out. Then they will be wise to the fact that they have another partner."

"Ha," laughed his companion under his breath, "you are streets ahead of them, Timmy."

Timothy wore his cleverness with little or no strain, and there was cool abstractness rather than triumphant gloating on his face.

At this point he interrupted the lecture. There was surprise and shock on everybody's face as they all turned to look at this ill-mannered, brazen individual. Dan O'Toole looked too, and was very surprised to see Roche there. They strained their ears to hear the argument that ensued between Argod and this 'student'. The talk was very difficult to follow, so little of it did they understand.

There was a man, said Roche, a Mr Archibald, whom he wondered if Mr Argod knew.

"He is a gentleman," Roche continued, "who is the leader of a group of surreptitious people in this city who are up to no good. He is a man of the subversive type, sympathetic to violence and instigations and with no respect for the legal and decent customs of the country. He hides his real identity behind a cloak of respectability. Society at-large does not know of his real intentions. Around him are unscrupulous people like himself, only too willing to listen to his machinations and to help him carry out his insidious deeds. If he is allowed to continue his underhand activities, undermining the foundations of society, we will be a very sorry community at the heel of the hunt."

"Who is this Mr Archibald?," shouted Mr Argod angrily, "I do not know him."

"You do not know him," replied Roche civilly with no trace of emotion in his voice, "and that is his secret. His very strength lies in his disguise. Yet he is a man who lives and works and plays in the midst of us. That is how he sets about his deceiving. You do not know him, Mr Argod, but you can be sure that he is known to at least one person. And if that person has his way pretty soon Mr Archibald will be known to one and all, and to the authorities as well."

This was not the end of it; it was evident that Roche was very much affected by the sayings of this Mr Archibald. As a consequence he appeared to have lost faith in the natural ordering of cause and effect – he was worried about the unpredictability of happenings in the world. It was up to Mr Argod and his likes, he said, people who were in responsible positions, to speak out against Archibald and expose his falsehood.

There was great annoyance in the hall at Roche's continued interruption and Mr Argod himself was visibly angry. He eventually resumed speaking, but his voice was now without much of its previous confidence. A tenseness overcame him, causing him to tremble and leaving as its testament beads of perspiration on his brow.

Michael Argod was never more glad to be finished with a lecture as he was that day. You could almost see the relief on his face as he walked stiffly from the hall. In the staff lounge he went straight to the cabinet case and took out a glass and a bottle of sherry. The sweet taste of the drink calmed the man, and even gave him a feeling of momentary well-being. Slithered down in a chair, he took deep breaths of air to relax, and his pronounced silence gave his colleagues cause to wonder quietly to themselves. Profound, witty and learned comments were running around in their minds as they watched him. As he sat there Michael remembered that last night during the performance of the opera at Rathgar he had been overcome by the same nervousness and feeling of despair. He now began to worry about the state of his health, and it was not his physical health that he was worried about either.

* * *

"That Roche is a demon," said Dan who was addressing the still-prostrate form of Heeney on the bed;

"he did his very best to insult Mr Argod, who is a gentleman. Everybody could see how upset Mr Argod was today at the end of his lecture. He said some terrible things about Trevor – and us too – right there in front of everybody."

Dan shook his two clenched fists in the air; in the dark they were the hammers of blind justice.

"I will wring his neck," he shouted loudly.

Nick straightened himself up on the bed and muttered about the state of his head. He asked Dan to pass him over 'a little sup'.

Dan slowly recovered his composure and handed Nick a glass.

"This stuff is for the Guinness Book of Records," said O'Toole jokingly;

"well, getting back with the poteen is good news, Nick. It's enough to make the devil forget his troubles. Well done. Life wouldn't be the same without it. Tonight now, sitting here with this, I couldn't care less about anything. It's good, honest-to-God stuff. Do you remember the time when it was only the whiskey we had to drink, and not a penny between us to buy it with? Those were hard times; then you said there was a better drink that could be had for nothing! I thought you were gone off your head that time, Nick. Honestly, I thought you were mad with the hunger and the thirst, that's the truth, but I didn't say anything. And then you came back from Galway with it and I saw it was poteen; sure wasn't I brought up on it? I didn't think it was to be got anywhere, for hadn't I asked in every shop and pub in Dublin for it? I never knew it was called 'poteen', or that the gardai had declared war against it. We called it Uisce Beatha, and it is sold fine and legal where I come from."

He drank again from the glass – with each sip he felt his spirit expand. There came an enlargement to his mind which was new to him. He was able to look at higher, more distant and more inspiring horizons. He was uplifted by this new freedom, though he also felt a bit dizzy.

"I'm telling you, getting to know the ways of Dublin is hard work. The place takes some getting used to at first. They said it was the Danes who invented the city and I can believe it. Only those foreign people could have made it so complicated.

There is no doubt that they put up some fine buildings though. There are some magnificent places around alright and I never get tired of looking at the buildings of Dublin. And the parks too are a joy to take a walk or rest in. Do you remember I was always finding myself in out-of-the-way places and complicated alleyways and not knowing from Adam where I was? It was no joke and I don't think the guards thought so either. They were always telling me they were going to 'ship me back'. I was afraid of the guards in those days, Nick. Anyway, I am probably a wiser man now."

He looked down at his friend, who now sat silently drinking.

"There was an awful fuss at the university after the lecture. Trouble seems to follow me around, like a curse. When Mr Argod had finished I went to the Registrar's. There was this big sign on the door that said 'Office of the Registrar' – it looked so foreboding I felt as if I was going to my doom. And the woman in there was another of those snobs who seem to be everywhere in Dublin. I could see at once that she didn't like the look of me. 'Get out', she shouted, 'do you have a Registration certificate? Where's your birth certificate, you people don't bother with them, do you? I'll call the guards. . .'; she was carrying on like anything."

Dan paused for a moment and then said in a resigned, philosophical tone;

"You know the trouble I went to , to try and get one of those certificates, with no luck. I don't know how she knew about the birth certificate, Nick."

It is not difficult for the unChristian type people who abound in offices to see at once the particular vulnerability of individuals such as Dan, and to vilify the unfortunates for it. It is a condemnation imposed – not so much by society as a whole as by the individuals who compose it – on those people who are unfortunate enough to be different from the rest of us, or to be unregistered.

"In came these fellows in queer white uniforms and they all started to bundle me out – that snob had a big smirk on her face. There was a whole army of these fellows and they did their best to make a prisoner of me, and to hold me so as I couldn't move. I blew me top, Nick. I told them what I thought of the place, and of the officials. They were upset too by what I said, for they tried to shut me up, sticking their hands in me gob. I let them have it, Nick, good and proper. I told them what I thought of them and their university. I forced them to let go of me; there wasn't one of them ready to take me on after that. I was escorted to a place outside the university gate, and they could only boast that if ever I showed my face in there again they'd lock me up."

"Lock me up, is it!," I roared at them, "I'd be better off in jail or the asylum than in that pigsty of a university. Ye're a lot of madmen!"

Nick Heeney was somewhat surprised at Dan's vehemence.

"That old curse is still on me, Nick. But I am a wiser man after today. Have you heard of the elixir of life? I know where it is not to be found. I am not going to waste my time with the people of this city any longer. I'm going to go out and discover it for myself. Do ye hear me Nick? Are you going to come with me?"

There was no immediate answer from Heeney.

"Ah well," said Dan, "at least I feel a stronger man now with the poteen, praise be. Do ye remember that doctor telling me, when I was low, that my days were nearly up? And he with a happy smile on his face? You are fit for the grave, he says, rest your poor bones and prepare yourself. Well, I feel fit enough to take on the devil himself now. It's a bit of a miracle that I'm still alive, all right. Do you think Good Fortune is watching over me, Nick?"

He paused in his talk and expanded his chest in a feeling of well-being, grimacing so that his face showed a mixture of both pleasure and pain. His raw face glowed in the dark and his grey eyes were alight.

"Yes, I am a wiser man after hearing Mr Argod. That is a man and a half. Did you know, Nick, that Mr Argod and Trevor are very alike? You would be amazed at the likeness between the two of them."

Nick Heeney, not taking the poteen as smoothly as Dan and wondering whether to take the next sip or not, did not reply. He was indeed secretly surprised at the events of Dan's day, though he could not adequately marshall his thoughts or feelings to express this fact. At the back of his mind, unacknowledged and as yet unspoken, was the belief that Dan was on the right track in giving up his fruitless pursuit of books and learning. Such things in any case Nick did not understand, they never came within the orbit of his interest or comprehension.

"Do you have e'er a bit of old food in the place, Nick? I'm starving," Dan suddenly asked in an earnest voice.

There was nothing in the 'food cupboard', Nick having already demolished his mother's 'week's supply' of food.

"I will have to try and find some bread in the morning, then," said O'Toole.

They drank on until the darkness waned. At last there appeared a faint light, growing ever more glaring to nurse the two drinkers into the reality of a new day. It was a day that to them was already quite old in its tiredness and greyness. At dawn O'Toole walked out of the Heeney abode with a slight stagger, under the hidden and speculative gaze of Mrs Lee. The early morning street was in a grimy condition after the rain, but as is so often the case in the aftermath of storms, the sky was clear and was without much of its customary cloud cover. It was even possible to see the glow of the rising sun in the distance. A clergyman cheerily said Goodmorning to Dan as he passed by, but the latter, busy getting adjusted to the light, neither saw the man nor replied to his greeting.

Chapter Five

In Bell's Fred Dunne was talking away to O'Reilly and Heeney about the episode on Saturday of Dan down in the town when Mick Bell, the big son of Andy, more or less flowed in through the door. He stopped with them a while and they listened interestedly to the fresh blood of his talk.

"Me and Sean went to the dance in the Four P's on Saturday night. The bouncers were there in strength and they blocked the doors when they saw us coming, not letting anybody in. There must have been a thousand of us outside wanting to get in – and more of the lads were turning up every minute. Sean was in an old woman's get-up and I had this huge red towel rolled up on the top of me head, like an Arab or Turk or what! It was a miracle the building didn't collapse, with all of us pressed up against it and shoving away, banging on the doors and screaming like maniacs. The bloody bouncers had to call for reinforcements and they armed themselves with clubs and sticks. We were all shouting

'Let's in Dick' and 'C'mon Moses, give up' – we were fighting like mad but tonight I'd never seen 'em more determined. It was a real riot, and people were getting injured and fainting by the score with ambulances coming and going all the time. It was going to be the best dance for many a year! The shouting was fierce and those bastards of bouncers were enjoying themselves altogether, punching everyone and cracking with the sticks left, right and centre. Not one of us could get past them – they wouldn't give up this time!

That was a fierce crowd we were but it was good-humoured punching and kicking until suddenly one poor skinny guy who had made his way to the front was grabbed by Moses and Dick. They beat him unconscious and flung him right back over our heads. The mood changed after that. Now there was a real bad feeling – and we were boiling for it! We started to heave up really hard against them with me and Sean at the front taking the brunt of it and giving it to them. Moses was pulling my head and kicking me in the stomach, until I lost my temper. I grabbed his arm and bloody well yanked it off! Sean was kicking Dick's head in and you should hear him jeering! I looked behind me once or twice and it was real great sport – everybody was mad. There were people on the pavement being trodden into pulp. The rest of the bouncers were using everything they had – sticks, boots, metal bars, the lot, but it was not enough. . . . Well the doors gave way and we poured in, shouting like it was a thousand maniacs escaping. We were in and the sight in that dancehall would have made you laugh! Everybody was dressed up for the Rag Ball and they were whooping it up like billy-o. I was sure glad we got in.

Sean and me parted and a little later I seen him with two mots so we were fixed up. The one I had danced close as anything and she was real impressed when I told her of what

I did to Moses. It was a laugh. The best night for a long time! Them students put on the best dances in town. Do you know who was taking in the money there, that fellow who does come in here sometimes, the Corkman? The band was terrific with the Hucklebuck and by the hokey, we danced till we were sick and blue. Anyway, we took the two ones home and finished off the night grand."

Fred Dunne laughed and said that it must have been a lively evening. It was really good that they had got in but, he said, one should always be careful not to get into trouble with the Law, since any entanglement with that institution was never worth the cost. It was true, he said, that he had found in his experience in the force that too much time was spent on needless assignments to counter harmless devilment instead of investigating the more important and 'respectable' crimes. He would even go so far as to say that hooliganism as such was not a crime but was of beneficence to mankind, for it released the oppressed spirit and even increased the numbers of gardai who had to be employed. However, even though his sympathy more frequently lay with the perpetrators of crime than with the perpetrated-against, his feelings for the underdog were too often by-passed by the sight of the accused getting more than they bargained for in the courts.

"It used to hurt me to arrest people, more often than not. The fact is, I am glad to be out of that line of business now," was the summation of his discourse.

They listened with respect to Dunne's words. As a former active policeman some might have thought that he had not lost all of his previous 'bad habits' – however they had all been impressed by the worthy tolerance Dunne had shown to the wrong-doings going on all around him. Indeed his independence of mind and extensive human sympathies had won for him the trust and admiration of everybody.

"I am half-expecting Trevor Archibald to walk in," said Fred a while later;

"it is good fun listening to him. Did you ever see a man so serious? I do wonder if he is a spoilt priest."

"He says he is descended from royalty. He told me he is in direct line of succession to the English throne. That's what he said. I am doing a portrait of him," said Patrick.

"Did he now, are you now?," said Fred.

"The way he does go on about the wife, do you know what I think?," put in big Mick Bell, "I think he is a murderer. It's my opinion that he did in the wife and nobody knew or guessed a thing. And he talks about her now because he feels guilty about it all. That is what I think."

"He is a gentleman," said Patrick loudly; "he has encouraged me with my painting. He has ideals."

"I often wonder why he comes in here," said Fred, "as it's buckets away from where his type usually reside. And the look in his eye would tell you he is a card. That phony Dublin accent of his is another thing. You can see that civility is bred in him though. Look at the way he dresses, like one of the pauperised gentry. He is not like the rest of us, that is for sure."

Mick Bell stood up and said he was going out for the night 'to see his bird'. He warned them all not to drink too much as then they might not be able to get up and go to work in the morning.

When he had gone they ordered another round of drinks and in the meantime they had a short sip each of Heeney's brew, ensuring that it was done below board and without attracting the attention of anyone.

"Do you not think there is something weird about Archibald though?," Fred asked the artist; "he puzzles me that man."

O'Reilly thought about this for a time. He mused in his customary manner, with his arms folded and outstretched fingers over his mouth.

"Well there is no doubt about it. I find his face fascinating. As a painter I have a good eye and there is something unorthodox about him. There is a mystery there."

"Mystery? What mystery? Don't keep us in suspense," said Dunne.

"I can't really say as yet. I am hoping that my portrait of him will throw some light on the subject. But that will only be the case if it is a successful painting and I don't know if I am capable of a real work of art." "That is true enough, I suppose," said Fred, doubtfully.

"Talking about seeing strange things," Patrick went on, "do you know that story about the Plague in the Bible? Well, I have heard how it was a . . . green mist – the 'green plague'; they were terrified of it. It killed them all off, sneaking around the streets in the middle of the night, crawling under their doors and suffocating the life out of people. The greenness of Ireland is legendary and I have discovered that it is more than just a matter of natural colour. I have discovered a strange spiritual presence in it. Have you ever seen the green mist? It's hard to pin it down – it's a transient thing. It's as if it's trying to slip by unnoticed, but it's still there all right and it's very hard to see with the naked, ordinary eye. Drifting up the Liffey at evening time when people are having their suppers or down side streets in the early morning I've seen it. I am studying it very carefully now. It is becoming more active, perhaps malevolent, and our bad history may have been caused by it. I have on a number of occasions chased it and it ran away from me every time. Another time it went right down Grafton Street, over the quays and into the river where I couldn't follow, just as I had caught it up."

As regards the presence of a mysterious – and mystical – green mist in real life the rest of the company there present were sceptical. Perhaps if Dan had been there he would have listened with more credence, even open-mouthed wonder, to O'Reilly's tale, though it must be stated that he too was considered a rather gullible individual at times, another result no doubt of the neglectful education he had received in early life.

"How much did you have of Heeney's concoction, Pat?", asked Fred laughingly.

But Pat did not take the rubbing kindly and he swore rudely at Fred.

"I wasn't criticising you, Pat," Dunne assured him, "it's just that what you were saying sounded a bit far-fetched and as a policeman of sorts I am trained to be sceptical of unusual stories. Nevertheless, I will admit that we are all cretins as regards these matters you are talking about. Who knows the mind of an artist? Tell us – do you plan any other new works?"

When Patrick spoke now it was with barely suppressed strength of feeling, a shaking voice and shining, staring eyes. He spoke of a series of wall murals that would be done out in what artists call a cycle. There will be four gigantic paintings in all, so huge that it will take people many days and weeks to look them over. The prevailing energy of each will be the very same green 'life force' – the green mist. They would illustrate the story of the Irish throughout the ages.

"When this has been sketched, I will transfer them on to the main walls of a public building in the centre of the city that is frequented daily by natives and visitors alike. This will be done at an hour when the authorities are least likely to hinder me and when it has been accomplished perhaps, they too, will gladly accept them for their artistic value and not remove them."

Patrick had to pause and catch his breath, so quickly and enthusiastically had he been speaking. In this pause Fred ventured to say that his schemes were very ambitious. He was not sure as to the extent of O'Reilly's seriousness; he looked at the youthful artist for signs of hilarity but saw instead the earnest if unsteady glint of two serious red eyes. It must be the poteen, thought Fred. Even if he had learnt that no man is incapable of a criminal act, vandalism of a deliberate nature was not something he would immediately associate with O'Reilly. If he were serious about this project, then he had underestimated the lad.

Trevor walked in the door and he was welcomed with loud greetings and shouts.

"Have you some poteen?," he asked quietly and was told that indeed they had. As soon as he had his coat and scarf off and was seated, he tried the taste of it and was delighted.

★ ★ ★

There was great joviality going on inside Bell's when Dan O'Toole came through the door, out of breath and exhausted. With neither a word of hello or by your wish he sank down on a seat. When they saw him they all worried that the fellow was sick.

"Give him a bit of that stuff," said Dunne, "and he will be all right again."

Nick Heeney shoved a vial of poteen in the direction of Dan.

"Leave the man alone to sleep," said an alarmed O'Reilly, for Dan was only half conscious.

The poor fellow indeed was hardly aware of anything and they almost had to force-feed it to him.

"For crying out loud don't make him sick," said Patrick.

"He will be more than all right in a while now," laughed Fred who ensured a liberal flow of poteen down O'Toole's throat.

They heard it gurgling away in his insides, making quite a racket. Within a short space of time a red colour came on his face and the life came back to his eyes. They were greatly relieved to hear Dan speak, if only in a rough, aggrieved manner.

"I wish they would clean that river up. There is a foul smell coming from it, and a dirty green fog. It took all my strength just to get past it. I very nearly didn't make it here," he said loudly.

"There is no denying it's like a sewer," agreed Fred.

"The poor man's Venice," said O'Reilly adding; "you too saw the green mist."

"I am going away soon. I am leaving this city," said Dan.

They were all surprised to hear this and a mystified Fred Dunne asked:

"Where would you go?"

Dan did not appear to hear this question, for his face was still screwed up with the unpleasant remembrance of a miserable day, some of it spent vying with the grey and white-feathered creatures for scraps of bread, to the not-inconsiderable and even understandable disgust of everybody who saw them there in the 'once proud' Green.

"I know what is needed," said Patrick, codding him, "you should get married. That's what! It's a wife you want and I know where there is one waiting for you!"

Patrick's face enlarged into a wide grin and a flush came over him. His eyes glinted with somewhat inappropriate, lewd thoughts and his voice quavered half in nervousness (one had to be careful when joking with O'Toole) and half in mirth:

"Have you ever heard of the beautiful Miss Jane Wood? She is really very beautiful. She's hot too you know. She was asking for you. You should soon get to see her. Don't let her go now, grab the chance, isn't that right lads?"

Fred Dunne and the others nodded their heads up and down rapidly in enthusiastic agreement, their lips drawn back in relish.

"From what Patrick says she is very keen," Trevor stated in an unfortunately patronising tone.

"That woman," said Dan O'Toole, "has been annoying me for a long time. She is a right hound and every time I see her coming I hide myself very carefully in case she sees me and makes a go for me. She is impossible to get away from once she grabs you. She is another good reason I want to get out of this city. If I was ever to get married, that would be the last woman on earth I would marry. In any case, a wife to me is forbidden. I would not even try to wish for one. For what do I have to keep a woman with, except my bare hands and poor health? She would be gone far from me before the darkness of evening had fallen. Nor would I wish such a harsh fate on any woman."

Dunne was the first in to console him:

"Ah, you are too modest O'Toole. Wake up man and see yourself for what you are. A fine fellow, and you will soon have a degree into the bargain, God willing."

"She'll be coming on Friday night," O'Reilly said, "to Nick's for the party."

"Things are happening now," said Fred excitedly, rubbing his hands together and preparing himself for another sip of the good stuff.

"I think there should be some music for the occasion and I'm thinking the fiddler himself is our man. What do you say?"

"That is just what we need to make it real lively," agreed Patrick waving his hand.

Dan drank a little more of the illegal brew and he cheered up with the rest of them. He did indeed relish the prospect of a drink and a music session and he said these words:

"If the fiddler comes I will dance a jig."

This statement caused loud laughter in the others and the whole pub turned to look.

"In which case," laughed Fred, "you can forget about the university and join up with the National Ballet instead!"

At moments like these it was hard to distinguish the fine line between jolly good-natured fun and a snide, underhand mocking of Dan. He however ignored their teasing and drank a little more until there was the sudden confusion of moving chairs and shuffling feet.

"Look what we have for you here," said Fred, and the four of them were standing up and looking down at him. Fred was holding his hands behind his back.

"Begob Dan, you are a bare man without the hat. You are like a new-born babe in the woods, and you will catch your death of cold. From the boys here, and Andy Bell over there too, a brand new hat."

He ceremoniously and with great satisfaction placed the new hat on Dan's head. It seemed to be a little too big, almost reaching down to his eyebrows. All around there were shouts of congratulation. A confused Dan O'Toole stood up, gradually bringing out a weak smile. He spoke a few words.

"I don't know what to say. . . . A new hat. . ., this is the best thing that has ever happened to me."

He was handed a glass of porter and encouraged to be the first to drink to the health of the new hat; then they all joined him in solemn gulping and celebration.

Meanwhile Andy Bell had been wondering to himself. He had not failed to notice the short and sweet appearances of the milk-water substance, being handled by them as if it were a potent and precious medicine. He wondered. Was it possible that they were all suffering from an illness and needed to partake of the same medicine? That did not strike him as a likely explanation. It was Heeney who had it, the

Galway man, where the stuff he was beginning to think it was came from. Andy felt a tug in his chest. What would the consequences be if all his patrons started going on that stuff? A shock and hurt came over him to think that his very best customers, whom he had always tried to please and gone out of his way to make feel at home, could be doing that on the sly, or even up to his face almost.

* * *

Grey-coated and cap-peaked Fred Dunne slid on to the moving bus like a strong, if harmless gust of wind. The vehicle contained the late-hour homegoers and Fred sat near the door where he could see everybody getting on and getting off. It was not that he was watching for anyone he knew or was even intent on spotting criminal types, but old habits die hard and amongst the post-midnight folk there are usually some strange characters who are worth watching just for the sake of it. Talkative eccentrics, gruff old philosophers, giggling girls going on about their sweethearts, furtive types either heading for or coming from places they wouldn't like the rest of the world to know about, the contented and the discontented, all can provide interest for the speculative eye.

The beverage taken in Bell's had raised Dunne's spirits to a high level, causing in him an unusually heightened, if temporary, zest for life. The thunderous machine sped on and he obtained thrills of pleasure as it swerved round sharp corners or accelerated quickly so that he had to cling on for life's worth. He wanted to cheer and egg on the driver to even more daredevil acts and he had great difficulty in restraining himself. He saw the lights go flashing by and he tried to steady his jogging thoughts. At one moment he felt he was on a spaceship rocketing out into space; the next moment he was helplessly falling through space with a backwards momentum. Without realising it he had lost control of himself. It was a ranting and raving Dunne that the other passengers narrowly saved from certain death under the wheels of the bus, and placed on a seat to recover.

After a little while he settled down and wondered what Mary might have laid out for dinner. He suddenly began to brood with a feeling of guilt. It was a bit hard on the wife, he thought, her having to spend so much time alone and receiving so little gratitude for all that she did for him. Indeed it was simply abuse that she would more often and more likely get for her troubles. He began to think now that he was lucky to have her as a wife. Few were the headaches she ever caused him, and when you look at the 'better-halves' of other folk you realise what an advantage that is.

It was not really the case that he had to be away from home so much. If he had happened to be an Inspector or Superintendent he might have an excuse due to pressure of work for his absences; home would then be of secondary importance to very prestigious tasks and the conscience would be clear. Even if he were just a rising executive, as it were, he would have the excuse of both work and ambition. But he was none of these things. He had not even made one arrest in all his time in the Special Branch. He was simply an ornament on the trappings of state, a useless item.

What would he have been if he hadn't joined the Force, he asked himself. As a small boy he used to imagine himself as the second-in-command custom's clerk at the famous ports of the Mediterranean or Asia. Here he would have a great time watching the ships and the fantastic cargoes and valuables being taken on and off. In those decorated shades, bereft of the responsibilities of the person-in-charge, among garnished shrubs and singing trees he adventured and was happy, grew rich, watching and resting under a bronzebright sun. So much for the dreams of boyhood – he had not even once left the shores of Erin.

Still, what was he complaining for at all? There was the comfort and simplicity of his life, which he should be grateful for. When he came to think on it, he was a lucky man. People who work hard usually shorten their lives through the strain – he was in sound condition. The boredom of long vigils was the sole content of his day's work; it was enough to be getting on with but it was not much of a strain on body or mind.

He got off the bus at his home-stop. At the corner of an ill-lit wall he casually relieved himself. Then he crossed the dead street and was glad to see the sight of his front door. When he got inside he found his wife dozing in the armchair in front of the dying embers of a fire. To his surprise he discovered that the table was not set for his meal. He found no sign of food in the kitchen either, and he returned to the living room a little distressed as well as puzzled.

"Wake up, Mary, it's me," he said in an anxious manner switching the light on.

She opened her eyes and looked at him, wordlessly.

"Where is the dinner?", he asked in a querulous tone.

She did not answer. There was a forlornness and laxity in her which seemed an inescapable part of that dimly-lit room, the late hour and a home bereft of any useful or happy activity.

"I'm starving," he said in a pleading tone.

He saw her eyes sharpen and then a current of anger coursed through her. There was a movement in her spirit that gave him cause to pause.

"Ah, don't worry about it, Mary," he said in a changed, softer voice before she could speak;

"I suppose you are just terribly tired. I have nothing to complain about, really – sure haven't you had my dinner ready without fail every evening these past fifteen years? Who can complain about that? You are not sick by any chance, are you?"

It was easier now in the better light to discern in her both virtue and attractiveness, qualities which would have made her pleasing to many men, if they were capable of knowing a good woman when they saw one. But it was only the anger in her that Fred saw now.

"There is no need to worry about me," were her first words.

"What?," said Fred, surprised by the sharpness in her.

"What I have said. Keep your concern for yourself."

"What is the matter? What has got into you – dear?"

"Don't patronise me. Sure what do you take me for? Only an amadan would put up with it forever."

He listened to these words and experienced a great perplexity.

"Is it something I have done? I will make it up to you. Come on now, tell me what it is."

"I am not going to tell you anything, my dear Fred. I will let you work it out for yourself. Let me just say that you will no longer find a meal waiting for you when you come in from your gallivanting in the middle of the night. It's even possible that you will not find me here either, and that's a fact. Oh, you probably find the change in me very puzzling, my poor unfortunate husband, but it has taken place nonetheless. I am not your dependable housekeeper any more. You will have to find a new cook, or cook your own meals. And I would not advise you to start coming home early in the future for you will find me a poor conversationalist. It's hard to teach an old dog new tricks."

Fred listened to her words without fully comprehending them. He had always found arguments, when they took place with his better-half, a waste of time if not downright boring.

He was greatly concerned now at the threat of a disturbance to his domestic routine. He spoke softly, trying to appease her:

"C'mon to bed darling. We'll talk about it later – I'm no longer hungry."

"You can go to bed by yourself, Fred Dunne. Leave me to sleep with my memories and dreams. And another thing. You needn't come up with an excuse for not being home to welcome your sister-in-law today – all the way from Africa – her first visit in fifteen years. I suppose it was work that kept you busy? Well, let me tell you, she saw you with her own eyes going into a pub with a disreputable character, when you should have been on duty."

He wondered at this fortunate 'chance' on the part of Sister Ann, or was it a case of sophisticated family espionage? Fred departed from the room sad and in a state of some bewilderment. It looked as if he had fallen out with the wife, all right. He had never imagined that would happen. It was a bolt from the blue. He had a clear perception that life would never be the same again.

Later, as he lay on the bed alone, he thought that for the first time since his wedding day she was not there beside him. It was an unusual feeling and he dreamt as soon as he closed his eyes that he was a castaway on a tiny island in the ocean with no one around to give him company or succour. On many occasions in the future he would dwell on the missing comforts and he would be heard to remark more than once that if a man had got used to a woman, it was hard to do without afterwards. A sense of unreality came to Fred, which increased the next day when she removed all her belongings from the bedroom, and her talk to him became simply a series of 'yes and noes'.

Chapter Six

They were all looking for Dan. Heeney was the first to inquire and by Friday evening everybody was asking questions. The disappearance of O'Toole was aligned to a series of big and unexplained fires in the city, and this added to the general excitement. Nick had searched all over town; he had gone to Dan's room and had visited every park and pub on both sides of the river. Even Dunne was stuck for words, at first. Surreptitious enquiries were made at Garda stations, hospitals and at the City morgue. These searches produced no results.

In the early morning light that Wednesday Dan had lain on his bed feeling happy. Nobody looking at his peaceful features would have imagined the fuss and controversy that was soon to surround his person. He felt happy and he had a new hat. The act of generosity of his friends was a revelation to him – it was a really pleasant surprise. As he lay there, he suddenly saw before him the form of Timothy Roche.

Roche must have been there for a long time; he was slouched at the table, reading a book with a cup of tea beside him and a fag in his gob. The curls on his forehead were restlessly questing and he was studiously ignoring the presence of O'Toole. Dan was immediately put off by his presence. It was seldom that they met here and even more seldom that they chatted. And when conversation would occur, Roche's talk would more often than not be scathing and disrespectful of Dan. His habit was to sit in silence until O'Toole spoke first; then Roche would pretend that he hadn't heard and would not reply but maintain a pointed silence. When at last he would condescend to speak he dropped his words scornfully at the feet of the Wicklowman, like alms to a beggar.

Now they looked at each other and there was a long silence. Eventually Dan said:

"It's a while since we met."

Roche, perusing a page of his book, breathed slowly through his teeth. It took him a long time to formulate his thoughts and answer. At last he said:

"You are looking the worse for wear. I suppose you have been spending your time in the pub."

"Yes – but not so much lately. I have also been going to the university."

"You have been going to the university, have you now? Well I didn't know that. That is a good one. And what do you wear while you're there, may I ask? Do you go dressed in rags?"

It was the same scornful Roche, but Dan was not too concerned. A craving for food had come over him making his stomach hurt badly. He got off the bed, his tattered pyjamas (a gift via Miss Wood) barely hanging on to him, and Roche turned away with exaggerated disgust. O'Toole, holding his clothing tightly in one hand, went across the room and with his free hand rummaged through the cupboard for food. All that he found was an old crust of bread, which he seized hungrily. Roche was on his feet in a flash and grabbed it from him.

"No you don't," laughed the Corkman, "that is my bread. Buy your own."

Dan felt his legs weaken and he found it difficult to talk. He was almost fainting with the hunger.

"I'm starving; I'll pay you back," he said in hollow tones.

"You poor bogman," was the reply of Timothy – that and a derisive laugh.

Dan swore a curse in Gaelic.

"Impudent too, a yokle like you. Well let me tell you my philosophy, seeing as you are interested in learning. I am against charity. It spoils the lower classes and makes them lazy. The lower classes and tinkers – that is what I am against."

"Let me have a bite of it."

"Ha ha," laughed Timothy, "you would like to eat my bread would you? Is there anything else that you might require – like my clothes for instance?"

Dan looked at him and said nothing.

"Well?," Roche insisted.

The smile was gone from his face and he glared at O'Toole.

"My clothes – that is what. Do you clean them after you use them?"

Dan was silent. He went back to lie on his bed. Roche flung the lump of bread on the floor:

"If you go near that," he warned in a loud voice, "you will be sorry."

Timothy continued to taunt him as he lay on the bed – explanations were demanded in the matter of his wearing clothing that did not belong to him; threats on the one hand and mockery on the other were delivered in malicious tones to the Wicklowman who, with a kind of stoicism, just lay on his back with his eyes closed, not apparently listening.

After a while Timothy changed his attitude and a spirit of forgiveness seemed to swell up inside him. As O'Toole lay there, seemingly in another world, the tone of Roche's voice took on a new pitch.

"Listen, O'Toole. I am not as hard as I might appear. I am even willing to forget about the suit and you can have the bread. All I want is for you to do me a little favour. Are you listening?"

Dan O'Toole remained silent.

"Oh, all right," said Timothy, impatience in his voice, "I was only having you on about the bread. It was a joke – see? Listen, will you? There is something I am interested in and if you help me out, I will make you a promise. I promise you that from now on – and this is my sincere word of honour – you can take anything you like from that cupboard. Any time at all. It won't matter to me what you take, chicken or ham or steak, stout or cake. Do you hear me?"

"What would you want for that? It's not like you to be generous."

"Here, have the bread," a cheery Timothy almost sang out as he collected the crust and handed it over to Dan.

"What I want, old pal, is something quite simple and harmless. I know you do be drinking poteen, for I have seen and heard enough. All I want is a drop of the stuff. Tell me where you get it. Is it Heeney? Ask Heeney to see me."

Dan was biting the hard crust and chewing it with considerable effort. He could not speak as his mouth was full, and he used this respite to think out an answer for Roche. In the end he issued an invitation to the Corkman.

"How would you like to come along to a bit of a hop on Friday? It will be at Heeney's place."

"That sounds a good idea. I don't suppose it would do any harm to tag along with you. As long as I get the important information – you know what I mean?"

The crust was extremely stale and proving difficult to swallow. As Dan contended with the task of eating there was a look of complete unconcern on his face which irritated Roche so that he became filled with exasperation. As a Corkman, he could not understand the dreamy and impractical world which O'Toole seemed to live in much of the time. It seemed to him that mankind would be far better off for being without individuals like O'Toole. Suddenly there was an impatient shout from him:

"Go and eat that bread somewhere else. The sight of you is making me sick."

Then, his patience having been extended to the last possible measure, Roche arose and prepared to leave. When he had brushed himself down and examined himself in the mirror he departed from the room, without even so much as a parting glance or goodbye for O'Toole.

Dan put on another of Timothy's suits and went out into the mild and sweet-aired day. He headed in the direction of Pearse Street where the Registry Of Births And Deaths had its headquarters. At the canal he met Fred Dunne again. Dunne was mumbling and complaining about life in general and the wife in particular; it was rare to find him so morose. They both went to Bell's.

Much later Fred's bad mood had lifted and he and Dan enjoyed themselves. By the time O'Toole remembered where it was he should have been going, he was well-on, as they say. Finally, he dragged himself away from the company of Fred and continued with his trek to Pearse Street.

The Registry Office appeared in front of him and he halted before it, staring at its great height. He had to gather up the courage to go in. At last he found his will-power and he cautiously entered the cavernous building. There was an elderly lady behind the counter, who scrutinised him severely as he came through the door.

Her reply to his query showed unreceptivity.

"I don't understand a word you're saying. Look at the state of you. There is a reek of alcohol from you fit to kill a skunk. And you look as if you are about to collapse in my clean office. It's a disgrace to this city that there are the likes of you about."

She continued to stare critically at him; her eyes bored into him. Dan stood in silence, and indeed looked around him to see if a mysterious and obnoxious presence had attached itself to him. He might have expected to see the devil himself standing there too.

"Papers – what papers?," she was shouting at him so that Dan jumped back with fright and pushed his hat almost off his head with dismay.

He told her his name in as respectful a voice as he could muster.

"Where were you born?," she asked, speaking a little less severely now. There was something about him that made her decide to hold her tongue. A feeling of pity was aroused in her.

"I can remember the place very well, and all about it in every detail. But as to its location, that I cannot tell you. I could not find my own way back to it now, no matter how strong the urge is in me to go there. The name we called it was Bailedecoinin, but it is a name not known to the government or police officials, who have tried to discover where it is. They have talked to me and questioned me for many hours, and it was all no use."

"Do you know the name of the county that it is in?"

"No, I do not I'm afraid."

"This is the queerest story I have heard in a long while and I have heard many. I hope you don't think you are codding me now, for we are used to funny stories in here."

"It has been a hard life for me ever since I left that place. It would be a cure for some of my despair to leave here with those papers."

"You are a sad case all right," said the woman in a voice that had now lost all its previous harshness. Her sympathy for him increased. She began to realise that she might have a responsibility in this matter. Maire A. Crowley was a religious woman. Born fifty nine years previously in the town of Navan, County Meath, she had the staid virtues of that county, including an individualistic tendency to be proud and stuffy. What other people considered virtues she looked upon as faults, and there were certainly some things orthodox people considered faults which to her were virtues. She had never married and her relatives, who knew her least well, always said it was because of her 'aloofness'. She did not even take the odd drink. She was in fact a person whose circumstances in life had obscured her real personality. The boring office routine, the soul-deadening task of giving or refusing certificates, concealed truths about Maire Crowley even to herself. Behind the severe expression on her face was a reservoir of untapped gifts and extravagant ideals.

As she looked at Dan she began to see him more as an individual deserving of mercy. She began to feel that his troubles were her's. A softer look had replaced her previously stern countenance and a sudden wave of emotion came over her. Time became confused in her mind as she thought of the far-off days and their lost opportunities. Like an advancing ocean the rapidly-approaching years of age loomed up in front of her. She felt she would have to be humble in the presence of this hungry, wretched and bleary-eyed man. A memory passed in her mind of a day when, as a child, she had shared her lunch sandwiches at school with a poorer friend who did not have breakfast or lunch and who ate them hungrily, even savagely.

"Do you go to confession?," she asked him quietly.

Dan did not reply, and she went on speaking in an encouraging voice.

"You do not have to be all cleaned up or tidy for that, you know. No matter who a person is, or what he is, he can go there. Did you know that?"

"No," Dan slowly replied, "I didn't know that. I have heard some people talking about something that sounds like that, but I didn't know what they were talking about."

"You didn't know what they were talking about. . .?," repeated a puzzled Miss Crowley, "what do you mean by that?"

"I don't know."

"Have you ever confessed your sins?," she asked him, her voice rising.

"No. I do not know what sins are," replied Dan.

"That is the worst thing I have heard in my life. Do you go to church at all on Sundays?"

"I am afraid not," he answered sadly; "the religion of my place is not the same as it is here."

"What?"

"I don't think it is. There was a priest who came, but he did not give us lessons or talk like they do here. He used to help us bury the dead and some people who married came for his services, but he was always more anxious to leave than to stay and when he left he was always helpless for the poteen. He was a strange kind of priest, for he told me he had a large family and a pub in a place far away from Bailedecoinin. He told me that the people of Bailedecoinin were the most foolish people alive and that if it were not for the poteen, he would never show his face there."

"If that is so, Bailedecoinin is a terrible disgrace. It is a blight on this country. When the authorities get to hear about this, there is going to be a lot of trouble."

"The government is not known there. The people have not heard of it, and do not fear it."

He must be a bit astray in the head, thought Maire quietly to herself.

But she would persevere, and send him on his way a better man at least than he was before he came in. No matter what he had just been saying she would not fail him. Perhaps it was all a test, a test she must not fail. She was feeling increasing wonder at the change that had taken place inside her. She prepared to put Caesar aside and serve God instead of man. No matter what happened she would see to it that O'Toole got a certificate.

"I want to help you," she said, "for although you might not understand it, you have helped me. We have a problem now, though. You see there are thousands of Daniel O'Tooles in this country alone. That is the crux of the matter which faces us."

"I see," said Dan.

"Yes – and out of all those thousands of certificates, which one is your's?"

Dan thought about this for a while and then he came forward with a suggestion.

"Would it make any difference," he asked cautiously, "if you gave me one of their's?"

A look of pretended shock came over Miss Crowley's face.

"Oh! Is it joking me you are? That would be going against the law. It would be fraud. It would almost amount to a criminal act. I have never heard the likes of this before."

As she spoke she opened her eyes wide and there was a secret joviality on her face.

"I do not understand 'against the law'? What is the meaning of that?," said O'Toole.

Dan had the old, puzzled look on his face.

She realised that he did not understand. Already the law had been broken by his simply making the request; she was holding the office open past its closing time; she was putting up with the smell of alcohol; she was doing things she would never have dreamed herself capable of doing. Well, if it called for the taking of risks, then so be it.

"Will you wait a minute?", she said, "and I'll see what I can come up with."

She went back into the office while Dan stood waiting in hopeful silence. He looked around him, staring at the walls of the room.

There was a dark green colour, emitting an oppressive, threatening air into the atmosphere. The longer he looked at them, the more alive did they become. They began to move and tremble, and Dan became startled. He saw wild animals appear and move about, as though in a green pasture. To his amazement, they jumped out of the wall and by the time Miss Crowley had come back again, he was in a state of complete fright.

"By heaven you are as pale as a ghost," she said to him.

Dan was bent over the counter and breathing loudly.

"Are you ill?," she asked.

"I have just seen something that is not fit for the eyes of man. It was the Pooka and he came to me."

"The Pooka is it now? Good heavens above. Go and sit down on that chair over there and I will make you a cup of tea. And don't worry yourself anymore about the certificate, for I have got it here for you."

Dan sat down, with Miss Crowley gently helping him. She handed him a piece of paper. He looked at it and saw written the name Daniel O'Toole.

She went back inside again and soon brought him a cup of hot tea which she assured him would have him 'right' in no time at all.

"When I was inside there," she said after a while, "I made a little phone call to somebody. There are some friends of mine who I think will be able to help you. In fact I am sure that they will be able to help you. They are coming right now and they'll bring you to a nice spot where you will be able to get plenty of rest in a quiet, safe ward and have lashings of time to think about things. They are very used to dealing with people who have the problems you have. And you needn't worry about a thing, it's all taken care of. You just sit quietly there and they will be here in a minute."

A great dismay overcame Dan at her words. He stopped drinking the tea and dropped the cup on the floor. With a shout he stood up, and his eyes jumped out of his head with alarm. He waved his arms in protest.

Miss Crowley tried to reassure him, though she herself was very alarmed by Dan's behaviour. She told him not to worry and that he was to calm down and not panic. O'Toole found his voice at last and shouted in a frenzied tone:

"That is not my certificate. You will not make me take it."

He flung the paper to the floor and pushed Miss Crowley to one side. She fell against the wall, speechless and with horror on her face.

Dan fled from the room, in a half-run. Once outside, he was relieved to see the sky and air and was almost glad at the sight of the ugly, glum-faced street.

He went down by the side of Trinity College. He walked fast, his feet just keeping up with the rest of his body. He looked as though he was fleeing some great disaster, with his shoulders bent and his hands dug deep into his pockets. Round about him the air seemed to be affected by a turbulence; leaves and odd debris flew about his feet and fluttered past him. He was a strange sight, alone and quite oblivious to the critical stares of passing 'respectable' folk.

A kind of trance came over him. As often happened in moments of hardship and disadvantage, a song came from his lips, low and muffled and certainly old and Gaelic in origin. His eyes permitted a vague and misty entrance to the light's rays. It was as if he were caught in a deep emotion, or in a dream, but he was veritably empty of any thought.

He turned left and wandered through the tall columns into Trinity College. His walk became slow and he had to pause to catch his breath. Normally bereft of feeling, an emotion now filled him, like the sea come to lap against the shore. It seemed that sparkling diamond-shapes appeared like mysterious lights and glistened in the upper reaches of his mind. He looked about him; the light in the air was not as it normally is and the buildings were shining and glittering. All of Trinity was an astonishing sight, colourful and gay. He would have to find a place to rest and recover, for he felt overcome. He came to a bench and carefully let himself down on it. He lay calmly, mingling himself with the thoughts in his head, and after a while sleep came to him.

When he awoke suddenly, mind alert, he saw that it was night. A darkness, deeper than the night, seemed to have descended. There was an eerie, ghostly silence – a quietness akin to that of the tomb. He felt that he was a million miles from the world. He lay quietly for a long time, trying to get some order into his thoughts. Then he saw, far off in the distance, a dim light. It was so very far away that at first he refused even to contemplate trying to reach it. It would be a hopeless exercise to set out for it; it would surely only result in him getting further lost. Finally, after quite a long time and much deliberation, he decided that he had no choice but to head for the light. He arose shakily from the bench and set off on his journey.

To his surprise he saw the light shining brighter and coming closer; it was not so far away after all. Before he knew it he had reached it. It was shining extremely brilliantly, and he had some difficulty in recognising where he was. There was a familiar aspect about the place; gradually he was able to make out some features. It was the library of Trinity College. The brightness of the light was now so great as almost to blind him and he had to grip the wall in an effort to maintain his balance.

He stood there for a long time, motionlessly. Then he peered through the window and saw a number of people sitting staidly at desks reading books. They sat there in an air of studious concentration and seemed to be oblivious of the immense brightness around them.

* * *

They were very surprised when Timothy Roche came upon them and were quite taken aback when the Corkman announced that he had been 'invited' to the party that night. He said he was sure O'Toole would turn up. He had seen him with his own eyes on Wednesday , in good health and in good spirits, walking out of their house in Ontario Terrace with his (Roche's) best suit on; though he had to admit he too was getting a bit worried now. He wouldn't forgive himself if anything happened to O'Toole, for he looked on him almost as his own brother. He would stick closely to the company in the hope, he said, of seeing Dan soon again.

"That one is a right cod," said Fred of Roche, whispering to the others as they started to make their way to the party. They all crept upstairs to Nick's room as quietly as they could, in order to avoid disturbing Mrs Lee. But their 'quiet' progress was marred by their grunts and stumbles as they ascended the stairs, and the landlady herself watched them from behind her half-opened door. O'Reilly had met Jane Wood and had brought her along with him and Mrs Lee raised her eyebrows with extreme surprise when she saw a lady in the company.

Roche was bonhomie itself; he could hardly have been otherwise, considering there were certain members of the party not very happy with his presence, especially since they were wanting to indulge in their favourite pastime of sharing out and drinking the 'devil's brew'.

Fred Dunne made Patrick O'Reilly very angry because of his (Fred's) behaviour over Jane Wood. Patrick in fact thought he was a 'stinking domineering so-and-so' and told him this straight out. It was because he himself had gone to all the trouble of looking after Jane and bringing her there and now Fred had more or less taken over. Dunne, the mature 'man-of-the-world' was trying to put the young lady at her ease and make her feel comfortable in the midst of this rather disconcerting collection of people. He assured her that Dan would soon turn up; he was certain that O'Toole had just gone on a 'short haul' up somewhere.

Then, in a rather patronising manner, he went on to discuss his friends.

"The trouble with my friends here," he said quietly into her ear, "is that they are too fond of the gay life. They will find it hard to settle down to a solid existence. You know, there was a time when I did try to give them a little bit of advice. Sure, when I was a bit younger myself I was as bad. Yes, believe it or not. . . I learned the hard way! I sowed my wild oats, in many a pub and poker session. But now I am a wiser man for it. And I used to never let it interfere with my work. Did you know I was the best guard in South Leinster once? Now I don't think you can mention work in the presence of these lads here. I like them all, including Dan, but the trouble, when you come down to it, is the drink. Too much of it. You could say it has ruined their chances of making a success in life. They are failures. Not that I would hold that against them.

That Roche fellow there, he is another case altogether. As genial as he looks, I have a suspicion in the back of my head that he is involved in unsavoury activities in this city. Oh, they are a right bunch we have here all right, and I sometimes wonder what would be the predicament of them if they were to find themselves without my restraining influence. I think they would be a lot worse. O dear me, it's no wonder that poor Dan O'Toole takes to the drink when he's mixed up in the company of these rogues and daredevils."

There was mock-humour in his voice as he said these last words.

It was impossible to say if Jane had been impressed by Dunne or put-off by him, for she spoke very little. However she did ask Fred if Dan was among those whom he had tried to dissuade from too much drinking.

"Indeed yes, I have often had long chats with Dan, and it seems he's been drinking from a very early age. He was brought up on it, and little else. They say that he is not a healthy man, that he is marked for the grave."

"Do you think he can be helped?", she asked, her voice dropping almost to a whisper.

"I think we can pray about that," said Fred putting a hand on her shoulder and looking at her with a kind of benign, condescending smile on his face.

The stout was finished sooner than expected and so the poteen was produced, somewhat prematurely.

"Look at it, it's as pure as water. A dram of this is priceless. I did three paintings this week with it," said Patrick, his face glowing bright like a fire, as the happy Heeney silently raised a large white bottle in his hand and showed it to them.

"Good stuff," enthused Timothy Roche, adding, "though I hear the guards lately are a bit worried by it over there in the west and are clamping down on it."

"Sure aren't they always," said Patrick.

Roche turned to Heeney with a wink:

"The guards are great to sell the poteen to, eh Nick?"

Heeney replied only with increased silence.

They sat on the floor and soon they were sipping away and Jane was made content with a cup of tea. Nick Heeney took out an old pipe and filled it with a dark, heavy tobacco. He lit it with flaming paper and his face disappeared in a cloud of smoke. As the room became hazy, the Corkman looked somewhat uncomfortable in the company, turning his glass uneasily in his hand and his gaze was directed to a point that seemed to lie somewhere up on the ceiling. A heavy silence hung over the whole house.

How can one describe adequately the happiness of contented drinking? It is a pleasure to be recommended to all, especially to those who are unsettled in heart or mind. The Total Abstinence Society are people dedicated to counterbalancing excessive drinking which undeniably exists in plenty. Jane Wood herself was also a member of that Society and a strong believer in its principles. However Jane had sound common sense as one of her attributes, and she showed this in not refusing to join the company of 'roguish drinkers' and partaking in their evening of entertainment with them, albeit sticking to tea. Too much is lost in any case when Abstainers keep to themselves, as if pubs were in themselves evil places, and refuse to go in and join their friends over a lemonade or some soft drink. Drink has come between too many friendships in Ireland. All said and done, there can be no denying the pleasure of drinking poteen, even if it is not easy to describe it. The thin liquid is a fuel to the spirit, bringing each person to his true self in its own way.

Although nobody could say exactly what was going on in the mind of each one there, at the same time there was a communion of feeling that exhibited itself in an air of well-being in the room.

Roche looked at Jane and winked brightly. With a nudge of his hand he offered her a sip of the hard stuff, but she declined, smiling back.

"It's bitter medicine," agreed Fred, "it would not do you any good."

"I am not tempted. I am quite satisfied with what I have," said Jane.

Fred proceeded to give a further little talk on the evils of alcohol.

"It is really bad for the young and inexperienced. I remember my first drink. I was sick just from the taste of it. And when I first came across this stuff, I began to understand what the Total Abstinence people are there for. It can put you away for weeks, if not months. I can state quite categorically, Jane, that I rue the day I ever set my eyes on alcohol. That is the honest-to-God truth. I am as much against drink as I am against crime. But what can you do about crime? The criminal element will always be with us, and young lives will continue to be ruined by drink."

Jane listened to Dunne with some uneasiness, for the facts did not appear to tally with his words. He was enjoying his drink as much as the rest of them, and she could detect an insincerity in him. He was most likely the worst of them all; if he thought he was impressing her, he was greatly deluded. And there was another scamp there too, Patrick O'Reilly, who was certainly not to be trusted, and who kept looking at her legs, putting on the face of innocence whenever she caught him. How was she putting up with it all, sitting there defenceless under the gaze of eight questing eyes? In her opinion there was no end to the hypocrisy of men. More than once she had told herself she would be better off inside a convent. And such a prospect (eventual entry to a Religious Order) should not be written off yet.

Timothy Roche began to feel sick and his face was very pale.

"Let him be. He'll be all right in a minute. I'm not surprised," said Dunne.

They watched Timothy, who took himself off to a corner holding his head in his hands, muttering incoherently. It was apparent that he had taken only a small amount of drink, for his glass was still almost full. They waited for the attack to pass off, although they were secretly pleased by it and were not distressed to see the Corkman caught in an apoplexy. In any case, such a reaction was not unusual in those unconditioned to poteen drinking.

"It's the works," said Timothy when he had recovered himself; "but I feel like more though. It's the best I have ever tasted and I would like to offer my congratulations to ye for having obtained it. Ye have done a service to mankind. It's a credit to ye."

Roche in his life had told many tall tales and engaged in much brazen talk, but this time he had exceeded himself. He took another sip to prove his satisfaction with it. He rarely indulged in strong spirits so he was finding the fare this evening extremely heavy going. After he had taken another small sip he slyly put the poteen away and later on, when nobody noticed, he quietly substituted water for it. It was his aim to retain not only the good health of his body but also the keenness of his mind.

"Does he always go around dressed up like that," asked Jane who was quietly talking to Fred about Patrick O'Reilly.

"Oh dear, I am so used to him in those bright coloured clothes I hardly notice now. Is it any wonder they call him names in the street? He is a painter and I suppose that has something to do with it."

"I know. I visited his place a few days ago – it is a real artist's studio. I think he may be spending too much time at it, though. He is too dedicated."

"I know what you mean, alright," said Fred with an intonation of deep understanding in his voice;

"but he lets it all out of him in the pub afterwards. Now in the case of Patrick I can't say whether drink is a good or a bad thing for if he didn't drink he might be worse."

"It's a dangerous thing, this art business. I think we would be better off leaving it to foreigners, for they don't seem too concerned about saving their souls. It's a bad sign when an Irish person takes up the art business."

"There is no luck in it. O'Reilly does cause an uneasy feeling in many people."

As a boy in school it was always the same with Patrick O'Reilly. He was supposed to be a bit of an eejit. Even then his body was slightly awry, as if his head was on crooked. His bones stuck out at right angles and he often looked like a little boat caught in the swirls of floods and rapids. On the other hand he seemed unconscious of those normal obstacles in a boy's life and was always trying to do silly things. He would say the most foolish things and laugh his head off at nothing. He was laughed at of course, and given nicknames. He had a fondness for sticking paint and crayon markings over his own books and everybody else's, the walls etc.. The teachers considered him a nuisance as he would speak out in class and ask questions without being asked to; then he did not understand you when a straightforward question was put to him. He was in the habit of dropping things out of his hands, with a loud clang to the floor. Consequently in order to be free of him his teacher would send him on unimportant errands out of the classroom, which meant that he missed most of the lessons. He learnt about the world instead from the multitude of different things to be seen in and around the school grounds, in the teachers' room, in their coat pockets, bags; many times he ventured out into the street of the tiny Cavan village, where he spoke to and learned from the 'passing-through' types.

When he turned thirteen a discovery was made. It had been believed that he was not only the worst pupil in school, but the worst art pupil, for whatever he did appeared to be only scribbles and blots. He was not able to draw a straightforward picture. Nobody minded him and he was put in the far corner of the art room where he disturbed no one but himself, and was left to dabble away to his heart's content with his paint and brushes. Not even the teacher came to criticise his work. But he was happy to work alone. Indeed this so-called disciplinary measure was perhaps the salvation of Patrick O'Reilly. In his corner, he was not exposed to the philistine mentality or comments of either fellow-pupils or teacher. And great indeed was the teacher's surprise one day when a glance was taken at the desperate lad's activities and it was seen that he had produced a remarkable drawing of a naked man and woman. The standard of this work in its detail was surprising. From that time on, the authorities and everybody treated him with more circumspection, with greater respect and a certain amount of awe. He was spoken of as the most unusual and brilliant pupil ever to darken the doorway of a Cavan school, and by the end of term he was being recommended to be taken out of normal school and sent away as far as possible; to the finest Art Academy that Ireland, or even abroad, had to offer, with a testimonial from every member of staff.

It was Patrick himself who recounted these incidents now to the amused listeners. When he told them about the painting of the naked man and woman everybody burst out laughing. Even Fred Dunne could not contain himself. They rolled about on the floor, holding their sides. It must have been the poteen that caused them to collapse in laughter, in uncontrollable hysterics. Patrick himself rolled about too, kicking his legs. Timothy Roche felt a giddiness, due to the small amount of poteen taken earlier, and he was holding himself in a somewhat contorted way. However he was not as amused as the others and he watched them with a critical objectivity. For quite a long time the room was a noisy place.

Fred Dunne began to call Patrick names, insinuating that he was something of a sex-maniac.

"Shut up," cried the artist, suddenly angry, "or I'll make you."

Least affected of all was Jane Wood. When a state of normality had returned to the room, there was an expression of distaste and disapproval on her face.

"Oh don't be laughing at him, he's better than the rest of you put together. You people have no sensitivity. I am used to your sort of mentality for I have come across it often myself in my capacity as a worker for the Saint Vincent de Paul Society; no to mention also as a Total Abstainer. It's the usual thing to mock people who try to do something constructive with their lives."

"The Total Abstainers are an admirable group of people and they do a lot of good," said Fred Dunne; "they were founded by a Father Matthew who was not averse to a pint in his young days, but he decided on the greater good and gave it up. He saw what it was doing to the people. Do you know his statue?"

"Oh yes, it's in O'Connell Street," said Patrick.

"Well he founded the Temperance Movement in a fit of pique," continued Fred;

"I reckon that with a bit more success he could have changed Ireland more than any man before him or since. He had the right idea."

"I don't know," said O'Reilly slowly, "if it is possible at all to change Ireland. Trevor Archibald says they laugh at us abroad."

"At who?," asked Fred.

"At the Irish," answered Patrick.

"He says that?"

"Yes."

"How does he know?"

"He was abroad. In England at least. Maybe even farther."

"The English have always laughed at us. We should not be surprised at that," said Fred.

"It's not just in England, Fred. It's all over. Even in America the Irishman is a joke. And it makes you wonder what they do think in Russia and those other places."

"Yes, but Irishwomen are not laughed at," put in Jane Wood; "many world-famous people have had an Irish mother, and the work of our women in the hospitals and missions of the world is appreciated."

"Right, true, to the point," Fred agreed in a chirpy voice, "and the Irishman is the first to testify to the worth of the Irishwoman. After all, who was it who bore him?"

"Let me tell you all a story," said the Corkman.

"About these fighting men in a war in a far-off place. It was a particularly dirty war, eating of human flesh and death a sweet song. Needless to say there was an Englishman, an Irishman and a Jew fighting in this war. And they got on together like billy-o, never a harsh word between them at any time. They were the best of chums, taking great delight in killing and mangling the enemy. Now it happened that they were captured by the other side and recognised for the blackguards they were and sentenced to a particularly horrible form of death. This is a true story for it is the story of a man who won fame and glory in that war – my very own father. Well naturally the boys didn't like it when they heard the bad news and they began to think of a plan of escape. 'Abraham' had a pile of money hidden away and the Englishman had his cute brains, see? What about me, asks the poor Irishman. "It's too bad, Paddy; it's every man for himself now," they said.

So up with them to the general and the lad from Jerusalem offers to give him all his money and the Englishman promises to spy for him, and there the two of them are, grinning like Cheshire cats, while the Irishman has his eyes to the ground, as glum as any person could be.

"It's nice of ye to offer," says the general, "but I need neither money nor spies. However I will tell you what. Whichever of you sing for me an Irish song, I promise I will set free."

Roche paused a while in his tale. They all laughed and agreed that the Irishman would have the better of the day.

"Well didn't the Jew and the Englishman get up and sing 'God Save Ireland' and 'Mother Machree' between them and not a note was heard from Paddy. You see the first two had Irish mothers but poor old Paddy's mother wasn't Irish at all."

"I am interested," said Timothy Roche finally, "in buying some of this poteen. I have never tasted anything like it before. I can pay a decent price."

He had not addressed this request to any one particular individual, bit it was within earshot of them all. Fred Dunne gave out a hollow, ironical laugh and said that it was impossible as he had not the faintest clue as to where the liquor in front of them had come from.

"Not the slightest idea. . . , you might as well be asking me where is the Wicklow gold or where to find a million pounds. The manufacturing and transportation of poteen, as it is at present constituted, is something that I would like to see an end put to. It has given rise to too many malpractices. Do not misjudge me – I am an easy-going person usually. The trouble is, I just cannot bring myself to break the law. That would be going completely against my nature. Now, whether the production of poteen should be declared legal is another question – in my opinion it should be. And that explains why I am drinking it here tonight. I have actually accused myself of doing wrong over this, but no matter how hard I try I cannot find that it is against my conscience."

"Come on now, old boy, it must come from somewhere," said Timothy, a little too jollily.

"Ask somebody else," Fred angrily replied, muttering a silent curse to himself and reaching for his glass.

"I will tell you," said Patrick, introducing a note of jocosity into the talk; "if you promise never to let out a word about it to anyone."

"You have my word," Timothy said.

"It had better be because everything would be ruined if the authorities get an inkling. It would be goodbye to a good thing."

"You need have no fear."

"It is a complicated procedure. We have to see whose birthday it is that falls nearest to the date we want the poteen. He, or she, becomes the chosen vehicle of communication. Then the word is sent out, and this is done by a very involved process of posters and newspaper advertisements. I'll give you one example. Sometimes the poteen is referred to as the 'Communist Party'. Now this is because the party that goes by that name here is a very small and not too-important party. Therefore you can easily get away with using its name, for nobody pays any attention. Posters are put up; 'Vote for Me', 'Vote for So-and-So' and, if you check it out, the candidate's name is a fiction, but nobody checks it out. With the exception that is, of one sharp-eyed person. That is where the poteen people come in.

Anyway to cut a long story short the message is sent out. The appointee spends the next day in a public library. It doesn't even matter what library it is or where it is. It just must be a public library. At least twelve hours is spent in the same seat, without as much as leaving it once. Another message will then be received, the manner of whose arrival is different on each separate occasion. It is always given in the form of the election result with a play on the candidate's name, which makes up the name of a certain place. This place could be anywhere in Ireland or the islands. Once it was the Isle of Man.On arrival gifts or money are left at the chosen spot and lo and behold, the next morning the poteen will be there. If, however, the Communist Party candidate loses his or her deposit, you have to go back to the same spot three mornings in a row."

The Corkman became rather sullen after this and from then on gave his attentions to the lady, more or less ignoring the others. Jane, who found as the evening went on that Roche was the only one in the room still able to talk, at least in a coherent way, was quite relieved and even pleased to listen to his sober words and opinions. His voice lowered to a conspiratorial whisper.

He began making revelations about the lives and deeds of Dan and his friends – of each of them drinking contentedly away there. He regaled her with tales of debauchery in Bell's and elsewhere; of their lives of idleness; he spoke of rumours and suspicions concerning each one of them.

He told her of Patrick O'Reilly's infamous sexual aberrations. It was the talk of the town. He was blacked from numerous places. Once the guards had hauled him in and he was certain of going to jail, only it was decided not to press charges for fear of scandal. Nobody else in the city would speak to him or be seen near him, except the lot he was with now. But even O'Reilly was not the worst. There was a man whom she might soon get to see who was said to be a fugitive. It was a fact that he had killed his own wife.

Jane felt a cold chill and her heart began to beat faster.

Archibald and the fiddler were speeding on their way to the party. Speed was the thing of the moment, for Trevor seemed to have gone completely mad and was travelling at a good seventy miles an hour through the narrow streets. The poor fiddler clung tightly for protection to his tool of trade, his fiddle, as if that could save him. His name was Larry Rourke and he was a simple man. He did his best to please people, and was normally happy to play his music for anyone, at any time or place.

"He pleaded with Archibald.

"I think you knocked down a cyclist there."

"I didn't feel a bump. He fell of his own accord if anything."

"Please slow down, we are going to crash."

"I don't want to miss the fun at Heeney's. Anyway it is your own fault that we are late. Why are you always late for everything?"

"My music sessions never end on time. People like it that way. Can you let me out of the car, please?"

"Hang on man, I can go even faster than this," laughed Archibald.

With that he pressed the accelerator to the floor and at the next corner he lost control of the car. They went across the street and up on the pavement. The car did not hit the wall but continued on down the pavement and eventually came right back out on the street again.

"Lunatic! Stop the car," screamed Larry Rourke.

Trevor regained control once they were on the street and, ignoring the pleas of the fiddler, asked:

"Are there any guards following us? Have a look."

With no recourse but obedience left to him Larry glanced out the back window and reported that no pursuers were in sight.

"I wish there were," said Trevor, "we could have a right race."

"You will kill somebody," said Larry.

"Do not dramatise. It's a funny feeling you get when you lose control like that. Did you feel it?"

The fiddler was not speaking.

"Time slows down so that everything is in slow motion. You have absolutely no control over anything. It gives you a feeling of liberation. Then there is a definite intuition that life itself is under your control, the whole time, and you have no doubt that you will come out of the situation unscathed. Did you get that feeling?"

Larry Rourke continued to sulk.

"Cheer up, man, I am going slowly now. No harm done. We can't have you looking sorrowful for the hooley, can we?"

Meanwhile the guards had been alerted to the presence of a maniac driver in the city and there was a standby on the part of every squad car in Dublin. Alerts were sent to Garda stations on the outskirts of the metropolis; at Clondalkin and Rathcoole; at Kilcock and Maynooth in the west; Swords, Skerries and Balbriggan in the north; at Dunlaoghaire in the east and as far as Naas in the south. Secure road-blocks were set up. However by this time the wanted car had already arrived at Heeney's and the occupants, both of them happy now, were let in.

Chapter Seven

"What have you been doing with yourself, Trevor?", asked Fred.

"Well, the old fiddler held me up," Archibald replied.

Dunne laughed.

"Have you ever known him to be on time? Anyway it's good to see you. We've missed you these last few days; the conversation here is a bit restricted."

"I have been thinking. I am fed up with my life, too much of the ivory tower. Can I have some poteen?"

"You don't have to ask, man; it's for everybody."

The fiddler, after a quick sip of the drink, played, and Nick Heeney for one was transported into bliss.

"I don't see O'Toole around," commented Trevor; "where is he?"

"He has disappeared," said Fred.

"I thought so," said Trevor putting on a wild expression; "I thought it could be him!"

"What do you mean?," asked Fred.

"The fires that have been started these past few days. Have you heard the latest? The library at Leinster House has just gone up," said Trevor with mounting excitement in his voice; "it must be O'Toole!"

"How do you know?"

"There is a strange look in his eyes these days. The places were all his old haunts. He is a great man."

"Indeed," said Fred, "if it is true, which I suppose is a possibility, I have greatly underestimated the man."

"I too have underestimated him," said Trevor, "more power to him. He puts us all to shame."

Fred was still nonplussed and wondered about what Trevor had said.

"Ah, a pretty young lady," Trevor cried out and went across to Jane who was still being closely attended to by the clear-eyed Roche.

"So you are Dan's friend? I am very pleased to meet you," he said to her; "welcome to the party. Have you tried the new drink that is in fashion here?"

Jane was frightened by the sudden appearance of this strange man with his onslaught of words. He looked like a foreigner with his beard; it was hard to believe that Dan could have anything to do with him. She felt even more dependent on Roche and clung to him.

"I do not drink," she said.

"I see you are in good company," said Trevor. He stared at Roche, straight into his eyes; Roche blinked.

"Whom," asked Timothy in a dry voice, "do we have the pleasure of talking to?"

"A good Irishman," was the reply.

"*That* is Trevor Archibald," Timothy said quietly to Jane.

There was a knock at the door and Larry Rourke put down his fiddle and quiet came to the room. Nick Heeney went to open it. It was Mrs Lee, who stood in the doorway, anguish on her face. They heard her speak in trembling tones:

"It's bad enough to be letting in thousands of strangers off the street, and now the whole house shakes to the roar."

"Come in, Missus," Archibald shouted and he went over and hauled her into the room. To say there was astonishment on everyone's face is an understatement. The poor old lady did not know what was happening and displayed a look of helpless stoicism on her face, though her feelings were obviously those of extreme shock.

"Let us dance," he said grasping her tightly; "play the fiddle and let's get this hooley started."

Even before Larry Rourke had struck up Trevor was moving across the floor dancing a waltz with her. Fright made Mrs Lee very stiff and she gave no reply when he asked her if she wanted a drink of the 'hard stuff'. The dance was finished and Trevor sat his new-found lady friend down on the side of the bed. He obtained for her a glass of poteen.

"Drink this, it'll make you feel better," he said.

She had to be helped with the task of putting it down her throat and she took in the fiery fuel silently, closing her eyes with the effort.

It was at this point that Jane had her bad turn and she suddenly collapsed on the floor. The small, crowded room, filled with dark tobacco smoke, was not the most recuperative of places and with much effort the four men dragged her to the window. This scene was misinterpreted by Mrs Lee who believed that they were on the point of throwing Jane out the window. She found herself unable to call out or help in any way. Jane's slender body proved surprisingly cumbersome and it was only after much grunting and panting that the window was finally reached and Jane's head given the benefit of fresh air. At this point Mrs Lee was weeping, causing general consternation and alarm.

"It must be the poteen," said Trevor lightly.

"It's no laughing matter," said Roche sternly.

Timothy Roche left soon afterwards, taking with him a weakened Jane Wood who, in a somewhat demoralised state, was not able to manage a word of farewell or even a parting glance. The others waved desultorily at Roche, glad to be rid of him and to be able to devote their attention now completely to drinking. They sat quietly, drinking and listening to Trevor's talk: he spoke to them of things elevated, mysterious, of matters urgent, impending. They listened with calm spirits to his words, which they did not understand.

Indeed, they would patiently wait for these matters such as he discussed and prophesied to come to pass, as he was certain they would come to pass. Movement in the room became minimal. It was like a sea-borne boat, a currach on the Atlantic waves and breakers, as a soft sea-shanty of the type popular in the fishing villages of the west filled the room. Nobody said much, as if desiring only to ensure a steady and prosperous voyage. It was a voyage to the dawn, Heeney at the helm and the others aft, lying on the floor, with Larry Rourke on a stool, astern.

* * *

It was the death-hour across the settled city. Nothing was conscious and even the spirits of the dead did not dare to move. Neither warmth or cold, light or darkness were apparent. The rigid corners of the houses and their walls crumbled in the death-air. The streets froze in a silent, bare desertion. The only remnant of nature, the black wind of night, blew, but only as itself too fled the dread minutes becoming transformed into the icy breath of a time that hated nature and everything in it. Stars and a bit-moon withdrew to a greater distance, their detachment from the earth being their only significance and their faint light could offer nothing to this world. Pillars and poles were like policemen in this limbo, keeping watch over all that lay still. If there had been a single being alive at that hour it would have seen the city tremble and the distant hills shiver and slink away under the cover of their shadows.

A terrible anger filled Dan O'Toole. As the first light of the sun appeared on the horizon, dashing the buildings and air with a pale look, he was making his way down O'Connell Street. His suit was crumpled and his hat was completely altered in shape. The bristles of his unshaven face, his dried lips which craved moisture, his limp, staggering walk made him appear very unpleasant, a strange, unwelcome visitor to the newly-dawned day.

Angrily, he put his hand into his pocket. After some fumbling around he pulled out a smooth, hard object. It was a small bottle, transparent and empty. He had run out of 'fuel'. His feelings were of rage and there was a strong desire for vengeance in him, an angry desire that was a new emotion to him, though he was not actually conscious of a change having taken place in his thoughts. It was as if this fury had always been a natural part of his character. The empty poteen container simply encouraged his frenzy-like feelings. It was the umpteenth time he had taken it out to look at it. He put it away again and returned to ruminating on the lost certificate. He could not care less about that now. He would tell them at the university what to do with themselves and their certificates at the next opportunity. He strode through the streets with a grim look on his face, like someone who had just done, or was about to do, a drastic deed. In Harcourt Street the sight of some gardai in their uniforms and their watchful demeanour put a sudden wariness into him; he crossed to the other side of the street and proceeded onwards, keeping his eyes on the pavement until he had gone around a corner.

By the time he had reached the front door in Ontario Terrace his mood had become a bit more cheerful. He felt relief at the thought of being able to lie in his own bed at last. It had been a long time since he had previously slept out rough. His bones had become unused to it and the nights had been distinctly uncomfortable for him. To his surprise the room door was locked – and he could not open it. A feeling of frustration returned to him and he struggled with the door. The sound of a muffled voice came to his ears; he listened intently:

"Is that you, O'Toole? Hold it a minute, you blighter," said Roche loudly.

"Open the door," shouted Dan in return.

His angry voice somewhat reduced Roche's jollity.

When entrance was finally gained Dan was surprised to see Jane standing there with Timothy. She had her coat on and looked ready to leave. She stared at Dan, a look of perplexity on her face.

"There was no bus home last night and Mr Roche kindly put me up. I hope you don't mind me sleeping in your bed! We have been worrying about you these last few days – where have you been?", said Jane, a little sheepish.

"I was away on a bit of business," replied Dan."

"It's good to see that you are safe, anyway," said Jane seriously.

"It's time to go to get that bus," said Roche hurriedly and firmly and both of them left the room without any further talk.

Dan was surprised that Jane should be with a person the likes of Roche. Although he was wary of her 'pursuit' of him he nevertheless respected her character and clearly principled nature. He was so tired and sleepy that all he could feel now was simple confusion and bemusement. He felt that Roche was one of the worst characters he had ever come across and that Jane had somehow fallen for his trickery. He thought that one day he might even murder the Corkman. He removed his now dirty suit, dropping it carelessly on the floor and slumped on to the bed. He fell fast asleep almost immediately.

A little later a strange dream went through his mind. He was floating in an endless, dark space and a cold mist was everywhere. Then he found himself back on the cranky old excuse of a bed he was accustomed to share with his parents. When his limbs had become too extended for this he went on to sleep on the floor where he was never loth to take in an infirm creature to share the night with him – he had nursed many a sheep back to health in this way. As he lay there an empty yet wistful feeling went through him and there was a tightness in his breathing. A wide array of life passed before his eyes, trees and mountains, birds of the air, fish in rivers and streams and the sparkling, stringy stars and the whole sound of the noisy air; the tiny creatures and the sheep of the fields. He turned uneasily in his slumber. There was a mystified, disturbed note to his dream. When he awoke later on, he saw that he was indeed alone in the room and he had an unreal feeling, as if he was still dreaming.

★ ★ ★

In the early afternoon Trevor Archibald went with the aspiring artist, Patrick J. O'Reilly, to the latter's studio (and home). They motored there from Heeney's, having decided that then was as good a time as any to work on the portrait. O'Reilly would probably even be able to finish it that day with a little extra effort. He would have a substantial reward through the medium of a promised fifty pounds, the sum of money by which Archibald valued the prospective work, and Archibald would have his portrait, a monument no doubt to his vanity. The task of painting proceeded with great, exaggerated flourishes on the part of Patrick. This was, he said, the most important work in his whole career; he was putting everything into it. Trevor sat on the stool with great solemnity. For a time he concerned himself with giving the artist advice, chiefly on the types of features and characteristics he wanted put in. 'Heroic aspect', 'directness', 'visionary look' were the terms he used. Patrick assured him that it would be as true to life as possible; that he would put into it all the fine features that he could see in him but that in the last resort it must be what he – the painter – saw as the truth.

"Agreed. Good heavens – of course – it is to be your creation, not mine. I would not dream of interfering in the work of an artist. Do it anyway you like, man."

Had he ever seen, Patrick asked him, the self-portrait that Picasso had done? It was painted in nineteen hundred and the cost was only a few pence. Now it was one of his most valuable works. He had been influenced by Van Gogh, amongst others, at that time. It was probably worth half a million pounds right now.

"I think, said Patrick, that money might spoil me. Still, I don't think I will ever be known. Maybe success would mean the end of any true art on my part."

"You have to be simple to be true, really," said Trevor.

"It's undeniable. All the same, one must have something to live on."

Patrick stood back from the canvas and raised the brush high in the air:

"Great – fine – it's beginning to take shape. Hmm, that's interesting; you are coming out a bit like Pedro Manach."

"Pedro Manach? I have never heard of him. Who is he?," asked a puzzled Trevor.

"He was an acquaintance of Picasso. Pablo Picasso painted him back in the nineteen hundreds."

"Can I have a look?," asked the curious sitter.

"Sure – it just needs a few finishing touches, that's all."

Archibald stood up and walked slowly over to the stand. He leaned over Patrick's shoulders, staring down at himself.

"I hardly recognise the person in that painting," he slowly said; "and still I think it is me. It is a work of art you have produced there. You can be proud of it."

Patrick was pleased with his achievement and his pleasure was doubled by Trevor's expressed satisfaction.

"A title, we must give it a title," Patrick cried out.

"Just 'Trevor Archibald' will do," said Trevor Archibald.

"I will put it up in that corner to dry," said a happy Patrick, "and then we can sit down and relax and celebrate with a drink."

They sat; Patrick now on the stool and the big chair going to Archibald. There was great satisfaction all round and they contemplated the work in silence for a long time. Then they talked, on many things, past, present and future. The red glow of evening appeared in the room and it was as though there had been no day at all. Such is the contemplative mood that all activity, however hectic and productive, is quickly forgotten and only the silent, inactive moments are remembered. Now and then Patrick would glance over at the painting and sigh and breathe heavily. Trevor, too, gradually said less and less, becoming more preoccupied with the painting until eventually he was completely absorbed in it. Patrick O'Reilly certainly appeared to have produced a successful work of art.

At seven o'clock Dan came in and they were very surprised and full of questions. He had been down to Heeney's, where he had drunk some poteen and his spirits were revived.

"We couldn't, for the love of Mick, think where you had got to," said Patrick; and the story of the misfortunate certificate was related sadly by Dan, who lay stretched out on the floor. He was still in some confusion and doubt of mind. It was plain to see that there was a great weight on his spirit; his face, hollow-eyed, appeared to have aged in the last few days.

"It is bad fortune not to have it. And I fear there is worse to come. There have been bad signs."

They asked him what he meant, but he was not able to elaborate. There were signs; there was something amiss; it was just a feeling he had like he would get in the old days immediately before a calamity; it would certainly do no good, only harm, to be talking about it.

There was a feeling of gloom in the room, momentarily. A vague, ominous presence descended and filled the atmosphere. For a long time nobody spoke.

In a conscious effort to break the mysterious spell that had come over them, Archibald suggested that they go out and have a hearty meal in a good restaurant, at his expense. It would be a double celebration – of Dan's safe return and the completion of a fine painting. The two prospective guests could scarcely believe their ears, or luck, for neither could remember the last time they had a decent meal, much less one in a restaurant.

"What are these things?," asked Dan later, when they had been seated at a large table in the restaurant 'Grand Prix', the best eating-out place in that part of Dublin, as well as the most expensive.

"That is a serviette," Patrick told him, casting a side-ways smile at Trevor.

To their surprise they suddenly saw O'Toole wiping his nose with the serviette.

"It is a table napkin. You are not supposed to do that," hissed Trevor, who was shocked by Dan's table manners. He saw that people were staring at them, and especially at Dan who was blowing his nose very loudly indeed, as if it hadn't had a good clean-out for years. Patrick O'Reilly thought it was very funny and his screeches of laughter reverberated around the restaurant, startling many of the guests seated opposite. He found it hard to control his mirth, which seemed to be semi-hysterical. Dan's uncosmopolitan manners as well as Patrick's ludicrous behaviour had a different effect on Archibald, who was in the throes of a sort of seizure. His face was beetroot-red, like the angry sun on a wet dawn, and a horrified gaze was in his eyes. That was quite a different Trevor from normal.

Big meals were ordered by the three of them and the host insisted that no expense was to be spared on this occasion. There were soups, vegetables, meats galore, various desserts and glasses into which they quietly poured poteen. Dan talked a bit about that morning when he had got in and discovered Jane in the room. He said that it was a strange thing but she had slept in his bed.

"Was Roche there too?," asked Trevor.

"Yes," replied Dan.

"With her?," Archibald wanted to know.

"Yes," said Dan; "it was he who brought her in and put her in my bed. She was not there when I woke up. It could have been that I dreamt it all, but I don't think so."

"The behaviour of these Catholic women," thought Trevor quietly, keeping his thoughts a secret from the others, "never ceases to surprise me. Who would have thought that that prim and proper young lady that we saw last night would end up like that? What with all the propaganda we get from the churches and convents, it's not what we would expect to find – cohabitation at the drop of a hat! I am surprised and disappointed. My poor, dear 'immoral' Protestant sisters are more upright betimes, I do think."

He looked accusingly at Dan:

"And where did you sleep, my man?"

"I slept in my own bed," answered Dan.

They looked at him to see if he was telling the truth, but his face was as placid as ever. Perplexed and disturbed by these revelations, Trevor was stuck for words. Patrick, too, was now feeling jealous and a spirit of recrimination welled up in him.

"That Corkman is a fast operator, no doubt about it. But she must love you, after all, Dan, for it was in your bed she stayed. She is your girl and nobody else's," he said.

Trevor agreed with this.

"There you are, you see. She is your's for the taking. You may find that your path will become more rosy if you put your faith in a solid woman. She is obviously keen on you to sleep in your bed! You are a lucky man. Many is the no-hoper who has been changed by the strong hand of a good woman."

"Ah, I wish that could be so!," said Dan, "but nothing will come from my life. There is a curse over me that worsens every day."

They did not mention what was foremost on their minds – the burning down of the eminent buildings, which they even more certainly attributed to Dan now, having seen the black and despairing mood he was in. They wondered about what had happened in the days he was away – it was something he was not talking about. Nevertheless, they were there to enjoy themselves and there was no use in letting the strange, fatalistic mood of Dan spoil it.

"Let us eat up and enjoy the food, for it is rarely that we get its like," were the words of O'Reilly.

Sunday is a day of rest and that is what O'Toole and his friends made of it. Each man (including Trevor whose excuse to his wife was that he was down with 'flu') spent it in bed, a secret bottle by his side and not a care in the world to disturb him. Solid food had brought peace to their stomachs and drink removed all external stimuli from their minds. They slept and dozed and slept and rested. There was no passage of the hours; only light, darkness and various shades of light and darkness in between. The peace that reigned was a peace fortified against the external world and all its noises and concerns; its gabble of semi-intelligent sounds and its traffic of men, cars and gossip. Instead of the groping hopefulness that makes up the normal content of a person's day, they lay in an accomplished detachment that did not grope, was not hopeful and was barely conscious at all.

★ ★ ★

It was on the Monday that it happened. Out of the blue it came. One moment and they were living their lives happily and peacefully and the next – everything was upturned and their lives had changed irrevocably. It was Patrick who brought the first warning, as they were drinking peaceably in Bell's. He came rushing in the door, panting and holding his side with the pain of a cramp caused by too-fast running. He told them breathlessly that 'they' had tried to arrest Heeney, but Nick had got away.

"Who tried to arrest Heeney?", they demanded, with some annoyance in their voices,for they were all wondering if Patrick was not just having another of his 'visions.'

"The guards did – the police," he answered in a slightly hurt voice, though he was also somewhat proud at being able to deliver this bit of important intelligence.

"Are you having us on, Pat, or what is it? What would the guards be wanting with that fella at all?," asked Dunne, a man who kept cool in all situations.

"I met him on the way here. He told me what happened. They arrested him but he broke away from them. He has gone to hide. I think he's gone to your place, Dan. He didn't say where he was going but he was heading that way. He's probably hiding out there right now."

At this point Trevor impatiently stood up (he had had a severe argument with the wife earlier in order to justify , once again, his going out for a 'cure').

"You dumbclucks," he shouted at them; "isn't it clear to you what they are after? Somehow they have heard about the poteen. And how did they know to go to Heeney's? Somebody told them. And where do you think they will go next? Use your brains. They are on their way here."

"I think it would be wise for us to leave now and quietly go home our separate ways," said Fred seriously.

They gathered their coats and caps and went to the door. Big Mick Bell was standing there, barring the way.

"Hold it fellas," he said, "you are going nowhere."

They were taken aback by this unexpected confrontation.

"Move out of the way," said Archibald bravely.

"I will move when the guards come. Now you lot go back to your seats and wait. This way no harm will be done."

They looked at Andy Bell behind the bar, scarcely believing this change from the courteous treatment they normally received at Bell's. The publican was standing behind the counter, his arms folded and his face unusual for its blank expression.

"I inform you once again that you are in the way," said Archibald as commandingly as he could.

"Ha ha," laughed Mick Bell, a smile on his broad face and the hairs and muscles of his red, massive body gleamed brightly.

The others looked at one another in puzzlement. It seemed as if there was no way out, for none would have considered tackling that big and surprisingly hostile man in front of them.

"We are armed," warned Archibald, hoping to frighten Bell with a bluff

"With what – your sweet words?," laughed Bell.

"Use your gun, Fred," pleaded Dan, worried now at the prospect of more close-dealing with the gardai.

"What gun?," asked a puzzled Fred.

There was a sudden, confusing movement and commotion and the next minute Dan O'Toole had pulled the revolver out of Dunne's coat and was pointing it at Mick Bell.

"Now you will move aside," smiled Trevor Archibald with much satisfaction in his voice.

Bell dropped his arm immediately and moved quickly aside to let the foursome through. There was great astonishment on his face. Everybody else in the pub, Andy Bell and the other customers, had fallen to the floor with great haste. They did not arise again until the arrival of the gardai a few minutes later.

The fugitive party, instead of going their separate ways, decided it was safer to go to Dan's room and quietly sit it out there for a while. In the gathering dusk they hurried along the street, saying very little and looking out for the approach of any gardai. They travelled in a line, Archibald the leader, Dunne next to him, O'Reilly a few feet behind and last of all Dan O'Toole, who was finding the pace a bit hard. Trevor shouted back instructions, assuming command with the pride of a great leader. In Charlemont Street they had to huddle together in the corner of an alley as a garda patrol car went by. When the danger had safely passed they crept back out again and proceeded to silently march on. Dan was now a bit further behind and falling further back with every step. He still had Fred's revolver in his trousers pocket; if he were picked up now there would be little or no freedom for him to drink poteen for a very long time. And he did not look as if he had any energy left to even fire the gun. If he were accosted, it was very doubtful that his friends ahead of him would be keen to come back to make any rescue attempt. They were far ahead of him at this stage and it was only the pleading of Patrick O'Reilly which eventually persuaded them to slow down and wait for him to catch up.

O'Toole said that there was no need to wait for him, he was well-able to look after himself.

"I would never have thought," said Patrick, "that Mick Bell would ever takes sides against us."

"You do not know your friends," Dunne replied, "until you are in severe danger."

It seemed as though Ontario Terrace arose suddenly out of the dust ahead of them. It was the most attractive place on earth to them now, a dirty but welcome haven. The non-descript, anonymous terrace, which appeared to have its own special aura of decay and pollution, was now a place of some beauty in their eyes. They were all glad to be there, though in normal times they would hardly have wished to pay it a visit.

"It's a nice street you live in, Dan," said Fred; "I've always been meaning to visit you but I never managed the time to come round. It is certainly a welcome sight to see your house at this moment. With your permission it will be a temporary resting-place for us all."

"Let us go in there," said Dan, "for the guards are someone who know me for my looks and I have no wish to meet them. Let us hide ourselves where we can drink in peace and be a victim to no one."

The brooding figure of Nick Heeney was lying on Dan's bed and he scarcely moved at their entrance into the room. He was tranquillized in the shadow of one finished bottle of poteen.

"If we were guards, Nick, you would be in handcuffs by now," joked Fred to no one else's amusement.

When they had settled down over a brand new bottle of the illegal liquor, Trevor asked what did they think had been happening.

"Can ye make any sense out of it all?," he inquired, looking at each of them in turn.

"Well, the way I look at it," said Fred, "it's a matter of this poteen, perhaps. We all know that some diverse persons would like to get their hands on it, and they have brought the enforcers of law and order in on it all."

"Do you agree?," Trevor demanded of the others with some scorn.

Dan nodded and Patrick said he was only interested in getting a drink and forgetting about the whole affair.

"You poor creatures," shouted Archibald, "that is poppycock. Have you no idea at all? Where are your brains? Do you not see it?"

"Aw shush," said Fred, "don't get yourself all het up about it. If we keep quiet the trouble will pass and we can get back to normal."

"Well," said Trevor slowly in a grave voice, "I have some news for you that you may not take to at all. I have a surprise for you, and a shock. There it is, and not a bit of it did you know."

Still, the others did not seem too interested.

"What is that?," Patrick eventually asked with a minimum of curiosity.

"They are not after you – they are after me," Trevor informed them.

"Is that so?," Fred inquired with increased interest; "why?"

"I have been thinking as we came up the street. Somebody has been telling them about me. For a long time they have been wanting to get their hands on me."

"But why is that, Trevor, if you don't mind me asking?," inquired Fred again.

"They have been wanting to find out who I am. They are afraid of me, and most desperately wish to learn of my views. Isn't that good reason enough?"

"You are imagining all this, Trevor, if I may say so. It is the poteen they wish to know about, if anything, and about Mr Heeney's provision of it," was Fred's reasoned opinion.

"I am surprised that a man like you, Mr Dunne, experienced in the ways of the world, can come to a simpleton's conclusion. Their whole plan was to get you lot behind bars and so isolate me. They wanted to reduce the danger that, in their opinion, I am to the world. For believe me, Fred, they do hold and consider me to be a great threat."

"Have a good sip of the poteen, Trevor, and it will relax you. There is nothing much that we can do now," Fred advised him; "we can talk more about this later."

They didn't say much for the next hour or so, just sitting quietly finishing their drinks and then having some more. The darkness of the night closed in, with a slightly ominous touch of silence, and in the quiet of everyone's mind there was an occasional flirting with the disturbing thoughts of the evening's happenings. The images of those threatening shadows, of the gardai and Mick Bell himself, were like ghosts which had come to haunt them. Not even the strength of the liquor seemed able to relieve them of the memory.

"When that Roche fellow comes in here, I am going to shoot him. He is the cause of all our troubles," said Dan suddenly.

They all laughed at him.

"You are a real desperado all right," said Fred, in a mocking tone that was yet full of praise; "don't shoot the rest of us into the bargain. Do you even know how to fire that thing?"

They all laughed once again.

"Yes," said Dan, "it is simple. You just pull the trigger."

Laughter seemed to fill the room with its hilarity and Nick Heeney woke up with the noise.

"Let me show you," laughed Fred, bending over to assist Dan with the revolver; "a few things which you need to know about these dangerous implements. And, the first lesson is to learn how to point it at that which you wish to shoot and at nothing else."

There were shouts of agreement from the others. There would not be much space for loose play if there were target practice in that room.

"You would never fire that thing off at poor Roche, would you Dan?", asked Fred.

Archibald intervened.

"And why not? Roche has only been asking for it. The country would be a better place and worthwhile living in if people like him were all dead. Fire it at him, Dan, and at some more besides."

"There is no need," O'Toole said seriously, "to give me advice on the matter one way or another. I know what it is I need to do. There is retribution coming on all those who stand in the way of justice – on those who spread wrong over the land! They have quenched the light and attempt even to blot out the very existence of life and wisdom. They will no longer rule the world, for they will be driven out of their hiding places for all time!"

"Those are words after my own heart, Dan," said Trevor; "it has done me good to hear them coming from your mouth, unaided by any prompting from me. Good show! It is a sure sign that you, if nobody else, have discovered the truth, and also that you intend doing something about it."

There was a knock at the door and it was only after shouted identifications that Jane Wood was allowed entrance. Everybody was surprised to see her, but none was too concerned with the reason for her coming, they being too preoccupied with putting back poteen to bother much.

"Hello lads. I hope you don't mind me calling in like this. I only came to have a word with Dan O'Toole," she said in a nervous voice.

She was a bit put back to see them all gathered like that together in the room. She was confused and there came upon her a despairing feeling that, once again, full access to O'Toole was impossible, due to his being surrounded by this unruly bunch. It was too much for her and she felt like giving it all up.

"You have a gun in your hand, Dan," she blurted out.

"Oh indeed, have I?," replied Dan, "and a very handy weapon it is."

She looked at him, not believing either her ears or eyes.

"I am not the person you saw in the hospital at all," he said after a short pause.

He waved the gun around, causing consternation.

"You see this," he shouted, "I am going to clean up the country with it. I see the truth, which is shining clear before me. There is a false philosophy in this land, and a wickedness along with it. They who teach untruth had better watch out! He of the false identity – beware!"

"Is he putting it on?," asked Patrick quietly.

"Putting it on or not, he means what he says he is going to do with that gun; I can see it in his eyes," answered Fred.

"What do you think this light is he's talking about?," a perplexed Patrick queried.

"I do have a faint idea what he's getting at, but believe me when I say this: O'Toole is a kind of mystic, and a dangerous sort of one. His kind only know in their own mind what they mean," was Fred's opinion.

"You are a good man, Dan," said Trevor Archibald, "what you say is very true, indeed. The more I hear you speak, the more I realise that you are a man after my own heart. That is why we are here, in this predicament. Some people out there think that we are, indeed, too knowledgeable and they would prefer to see me and indeed you, too, cut down to size."

Trevor was nodding vehemently as he spoke and his false beard came away and almost at the same time his hairpiece and moustache became twisted sideways. Never before had he stayed so long in their company, and he had become careless in his 'camouflage'. What with all the events of the day, the poteen and the general excitement, this further development left everybody speechless, and even Trevor himself said nothing at first. They all sat there in wonderment.

At last Archibald recovered his senses. He looked around him slowly as if he was waking from a dream. He removed the wig and moustache and gathered up his beard and put the whole bundle on the table in front of him. He smiled, his teeth and general appearance looking radically different now. This new man had a surround of golden locks and brown eyebrows, protruding from a no-longer pale white but a shiny, bright pink skin.

"What in the blazes have we here?," were Fred's first words; "can you explain this play-acting, Mr Archibald?"

Dunne seemed to have become very agitated and his words were spoken in a high voice.

"I know him," said Dan O'Toole; "so it is he. His name is Michael Argod. His tricks had me fooled for a long time. He is a cod who has been using his knowledge of books as a means to increase his own importance. He is a liar and a trickster who has dressed up in order that he might sneak in among us and work his devilment. . .".

"Let me explain," said Trevor; "behind every mystery there is a clear moral, even a very precise logic. Suffice it for me to say at this moment – trust me; it will all be clear soon. . .".

He was interrupted by O'Toole.

"I am going to shoot this informer," shouted Dan, pointing the pistol at Trevor whose face now took on a very worried look. The intended victim was stuck for words for an instant; then he found his voice.

"Don't do it, Dan," he shouted, "I am on your side now. I am very embarrassed by this whole thing. I should have come out with the truth a long time ago. I will admit that I put on a bit of a pose in the beginning. It's true that I fooled people by my appearance. In the university I always spoke baloney and led my pupils astray; I did not believe my own words. I was dissatisfied with my life and I came to Bell's to find enlightenment. It was you people who eventually made me see the error of my ways. O'Toole I could see has a special wisdom. From the first I held you in some awe, Dan; I could see that you were different. You put to shame the sophistry of my bookish learning – I was envious of your independence and your lack of entanglement with the things of the modern world. Some said that you were just a country bumpkin; I saw differently. When you came to my lecture, I realised that I was faced with the ultimate test. I could no longer accept my own falsehood. Your presence, there, made me see all the more clearly the absurdity of my job and of my position in life. I felt that there would have to be a radical change in myself; a cutting-off of old links and a forging of new. I have decided to quit my job at the university and leave my wife. Originally I had joined your group on a subterfuge, to learn your ways and to get to know your viewpoints. Now I feel I have become one of you. That's the truth, lads."

"All that sounds like a made-up speech to me," said Dan; "you are still spinning words in order that the truth may be concealed, Mr Archibald, or shouldn't I call you Mr Argod? But you are no longer able to hoodwink us."

He pointed the gun at Trevor.

"You will not be shooting anyone. Put that gun down, Dan O'Toole," cried Jane Wood; "is it gone off your head you are?"

She attempted to pull the revolver from Dan's hand, but he pushed her away and she fell back against a chair. Everybody was shocked by this rough behaviour. Previously this was a man who wouldn't have said 'boo' to anyone. They thought now that maybe Dan was serious in everything he said and perhaps he would shoot somebody.

The sound of a loud shot filled the room, and to their horror they could see that Archibald was hit. He was holding his bleeding arm and there was severe pain on his expression. They could see blood running down his arm. Jane Wood ran to him, blocking off Dan's line of fire.

"Give him a chance, Dan," shouted Fred in a very high voice.

He stood beside O'Toole, having inched himself up closer to the Wicklowman and he extended simultaneously his aura of authority as he spoke, expanding his chest as befits a member of the Garda. He tried to look stern, while at the same time he put on the pose of a mediator, one who does not judge, a knowing and sympathetic observer of the wayward ways of mankind. To achieve this effect, he patted Dan on the back even as he tried to restrain him.

"I have my blood on me now as a sure sign that I am one of you," cried Trevor; "I hold nothing against you, not even this. Isn't that proof enough? You are all still my friends, as far as I am concerned. I didn't inform the police of anything. Fred, you would know; you would have knowledge of any such underhand dealing, wouldn't you?"

"Not necessarily," replied Fred, neutrally.

"You are the kind of man I am speaking of," said Dan in a low, almost muffled voice to Trevor; "you will be the first to be executed. We will leave you as a warning to all others like you, especially those cheating authorities at the university and the busy-bodies who work in the offices."

He was on the point of finishing off Trevor when Patrick, who was standing at the window, gave a loud shout.

"Look. It's Roche. He's out there with a whole lot of guards."

"Guards!," at least six voices shouted in unison.

"He's showing them the house. Isn't he a sneak?," said Patrick.

"That proves it was he," said Trevor excitedly.

"Does it now, you blithering idiot?," shouted Dan angrily; "if you don't shut your mouth, Mr Argod, I'll shut it for you."

"You had better stay quiet, Mr Archibald, at least for a while," advised Jane.

"How many guards can you see?," Dan asked Pat.

"I can see at least ten clearly in the light, and there are dark shadows which could be others. Roche is looking very brave out there in front of them."

O'Toole crouched at the window and fired a shot off at Timothy Roche. The Corkman fell down at the spot while all the gardai ran every way. It was clear that Roche was badly hit.

The six people in the room stared out at the sight below.

"That's two murders now, Dan," said Jane.

There was a note of satisfaction in her voice.

"When was the other one?," inquired O'Toole sarcastically.

"Mr Archibald here," she replied.

"He is not dead," said Dan.

"Premeditation is the important thing. If you keep this up, you will go to Hell, Dan", she said emphatically.

"Where is Hell?," laughed Patrick O'Reilly; "are we going to have a sermon preached to us? What has the Church ever done to solve the world's problems?"

Pat's emotions had been greatly aroused by the presence of Jane, especially since he still felt guilty over his recent behaviour. Also, the poteen made him argumentative, giving him cavalier feelings. He felt capable of great things, of winning fights against overwhelming odds, or righting wrongs in a wicked world.

"We have a better use for Mr Argod now," said Dan; "we will make a bargain over him."

O'Toole opened the window and shouted out:

"We have Mr Argod from the university here. If you do not keep away, I will shoot him too."

With that he closed the window and looked straight at Trevor. There was a cold look in Dan's eyes. Trevor Archibald felt trapped, like a noble animal in a net. Nick Heeney was standing at the door, and it was clear that he was supporting Dan in everything he did; he was not going to let anybody in or out of that room.

"That's a good idea," said Fred, "for he is more use to us alive – remember he has all those brains. He says he is our friend. Let him help us then."

"Right," said Trevor with enthusiasm, although he was still feeling the pain of his roughly-bandaged arm (modified by poteen which was even still being handed to him), "I'll just pretend that I'm your prisoner. I have got a wife as well and she is with child. They won't dare to come near us if I tell them that. Remember I am an important man at the university. Let me go to the window, Dan."

Dan said nothing – he went over to Heeney. The two huddled together in mumbled conversation, then Dan came back to the middle of the room.

"All right. You may go to the window. But don't try any funny business," he said.

"It's thirty feet down," said Trevor.

"That's not so far for a desperate man," interjected Patrick O'Reilly thoughtfully; "I'd keep an eye on him if I were you, Dan."

Trevor was escorted to the window. He waved wildly, shouting at the quiet street below. Patrick had another idea and ran to give him a white handkerchief.

"I have a wife and child. I am a professor at the university. These wild people have captured me. Don't shoot us. Save me."

His words sounded desperate; the others were pleased.

"Very good, Trevor," said Fred; "that was very convincing and good."

"There is Roche's volkswagen car down there," said Patrick; "we can get away in that."

"Tell them we want the keys to Roche's car, "said Dan.

"You are to deliver the keys to Mr Roche's volkswagen up here immediately, or they will kill me," Trevor shouted down.

The tension was reduced when they had shut the window again. In the street below the guards themselves did not know what to make of the matter and they were glad to listen to the wise words of their commander, Mollusc.

Inside the building they sat back to await developments.

"We can make laughing stocks of those guards," said Trevor, doing his best to restore his once-familiar and friendly relationship with the group; "they are the easiest people in the world to fool."

"Don't be so sure that we are all against the Gardai here, Mr Archibald," said Fred; "I would remind you that until today I was a member of the same force myself. They do a good job, most of the time. I am only sorry that my own service with them should have run into serious problems and that it came to such a sorry end."

Fred turned to address them all.

"You see lads, the fact is since this morning I am no longer a sworn-in, fully-fledged serving officer. I am a civilian now."

He told them the story of the events that morning. He had been called to his superior's office as soon as he arrived at the station; the Superintendent glared at him as he came into the room. Fred was looking thin and miserable in his sombre, dark suit, which somehow appeared to imprison his body. His hair, as usual, was combed back and parted with a sweet-smelling hair oil. He strode in lackadaisically, his hands behind his back, thereby avoiding the need to make any sort of salute.

Fred knew that this was to be a showdown. He had been warned many times about his lateness and neglect of his duties. It was Superintendent Mollusc who was in the office that morning. Mollusc was an imposing, foreboding officer of state. He was almost seventy and he had been requested to remain on in the force well past his retirement age, indeed until his death. As a young man, said Fred, he had been noted for his skill at killing members of the enemy – he was known to prefer the knife to the gun; he had consistently supported torture as a most useful police weapon and was continually at odds with successive Ministers of Justice in trying to have torture implemented throughout the land. He was the man who had killed the plainclothes British officer in front of thousands in Croke Park by stabbing his stomach with a blunt knife. It was not the first time Dunne had been carpeted before this man; it had happened a number of times previously and Fred had always laughed in his face.

In the chill of the morning he felt cold and a bit bored as he returned his Superior's unfriendly gaze. He was told to sit himself down and they would get straight to the point.

Frankly, Dunne was told, he was a disappointment.

Mollusc's heavy eyelids opened and closed like trapdoors as he spoke in a pompous voice.

"Do you think," he asked, "that it is beneficial for this country for one of its security officers to be continually drinking with the lowest scum this side of prison; and an even worse matter, to be seen to be continually drinking with them? It's no good asking you where your self-respect is, Dunne, for it's obvious that you have none. That is not the beginning or the end of the matter. It has been reported to me that you are neglecting your duties; leaving public buildings unguarded and the like, just so you can go drinking. Let me ask you a straight question – is it poteen you drink?"

"I laughed in his face, lads. He must have realised what I thought about him and his stupid job, for he asked me what was the smirk doing on my face."

Fred and his boss sat in the cold office and for a while nothing passed between them but silence. The Superintendent was trying his 'cold treatment' technique, and Fred knew it. With nobody was the boss so ruthless as with his own misdemeanouring officers.

"Nothing you do is any secret to us. We have been having a long inquiry into your case," said Mollusc.

"Is that so?," was all Fred could answer.

"You will never work in this country again. You can just forget about your pension. Your wife has told us that you are despicable; she wants nothing more to do with you. We told her everything, including your more than businesslike acquaintance with a certain young lady by the name of Miss Wood."

They all stared at Jane, who was mortified by this calumny.

"Yes," said Fred, "he doesn't even stop at slander that man."

"I have here a special revolver, Fred Dunne," continued Mullusc, "you can put your own there on the table. Then, if you like, I will take you down to the butts and shoot you clean in the head. You won't have to worry about anybody being upset; your wife has given the go-ahead and we will easily dispose of your body. That is one thing we never get tired of dreaming up ways of – disposing of bodies. It is an extremely eclectical job. Once do you know how we did it? We skewed it up into a round ball, coated it with fertile humus and produced the best, prize-winning vegetable and flower patch of all the Garda stations in the land. With your immortal remains, Dunne, there should be even less trouble in disposal, but I fear with much less beneficial use."

Fred spoke back in a quiet, dry voice.

"I think it is pathetic, the crudity with which you think out your plans and schemes for solving the problems of society. You never were much of a policeman and the word Intelligence applied to your department is the most laughable thing in Christendom. I will tell you now, so-called Commander, you can go and get lost as far as I am concerned. I am not afraid of you or your scatter-brained followers. Neither will I voluntarily return my service revolver, for I need it for protection from you and those gangsters behind you. There is one other thing. If you want to make anything of it, then you will find yourself having to explain to the newspapers et al that case of the missing police funds and me having to extricate you from that embarrassing fix with those tinkers down in Wexford."

There was a further silence.

The interview came to an end, with an uncomfortable Superintendent trying to restore his dignity with the words:

"You can go now. Consider yourself dismissed from the Force. You could, I only say could, be hearing from us."

Fred had departed from the station in a cool, relaxed fashion, smiling at those he passed and greeting fellow-detectives with warm 'hellos' and 'soon-be-seeing-ye's'.

They were astounded at Fred's story, not knowing what they might think of it. It was hard to visualise Fred as anything else but a guard and they all felt a little strangely about him. He was now like a minister without a holy book – they could not see him without the insignia of office, or visualise what he might become.

"You are not a detective any longer, Fred?," asked Patrick with a mixture of surprise and disappointment.

"I was fired," said Fred.

They drank to Fred's demised career and before they could finish the drink they were interrupted by a loud voice on the stairs.

"The keys are here. I'm coming up," the voice said in a shrill tone.

Instructions were shouted down by Dan. Everybody in the room was tense, straining to catch each word and detail.

A uniformed arm appeared through the door, holding a key ring. It was taken by Heeney and the arm withdrew. Trevor asked them if Jane was staying. Everybody agreed that she was doing a good job looking after Trevor's injured arm, and it was said that the police were less likely to shoot at a group of people that included a lady. Despite her sharp criticisms of them all, they felt that she was doing little harm and in a way her idealism was admirable. As they discussed her in slow, somewhat slurred voices, the 'Good Samaritan', who still sat beside the injured Trevor, looked at them with wide, emotional eyes. She had determined all along to keep quiet and do all she could to cool down an explosive situation – she did not intend to speak, and at first she did not even realise that it was her own voice that was saying these words:

"Christianity is what will save the world – it is all that I live for. I believe that when the Lord walked on earth, he saw quite clearly who were the hypocrites and who were the sheep. He separated the sheep from the wolves; kept the grain and threw the bad chaff away. By sticking with you fellows I am probably doing great harm to my family and my future. I really had hoped to be accepted into a convent but that has had it now, and even my reputation. Your behaviour is everything I disapprove of – drink, idleness, no sense of responsibility, bad manners, dirtiness even, and if I may say it, downright stupidity. You are exactly the type of fellows Our Lord came down on earth to save. Who am I to abandon you then? I am praying for you all the time. I know what the 'Righteous' will say – are they our judge? As long as the Lord sees what is in my heart, what does it matter what the world says?"

She was filled with emotion when she had finished this speech and tears were running down her cheeks. Trevor smiled at her and secretly thought that despite the bed incident and everything she was really the only decent person in the place.

They went down the stairs, and more than one was finding it difficult to keep their foot on the steps. They had blindfolded Trevor with a white cloth tied round his face. His progress to the street was most bumpy and precarious, being led by Fred and pushed by Dan. The volkswagen stood there, its doors already wide open, as welcome as daylight. Fred took the steering wheel and Dan said he would tell him where to go.O'Reilly annoyed everyone by being over-fastidious about the fate of his coat and over whether the seat was dirty.

The whole operation was watched by a band of gardai who were hiding in a quiet side-street; the jollity and cheerfulness of the departing group was such that they could only look on with wonder. At their head was an officer of the State Security Force – Chief Superintendent Mollusc. The car drove off, initially on the wrong side of the road.

"I wouldn't be surprised if Mr Mollusc, my former boss, is with those guards," Fred Dunne said; "he is a strange man with a compulsion for catching smaller criminals while he's full of admiration for the bigger ones. He's a queer one all right and you never know what he is going to do next."

Chapter Eight

An argument broke out in the car during the night over the crowded and uncomfortable seating arrangements. Six people was a large number for one small volkswagen, and there was much shoving and sweating. The cursing of Heeney was the worst part – he kept awake many of those wishing to get some sleep. This was a man who was ignored for most of the time (except by O'Toole). Their attention might be called to him only in the most rare of circumstances (usually some ill-mannered incident). Such a time was now. They asked him to control his tongue as there was a lady present. He swore all the more loudly and also threw a punch at the ceiling which put a hole in Timothy Roche's upholstery. Fred drove on, his eyes fixed straight ahead, a man intent on the task of going to wherever it was O'Toole was guiding them. Meanwhile, the 'guide' himself was fast asleep.

When morning broke they found themselves in the middle of a grey, bleak valley, not knowing from Adam where they were or even how they had got there. Fred would not stop the car, and it took much pleading and even threats from them before he was persuaded to come to a halt so that air could be taken in. As they tumbled out of the stifling vehicle, Dan remained asleep inside.

It was a rough road. There were no other souls about; just a dead silence in the air. They listened, cocking their ears for a while, not quite knowing exactly what it was they were listening for. The silence of the place, of themselves, of their car, was a surprise to them.

Pat O'Reilly appeared disorientated, and the next thing is they saw him running up the steep hillside, clambering over the healthy, rushy grass and making towards the misty top. They had been busy stretching their legs, moaning and groaning and taking in fresh air while letting out the stale which had accumulated over the night. Heeney took off his shoes and the smell was so strong that even he himself noticed it and he was compelled to remove his socks and throw them away. His feet and shoes he proceeded to wash in a conveniently situated nearby running brook. It was while all this activity was going on (Jane had meanwhile removed herself some distance from them), that the sight of O'Reilly up on the mountain gripped them and they stared.

Fred called – uselessly.

"Well, let him go. It's one of his funny moods. How is your arm this morning, Trevor?," he asked quietly.

"I don't feel any pain. I can't remember any pain even when he shot me. I am just lucky he shot me in the arm and not in the head! I don't blame him for it," Trevor replied softly.

"There is something I want to ask you. Why would you want to go and change your name like that? And dress up – is there a serious purpose behind it all, or was it your idea of a bit of a joke? Tell me, could it be that you are in a spot of bother?"

Fred's question was asked with concern.

Before he had answered Fred put in:

"People suspect you of being an eccentric."

Now Fred's voice had a new element in it, the attitude of an understanding confessor, a trace even of connivance.

"Some would call me that. It is true that I do not expect comprehension. That is not for me. It is better to be right and not understood. My problem is that I try to think. That is a mistake; to try to find solutions to the problems of the world is a fool's game. I am a fool. I do not deny it; in fact I admit it. I am the most foolish person alive. How many people think for themselves, Fred? Very few, I am afraid, for do you see where thinking leads us. . .? Not to a peaceful life I am sure. No, I do not expect that many people will comprehend."

At this point he moved forward and leaned on Dunne's shoulder. It was not clear whether this was due to a desire for sympathy or perhaps a weakness caused by the wound. Fred accepted the extra burden, but with much embarrassed forbearance.

"I am fed up with the books. The stale, old books have been driving me mad . . . , those dry, useless things. To stay at home; confined every Sunday between four grey walls listening to terrible opera music . . . has made me want to leave it all behind for good! It is Sundays that are worst of all, you know, a terrible day, when there is absolutely nothing to do except listen to your boring wife, who is like a prison warder to you. When it rains on a Sunday, and you peek out at the people going to church in their Sunday best with mournful faces, coming back again a while later with the same faces and in the same rain, it makes you want to be sick. You realise there is nothing worth living for in this world. I sometimes ask myself, on a Sunday, if I am alive at all. To find out then at the end of the day that your wife is pregnant and that there will be one more to make your life unbearable, is just about too much. As hard as I try, Fred, I can't find it in me to become a father. Perhaps I am unnatural, but I am not ashamed of it."

Fred spoke softly, trying to bring a little reason and cheer into the discussion.

"Your wife is pregnant you say? Well, that is great news. That should be something for celebration. As soon as we get the chance, we'll all go back with you and celebrate, man," he said.

"No, I am not going back," insisted Trevor; "I am keeping my new name and I am going to start a new life. It is what I have been wanting for a long time. I have been thinking long and hard, Fred, and I believe that at long last the answer is in sight. These people here are an essential part of the solution. They are a hardy crew; they know how to take care of themselves. All right, I agree that they have their faults and sometimes are a bit ignorant, but look – they are independent. They toe the line to no one. I admire them, for on none can it be said that the educational and social values of our society have had much effect. For varying reasons, they have reached their present state free of much of the brainwashing of society. Miss Wood is an exception, of course, but I think we can make use of her. They are free men in their way, and that is the important point. Isn't that true? It is all we need. All we need, Fred; we have our sufficient raw-material for the building of the new Republic – if only we keep out of the way of the gardai or they grow weary of trying to find us."

Trevor took his arm and weight off Fred – he seemed to have recovered his strength all at once.

"You will say I am mad, right?," he said quietly.

"No," replied Dunne, "in fact I was thinking all along you were planning on something. I knew you had a secret that you were hiding from us."

"If we could find a place which is quiet – a virgin land, if you like, I see tremendous possibilities in this, it's a kind of vision I have. We could start a new community, a family. Children would be untainted by the quite idiotic customs of this country. We even have a female member with us, providing us with an opportunity that we must not miss. Whom do you suppose Jane would take as a mate – Dan O'Toole? I think that she's gone off him and I don't blame her one bit. In any case, do you think he could have healthy children? Also, I don't think Pat O'Reilly would be capable of being a husband, do you? And Heeney – well – I myself would never let that man near anything weak or fragile. I know you are a Catholic, Fred, and that this may shock you – but I wouldn't see any problem in her having children by any number of us – a real variety. If only we could make it work. What do you think, Fred? Tell me."

"It is something that has been tried before, Trevor – many times. I remember reading once how they tried something similar in Russia and they had a free-love set-up but all it ever led to was Communism. It would never catch on here in Ireland. The whole force of church and state is against it for one thing. Then the attitude of the people would not be amenable to such an idea. But I am interested in your theories, Trevor; I am very interested, for I have never heard anything as advanced as this before. Have you written it down somewhere?"

"I wish I had, I only wish I had. If anything happens to me in the near future – and what with O'Toole after me at one end and the police at the other, I could be dead before the evening – if anything happens to me now, the idea will die with me. I was waiting to explain it to you all; I was gradually preparing you with hints and suggestions and I was testing you sometimes. I was on the verge of announcing my plan when the guards pounced. That will explain my 'playacting' as you call it, Fred. I knew that as Michael Argod I could never win the confidence of any of you. That type of man is always full of fancy ideas, none of which he would dare attempt to put into action; it is all Fancy Dress Ball stuff for him. Nobody knew Trevor Archibald – he could have been the 'Grand Old Man', or a Russian prince, or an exiled Polish poet – many people I imagine were saying these things about me. It is not to everybody that you can announce revolutionary ideas.

The ground and the seed must be prepared beforehand. Then, when you have made your first few converts, you can go out and announce it to the multitudes. It doesn't matter what is the quality of those first followers. The important thing is that the idea is at work in them. The idea spreads of its own accord. That is the first principle, Fred."

"This is astonishing, Trevor. I never knew that you were as deep as that," Fred said.

"Fred, listen. Will you do me a favour? I know that you are not the sort of man to get carried away by novel ideas; you are not impressed by people or events, high or low. In fact I have felt that your presence was the chief obstacle to my succeeding with these people. You would always have an answer for everything; or else an objection. But I am asking a favour of you now. Will you grant it to me?"

"How can I grant you something before I know what it is?," asked Fred.

"Not even a dying man's last wish?"

"Do not be melodramatic, Mr Archibald, or Mr Argod, whichever it is your name is, you are not dying.," said Fred.

"Do you deny what you saw O'Toole do to me last night?," asked an equally peeved Trevor.

"He was just warning you. He certainly did not mean to kill you. Your false beard fell off at the wrong moment, when we were all a bit jumpy. A bit drunk too, I might add. You are imagining things, exaggerating somewhat."

"If I die, I am asking you to pass on what I have said. Encourage them. Tell them to withdraw from corrupt civilisation and to establish themselves in a new setting somewhere, even if it's only an old bog, where nature is allowed more play than man. I believe in the natural setting. I am putting that message in your hands now, Dunne."

Trevor Archibald bowed his head. He looked almost humble. The golden locks and clear eyes of his white face made him look a complete stranger to Fred, as if he had just arrived there from a distant place. The once – neatly attired intellectual, now in unkempt clothing and stubby face, stood there in a solitary pose. He didn't look either like Trevor Archibald or Michael Argod; it was as if he had been changed into a new species of man.

A depression came over him and a further sag came to his shoulders. As hard as he tried, he couldn't see Fred Dunne as a loyal and enthusiastic successor.

"If O'Toole does anything to me, all my hopes will depend on others. Pat O'Reilly seems to me to be the best prospect now. He is at least idealistic and he doesn't seem to mind what anybody says about him. O'Toole on the other hand I see as a man who has a great spirit; he can be depended upon to go where others more timid or fastidious will not. O'Toole is a man who, with the right guidance, can be the cornerstone of the new society. He is a man of action; the only trouble now is he seems to have murder on the brain. Heeney can be used too, as long as he has his poteen; I see him as a solid labourer. Fred, there might even be a place for you – as our policeman. What do you say?"

"Ha ha," Dunne laughed, "I don't know what to think. I imagine I would be both head of Police and the policeman on the beat at one and the same time. It would be an appointment with many advantages. What else would you plan for this place?"

"Many things. There are O'Reilly's paintings for instance. I foresee a great Art Gallery; indeed that will be one of my main roles, as custodian of all art treasures. Art will be given pre-eminence over economics or anything else. Do you know that I have bought all of Patrick's paintings?"

"Is that so?," Dunne said.

"The painting he did of me is a magnificent thing. It is surely his best work. I can't wait to have an unveiling ceremony, with all of us gathered round and plenty to drink. There is only one problem though – the paintings are all back at his place, and we will have to go back to get them."

Their attention was distracted by the sound of O'Toole waking up. Dan had let out a loud mutter from the car, and Trevor and Fred both fell silent as they awaited his emergence from the vehicle. Heeney, sitting on a rock opposite and drinking away happily, raised his bottle of poteen in a salute to Dan. Jane Wood was kneeling down beside a stone wall further on, ignoring everybody and saying her morning prayers.

As Dan came out pulling up his trousers, both Trevor and Fred decided that it would be as well to greet him cheerily; attempt to brighten up his day so that he might recover his good spirits and maybe even erase from his mind the bad memory of the previous evening. Fred greeted him with a good-humoured sally, showing his teeth in a smile.

"Top of the morning, Dan. It's good to see you looking so bright and cheerful."

"The sun will shine down on us now that you're here," added Trevor, making his contribution, hoping that the fellow's temper had cooled down; "it's a bit of a rotten day that's in it at the moment, but it will soon clear up."

O'Toole just grunted and turned his back on them, staring at the morning on the mountainside. They watched his back, thinking about him and his ways. Fred felt he could not be blamed for shooting Trevor. The sight there of Michael Argod could not but have brought back memories of those lectures which had first so impressed O'Toole. He had been captivated and held spell-bound by the talk. He had believed in Argod; he saw him as someone who had answers to what he himself was searching for – the answers to life's riddles. In those early days he had not dared approach Michael Argod but was content just to listen. Later he tried a few questions and although he did not understand the answers, he was happy to wait – illumination would come later. He felt sorry for Dan. He had been let down by Michael Argod. During a ramble into the university not many days ago he had learnt that Mr Argod was no longer lecturing – he had been removed from his rostrum while lecturing in a drunken state. It was true to say that his reputation now really stunk with the students and professors. When Dan heard this he wondered. How could such a man be taken in such a fashion? That same person stood behind him now, exposed in all his decrepitude. Who would have thought that the modern, spell-binding lecturer was none other than the strange, heavily-drinking Archibald? As far as Dan was concerned, Archibald was simply another one of Bell's customers, a mere mortal and a man with no outstanding attributes who only liked to talk into his drink each night. He had believed that Michael Argod was a man who spent every evening wrestling in his mind with topics of immense import; with hours passed gazing at the sky as each conceptual issue was resolved in his brain. There was unrelieved pain in him now when he thought that the romantic philosopher did not exist; that instead he was just a drinker, a man exposed and disgraced in full view of those who had most believed in him.

"Old Trevor has been talking to me," said Fred, "and he has been explaining a lot of things. He has got a few good ideas – something really interesting. . Has he told you about it? It's a good plan, I think, and it will solve a lot of our problems. Come over here and we'll talk about it. Pat O'Reilly has gone up the mountain, for heaven knows what reason."

Dan came moodily over and they discussed Trevor's ideas about getting to a safe, remote place. After a while Nick and Jane came to gather round and there was still no sign of Pat.

"We will have to go and get him. Who knows what has got into him. There is a heavy mist coming down and the sooner we are out of this forsaken place the better," Fred Dunne said to them all.

There was general agreement, for they were cold and hungry.

"It is so easy to get lost up on a mountain," said Trevor, the climbing expert; "from experience I can tell you that you are in one place and then you find yourself to your great surprise in another. If you set up landmarks it doesn't help much either, for eventually you find that the landmarks too are not where you think they are. O'Reilly right now could be way over on the next mountain and getting further away with each step, yet still imagine he is approaching us and will arrive here at any second. It is a treacherous business and I doubt if that lad has any idea of climbing a mountain."

They were at a loss about what to do. The cool, hill air was blowing around them and there was an atmosphere of great impatience.

"Let the two of us go up," said Fred to Trevor, "for we had better get him down before he does harm to himself – I am going to have a fatherly talk with him. It wouldn't do to have him acting on his impulses every time he gets one."

There was agreement on this plan.

They set off, with grim if solicitous looks on their faces. They took the ditch and first few obstacles easily and began climbing. Both men were still in their fine suits and they looked rather like businessmen from the city out on a mysterious, countryside walk. The others sat down in exasperation to wait; they did not speak to one another, each silent in their particular exile.

It was a steep if mediocre hill. Despite their initial enthusiasm they soon got tired and they climbed the final stretch to the top in sullen silence. They clambered in half-crouching poses, using their arms as guides and quickly finding their 'natty' clothing to be uncomfortable and tight-fitting, giving little air or comfort to their bodies. At the summit they suddenly found themselves in a great, grey-greenish mist. They lost touch with one another almost immediately. Fear and terror set in as they individually groped and grasped around in the shrouded, bereft spot. The noise of the wind was loud and eerie and they vainly searched for each other, or for an opening of light. Each of them was unable to see more than a few feet and the eerie mist came at them and surrounded them in a suffocating fashion. After a few more yells and shouts they came together again and recovered their composure. They began, hesitantly, to make their way downwards. There was scarcely a glance sideways for a sign of the artist. Patrick was well-nigh lost in such a mist and their own skin was in considerable more danger than his, they thought. As they emerged out of the cloud, Fred turned and shouted the name of the artist as loudly as he could; they hardly bothered to wait for any reply.

Presently they came down in the vicinity of the road and at last they were able to breathe more easily. Once they were back, it took them some minutes to recover their breaths.

'That was a near miss," panted Fred, "we are lucky to be alive. That fog is dangerous – we could have been lost for good."

"Was there no sign of Patrick?," asked Jane.

"We couldn't see much up there. It was impossible to see anything. I wouldn't give much for his chances now," said Trevor.

They stood in silence, contemplating the lost artist and looking up at the hill.

"It's too dangerous to go up again. We will have to leave him," said Fred.

There were objections from Jane to this, but they were of no avail.

"Let us get into the car. We might pick him up along the way," Dunne said, trying to offer a little encouragement.

They were very relieved to be back in the warmth of the car and Trevor commented, in a half-joking fashion, that at least there was a little more room with Patrick absent. Nevertheless, he showed his concern for the missing lad, and made a number of suggestions as to where O'Reilly might be on the mountain. He was in no doubt that they would soon find him.

Fred was once again at the steering wheel and the car set off, everybody making themselves as comfortable as they could. They went round two bends and then along a fairly straight stretch. After a mile or so they came to a turning and then, round the next bend, they came across Patrick sitting, clothes-less, on a stone wall.

There was a wild look in his eyes, which were very red.

"Where the hell have you been?," shouted Fred out of the window; "you just about got us lost and nearly killed as well."

O'Reilly came over to the car, carrying his bundle of clothes in his arm. The door was opened for him and he squeezed inside between Jane and Dan. He spoke quietly as the car moved off.

"I knew you had to come along this road," he said.

His words came out modulated, with an air of high tension in them, and this had the effect of causing silence in the car.

"I went up in the mountain for a bit of peace and rest. I am all right now."

They took in this information silently, ruminating over it. There was still an air of cynicism in the car, emanating especially from Dunne and Archibald in the front.

"It's all right, Pat," said Dan, "take it easy and have a rest now."

Pat became silent and sank back against the seat in a state of exhaustion. No more was said on the matter. O'Toole made certain that Pat was comfortable and opened the car windows so that draughts of fresh air might come through. The others had an inkling of an unspoken understanding between Pat and Dan, an understanding that went deeper than words.

The car drove on, out of the mountains and on towards the distant horizon, which lay far ahead of them across innumerable flat, look-alike fields with scanty farms and poor, dark trees making a pretence at respectability. The sky stayed immobile during the long hours that they travelled, a white, unemotive cover whose only object seemed to be to keep out any glint of sunlight, a substance that might perhaps be unwelcome in such unobtrusive countryside. They journeyed on, with increasingly greater periods of silence and less chat between them. Evidently a long journey in a car was less stimulating than happy, chatty hours spent drinking in a pub.

"Try that radio and we might hear some news or some music," said Fred, pointing to a small car radio under the dashboard. Trevor twisted the knob and they picked up Radio Eireann, the local radio station. There was a lady speaking on it, in sombre tones, talking about the Youth

Macra clubs of the land and what they were doing to develop the country. Trevor commented after a short period that this was the kind of thing that the land did indeed need. The clubs helped to foster a spirit of unity among the youth of the soil, while bringing out in the young their latent talents for thrift, agricultural skills and a straightforward approach to life. Most people, he said, turn off the radio once that kind of programme comes on and turn it back on again when some modern music starts up. The trouble was that, even with an immense amount of resources devoted to educating the people and prime radio time, still hardly anybody listened and most of the people were in fact unimprovable. The lady spoke on the activities of clubs in different parts of the country. One in Ballysaggart had won a prize for its very fine exhibition of brussels sprouts which were absolute prize-winners; for next year they were considering investing in thoroughbred horses and eventually racing these in the classics.

"Did you hear that?," said Trevor enthusiastically, "that is what I call initiative. The whole thing has the touch of greatness which is so lacking in this country."

Project schemes in pigs, poultry and sheep-rearing in different areas were described and praised; special mention was made of a scheme in Ballyboru which was a pilot goat-rearing enterprise. There was a capacity meat-wise and milk-wise in this animal, they were informed, that was not realised by many people.

"Yes," shouted Trevor with glee; "that's what I have always figured. If they're good enough for the nations of Africa or Asia, then why not for us? I see the goat being the answer to many Irish problems. Let us get into goat-rearing, lads, as soon as we have the chance."

"Goat-rearing, brussels sprouts – what's all this about, lads?," asked Patrick, wide awake and now conscious that, due to his previous absence and then his exhausted sleeping, he had been missing out on the conversation.

Fred told him about Trevor's idea of settling down somewhere in the country and setting up what amounted to an independent state.

"Wow," said Patrick in wonderment.

They listened again to the radio programme, with heightened interest. It was stated by the lady that practical economic programmes were not the only concern of these clubs – that man does not live by commercial activity alone was the gist of her message. She had ample praise for those areas which had held poetry readings, artistic exhibitions and drama. These all had their place in the rural setting, and were not to be sacrificed for the sake of mammon.

"Exactly my sentiments," agreed Trevor happily.

The programme went on for quite a while and everybody listened with interest, if only varying degrees of enthusiasm. The movement of the car in its ceaseless journeying had a lulling effect on all their senses.

Eventually the lady's voice faded and the news came on, delivered in even more sombre tones in Gaelic by an erudite gentleman. They listened in surprise now to these words which came midway through the bulletin in a suddenly changed, angry voice and through the medium of Dan's translation:

"The gardai are puzzled by the mysterious disappearance of a gang of hooligans who have been causing great trouble in Dublin city. 'They are the worst bunch of scamps to come to this city in many a long year', a garda spokesman is reported as saying. He went on to say: 'That is saying something, you know. I have been arresting these sort of people for more years than I care to tell you, but none have ever got under my skin as much as this lot has done'.

It is a low-class, raucous set of trouble-makers led by a certain Captain Searchwell, a mysterious figure who is said to have been recruited from abroad. The whole aim and scheme of work of this small group of people in unknown. They have been carrying on their activities for some time now, in the midst of ordinary people who have remained ignorant of these activities. At least one among them is armed; he is Georges Braque, a little-known figure who wears a hat and who may have been responsible for at least three murders in the capital last week, the latest being of a certain Doctor Heifernan, killed by gunfire in the middle of the city last night. Doctor Heifernan is said to have possessed a brilliant mind, put to ill use. He was a scientist of sorts and was an associate of the gang. It is possible that he was killed in some kind of double-cross. Doctor Heifernan was notorious for his animal experiments, carried out in the laboratories of University College. Although the death of any man is a tragedy and diminishes us all, it is true to say that the demise of Heifernan has made the community a more decent and safer place to live in. Perhaps it will be seen as a warning to others who are tempted to take the same, perfidious path. Sources close to the police authorities say that all the available evidence points to a group of 'constitution subverters'. Their methods are vague and underhand. Instead of directly confronting the authorised forces of society, they prefer to unleash their attacks by sniggers and innuendo. They sit around drinking and talking, on the surface apparently no different from other men or women. But their secret, behind-the-scenes talk is something else and would not be suitable for the ears of decent men and women. They can do more damage in one night than a thousand regiments will achieve in a year. The whole search operation is being directed by specialists sent over from the Special Branch, whose representative has issued the following warning to the public:

'Do not approach these people under any circumstances. Leave them to us. If you see them pass by in a grey volkswagen whose license number at the last inspection was FIR 123, just report it to the nearest garda station, who will then inform us. If it happens that they come into the bar or pub you and your friends are having a quiet evening out in, ignore them totally, as though they weren't there. When they're not looking, make a quick call either by telephone or by person, whichever is quicker, to the guards. They will take the situation in hand. Good night and God bless. There is one other thing. These people are sinners and have no morals. Your women and children are not safe while they are around. Good night.'

The following descriptions have been issued of the wanted persons. Frederick Dunne, forty, of slight build and believed now to have a small beard. He can display a sly grin, and is said by his former employer to be quite a trickster.

Captain Searchwell, thirty to forty, who is known for his disguises but who is in reality quite a small man of no particularly striking physical appearance. The best description of him comes from an outrageous portrait believed to have been done by another member of the gang and discovered in the painter's den this morning. It shows a wicked-looking gentleman, with ill-proportioned features and a blank, characterless face whose eyes glare with cruelty. It is probably the truest picture of him yet to fall into the hands of the police. All reports of this man suggest that he speaks with a foreign accent.

Georges Braque, twenty five to thirty five, of unknown origin, occupation unknown; he is a dangerous character who, during his time in the city, was seen to frequent places of a sensitive security nature, wearing a hat.

Nicholas Harlequin, thirty to thirty five, of a rough and rustic appearance. It is said that this man loves to start a brawl wherever he goes, and he is never happier than when he is punching somebody and cursing at the top of his voice.

He is always on the lookout for trouble and his very presence used to be enough to make others get up and leave when he would arrive at a public place.

Sigaat O'Toole, a painter, probably still in his teens and most likely an innocent abroad who was led astray by these people. He is thin and fragile, and yet has been involved in some very unsavoury incidents. Many obscene drawings and so-called works of art have been removed from his quarters by the police, the most prized one being the portrait just mentioned of the said Captain Searchwell.

The last member of the gang is a woman, about twenty, name unknown, who is said to be dark but with a fresh complexion. It is not known if she has voluntarily gone with them, or is an unwilling victim.

The gardai are also looking into an unconfirmed rumour that these gangsters have kidnapped and perhaps even murdered an eminent member of the academic community, Professor Michael Argod, a social scientist of great renown. It is felt by the security forces that it is not by accident that the chief object of attention of some of these people happens to be the main educational institution of the land. In any society, it is these very bodies which are first destroyed in a revolution."

"Roche is dead," said Patrick in a loud voice, full of surprise.

"I told you he would be," said Jane in a cold, condemning tone.

"They are after us with a vengeance," Fred Dunne said in an intense manner; "they are trying to put the wind up us with all those lies."

"They have got all the paintings," Trevor bawled; "we will never get them back. Did you hear how they spoke of my portrait?"

"You mean your picture?," asked Dan.

"Yes, it was terrible, wasn't it?"

"You shouldn't be so bothered about a picture," said Fred in a critical voice; "why are you so bothered about a picture?"

"It is Pat's finest work of art. It has nothing to do with me. He could have simply painted a donkey if he had wanted to. There are pictures of buckets which are works of art, of stones even," replied Trevor.

Dan spoke again, sarcastically.

"Well the guards have got it all now. What are you going to do about it?"

"We have no choice but to get them back," Trevor said firmly.

"You must be pretty angry with the guards, Patrick?," said Fred.

"I pity them, that is all," sighed Patrick with a resigned air; "I don't see any need to get them back. I can always paint more."

"I am going back to Dublin to fetch them," Trevor said again.

He spoke in lofty tones about how important the paintings were; particularly his own portrait which had given him a true insight into his own self. He discussed the importance of art generally, in a materialistic world and of the superiority of painting over all the other arts. The car bounced along the rocky road and everybody listened, if only half-heartedly, to the suave voice of Trevor Archibald. His words had a kind of hypnotic effect on them, like a cool wind, and they felt a powerlessness in the presence of the man who, even as he spoke to them there in the car, seemed to have his mind firmly set on a distant, more important place. There was not one in that car who knew what to make of Trevor – except perhaps Dan O'Toole who believed that he, at least, had seen through the facade.

"I suppose we could trust him, Dan," said Fred; "and there is something he could do for me back in Dublin. He could have a word with Mrs Dunne for me, as she will be worrying about me very much. Go and see her and tell her I am getting on fine. Go and see your own wife too, Trevor, while you are at it. I am sure that she also would appreciate that very much."

"We cannot trust the man," said Dan O'Toole.

"I am a trustworthy man," said Trevor loudly; "I am a person of some repute and importance. I will tell you something – it is not just in this country that I am a person of note. There is royal blood in me and in England I would be a prince. . .".

His shouting and vehement air was a surprise and a shock to the others and they stared at him open-mouthed.

"Grab the bloody, tricky blackguard. Tie him up until we decide what to do with him," shouted Dan, before Trevor could get a chance to continue his tirade.

Fred obligingly brought the car to a halt with a screech of brakes.

"Hold him tightly," said Dan, "and don't let him wriggle out of this one."

They took a speechless Trevor from the car. O'Toole put his knee on Trevor's neck and pointed the gun at his head. There were few words spoken. Only the occasional bird nearby was a witness to the activity; the trees blew back and forwards with a gentle laugh – the rocks, stones and boulders were silent and mute. They bound his wrists quietly and tightly with dirty handkerchiefs (Fred was the expert at this) as well as his feet and then they lifted him up and carried him back into the car with a certain amount of satisfaction.

"We feel a little more secure with you like this," said Fred; "it doesn't mean that we are going to harm you or that we can't be friends in the future."

"I only pray," said Jane, "that you will soon give up this viciousness."

"It is about time that you thought about getting married," snapped Fred at her.

"And you should be at home looking after your wife," said Jane in return. The two of them went into a sullen silence and did not speak again for some time.

They slowly moved off, rounded an inconsequential bend and picked up speed to go away over a hill. Later, a valley brought them out into a more civilised part of the country and when they came to a cross-roads with signposts, Dan ordered the car be brought to a halt.

"Nick has invited us to visit his home in Galway," he said; "we will be welcome to stay there as long as we like. It is a good place to hide from the police and we will be getting more poteen."

"Galway is that way," said Fred pointing to the road to the left.

"It would be a great honour to visit your home, Nick," said Trevor, who had managed to make himself comfortable despite his cramped situation; "it is an honour in itself to be invited there."

They were pleased at the prospect of a place to rest and to have a good wash and clean-up, not to mention to get something to eat. They journeyed on for many more hours, passing towns and garda stations, as well as the occasional gardai (none of whom seemed interested in the passing volkswagen), until finally they reached County Galway. Just one hour later they were driving up a rather narrow boreen when they saw a small, white-washed cabin sitting on a large rock, with white smoke billowing from its unusually large chimney. At its door they could see a man and woman standing, farming types, and the man was smoking a white clay pipe. The man waved the pipe at them and the woman had a white cloth in her hand which she was also waving, even while they (the travellers) were still a good distance off. The welcoming attitude of the two showed that the visitors were expected.

Chapter Nine

Trevor Archibald was placed on a chair in the corner of the small kitchen which reeked of all kinds of country smells. He wriggled his nose in disgust and thought – what have we sunk to? Everybody else made themselves at home and even Jane felt herself a little relieved to be in the company of more stable, seemingly more responsible people; she felt that their presence might forestall any more unpleasant incidents. Mum and dad were very accommodating, asked no tiresome questions and accepted without any hesitation all of them. They even took no notice of Trevor's predicament. Mrs Heeney eventually brought him a glass of milk, giving him a wrinkled wink as she passed him by. When he tasted it – having to drink it with bound hands – he discovered a strong alcoholic flavour to it.

The parents were a tear-jerking sight in their adulation of Nick, whom they treated as a sort of god. They smiled continually at him and hung on his every word and movement. They turned in awe to look at him whenever he opened his mouth. This he did now, far more than he normally would. These 'words of the sage' were never more than simple requests for 'a cup of tae', or 'a crust of oul bread' or questions such as whether the lavatory was in use. The parents were apparently expecting to see in the eyes of the others a similar glow of respect and praise. When dad said that they were very proud of Nick and that he was a son the likes of which no man had ever had, they were all embarrassed; it was clear that he expected equal praise from them.

"He is a good lad," was all Fred could manage.

Mr Heeney Senior put his arm around Nick and addressed them all. Mrs Heeney left the pot on the hob and listened intently. Nick himself just stood there immobile, looking glum.

"Dis son of mine is a great man. We always knew he would be a success in the world. He is a lad who will change the world. His great doings in the fine capital city of Dublin are a legend here in his own neighbourhood. He is called 'Big Nick' which is an almighty honour and not even my own grandfather ever held such esteem among the community being known simply as 'Larger Sean' in the old vernacular. And that grandfather was the biggest basher of landlords in this part of Galway. He used an old hurley stick, which they buried with him. A famous man he was and still is, but listen – Nick has surpassed him. Nick has gone out of this village and has established himself in the places which matter in the land. He has always promised us that he would someday bring his influential friends back home with him, to show them the place where he grew up, little though it be. We have always been very proud of Nick's doings in the city, and we have had the special privilege on rare occasions to read of these in the newspapers. On every visit home we hear descriptions of new and even greater deeds. He walks with the mighty and the famous and he is on first-name terms with the President – isn't that right? I know you gentlemen are very important people in your own right, and I hope ye don't mind my humble cabin too much. Have a drink of fine poteen."

They did indeed drink the poteen and it was very fine – straight from the still. Jane herself was given the room at the back of the cabin for her own use and she went into this.

"That is a fine woman," said Trevor from his chair when she had gone; "she would be an asset to any man."

Fred spoke softly to Nick's parents:

"Jane is a very holy young woman and she prays a lot. She does not drink poteen at all and she keeps herself very much to herself. I think you both can help her if you speak encouragingly to her."

"I am thinking she would make a good wife for our Nick," chuckled old Mr Heeney,

"and I would be willing to give her family all my goats to make her so. It is about time he settled down."

"Goats," cried Trevor; "did you say you have goats here? Where can I see them?"

There was excitement in Trevor.

"That is goat's milk you have been drinking," replied Mr Heeney, "for we get everything from them."

A worry came over Trevor's face and he stared down at the glass of milk. Now, despite the extra beverage that had been put into it, it smelt very strange and over-strong. A peculiar feeling went through him and he became slightly dizzy.

"He is fainting," Fred said as Trevor fell off his chair on to the floor, his glass cracking to pieces on the ground beside him. They revived him quickly with a sip of poteen and by opening the cottage door – more to let out the smoky fumes than to let in blasts of fresh air.

"Let him loose," pleaded Fred, "for I am sure his having to drink tied up has caused this fainting."

No objections were heard from O'Toole and Trevor was released from his 'chains'. He said that he would love to see the goats. They all thought that this was an excellent idea. It was still daylight outside and they trooped out the back to where the goats were. There were three of the animals there, and Mr Heeney said that the rest were probably in the back field, making a total of ten goats altogether.

"A fine number indeed," said Fred.

"I would have more only for the weather lately," said Mr Heeney, "and there are other things I do be doing anyway."

"Aah," said Fred, "very wise in this day and age. What sort of things would you be doing as well then? Pigs like, or fowl?"

"Aye," replied Heeney, "that an' all."

They stared at the goats, which were black, white and brown-spotted in colour. One of the goats glared right back at them and Trevor was slightly uneasy. They were such.. alien creatures. But his greater interest overcame any hesitancy that was in him. All of the goats were female, they were informed.

"Do you have a ram then?," asked Trevor, "maybe out in the back field with the others?"

"Eh, no; well yes I have," replied Mr Heeney in an uncertain fashion; "I mean I hadn't but now I have. Two of them in fact and I am getting more."

"Mr Heeney sir," said Trevor in a voice full of respect; "I am asking you to sell me some of your goats. All of them in fact, or as many as you are willing to part with. We have a plan for them. Would you at all consider a sale may I ask, hoping at the same time that I am not insulting you?"

A huge grin broke out over Mr Heeney's face and immense happiness came into his eyes. He was hardly able to find the words for the trembling that filled his throat.

"Yes, surely. I would consider it an honour to sell them to you sir, who are a gentleman if ever I saw one. It's a deal. You can have all three of them at what I consider a real fair price. That would be fifty pound each, making a total of a hundred and fifty pound in all, and cheap at that price."

"What?," said Trevor, "a hundred and fifty pounds for three goats?"

There was a short, tense silence as both men considered the matter.

"A hundred pound sir," said Mr Heeney.

"Twenty four pounds more likely," Trevor answered back.

The old man laughed and said that Trevor was a good-humoured sort of person.

"Seventy five pound is my last price," he told the city gent.

"Twenty one pounds," said Trevor grimly.

"What?," cried the Galwayman, scarcely able to believe his ears.

"I'm going down a pound each time. Accept or reject, it's up to yourself," Trevor said.

"Twenty four pounds I'll take then," said Mr Heeney quietly.

"Twenty pounds I'll give you," was the reply.

"Done sir. You are a gentleman I can see."

"I will buy all the goats then at six pounds and thirteen shillings and four pence each. That is the ten goats."

"I can only sell you the three sir," said Mr Heeney glumly; "the rest are a bit diseased at the moment and I wouldn't suggest that you buy them at all."

"I see," said Trevor, "the three of them will be enough to be starting with and we should be able to pick up more later on – specifically a he-goat. Thank you very much, Mr Heeney; you got the better of the bargain then."

"I hope not, thank you sir."

The others laughed at this deal and asked as a by-the-way how they were going to actually transport the creatures. Trevor said that he had a plan and that it would be no problem.

Later they had tea and bread for a meal – a cup of tea and a slice of buttered crust was sent to Jane in her room. It was noticed that Mrs Heeney was a great hand at drinking poteen and she was able to put it back in generous quantities. Her face was grey-white and her eyes were watery, like pieces of glass. The poteen seemed to have no effect on her and she drank it as if it were some health-giving food. At the end of the 'meal' Mr Heeney asked them all outside for a smoke. They went happily out to see new vistas, with Nick staying inside to clear up with his mum. In the darkening of evening the wing-drop of swallows filled the rain-threatening air. They enjoyed a tremendous glow in their hearts, a glow fanned by the sudden influx of fresh, peat-infested winds. They sat down on the very large rock and listened to the odd dog-calls and other sounds of east Galway. For a while – which was prolonged enough to give each of them a private moment of daydream and fantasy – they were in silence. It was the hard, ringing east Galway accent of Mr Heeney that brought them back to reality.

He was once more talking about Nick. They were so very proud of him and of all the success he had had in the foreign city. Nick was never one to be satisfied with the poorer opportunities of a place like Galway city, big though that town was. No, it was Dublin or Chicago for Nick, where he would at least have a chance of using all the skills which had been his from childhood. While his younger sister was doing all the housechores (she was now married to a man of substance beyond the Bohorbron river), Nick was always out on more useful and more promising activities collecting garbage and old bottles that nobody else knew what to do with. He had always, from the age of ten at least, had his own private source of tobacco; especially known were his famous 'clipped cigarettes', always in great demand throughout the community.

Come Tuam races day or anything else like that when crowds appeared and Nick would be away and come back home at the heel of the hunt with a collection of a black eye and a sackfull of goods. The black eye was a regular feature of his young life, for nothing is ever handed free to a man and to make a way in the world you have to fight. There was no way Nick could fail to make good when he reached wisdom and the big city. They were so very proud of the fact that he owned so many businesses and factories. His frequent trips to France, Austria, China and other 'fareign' places were a most common subject for discussion in the village and fields. Every month brought a new, fantastic place to be added to the itinerary of their well-travelled son. On his visits home he brought them souvenirs and 'relics' from all these countries. These were much-prized items in that area and were in pride of place in many a spot. It had been confided to him by Nick that right at this moment the whole government itself was out looking for him in order that some highly crucial scheme that he was working on might be completed, but he was dodging the government so that he could get away from it all for a much-needed rest. A holiday was essential for the fevered brain. They would all get as much poteen as they wanted to take away when they left.

Nick's lies were not much of a surprise to them, as a sneaky, secretive manner was a fixed part of the make-up of the said gentleman. Heeney was his own man, stealthy and not the type of person who was of a straight nature to deal with. The poor parents were as proud as punch and it touched the others' hearts to see the spectacle. Patrick O'Reilly in particular was amused and he broke out in laughter. He grinned away uncontrollably, to his own embarrassment, and the rest looked at him sternly.

"Do you think it will rain tomorrow?," Fred asked the old man in a soft, even sorrowful voice.

He felt a certain sympathy for the simple countryman, the sort of sympathy he had always felt as a policeman for the victims and even the perpetrators of criminality.

"Do ye see them swalli there?," said Mr Heeney, proud that such educated men from the city should come to him for information or knowledge of a kind; "in three hours the skies will open themselves, but in the morrow it will all be clear again."

They rested in the certainty of his statement, letting the gathering dark lull their minds into a sort of peace. Soon they saw a firm, black cloud approaching at great speed at ground level, threatening and foreboding like an on-coming autocratic cleric. They went inside, culprits escaping immediate exposure. Immediately, the rain came pouring down. Fred commented on the swift passage of Mr Heeney's 'three hours'.

Mr Heeney replied, with a slight note of irritation in his voice;

"Dis rain is always sent to help us poor farmers and 'tis not always city folk can appreciate the ways of life out here in the country."

"He sends it to rain on city folk and countryman alike," commented Mr Archibald.

It was very late before they got to sleep that night (or next morning as it happened), the drinking, smoking and talking keeping them up till all hours. The big surprise of the evening was Mr Heeney inviting them to see the poteen factory outside; apart from the very large cottage chimney that had smoke proliferating from it, there was no sign as far as they could see of any factory in the vicinity; neither inside the house or outside of it was there a hint of any unusual economic activity. Trevor for one thought it must be all something of a put up job. The others were curious to say the least. They followed Mr Heeney when he signalled to them by means of a lighted candle (the wonder of electricity not yet having come to this part of Ireland), to follow him out the back. They went through the room where Jane lay fast asleep, slipping past her as quietly as possible. They had another surprise when they found that they were not going outside at all; instead they went through a trapdoor and down under the house. They progressed slowly and cautiously along a stuffy, narrow corridor, in speechless wonder. They held their breath in amazement – the only sound that came through the air was the voice of Mr Heeney saying that if everything was built underground nothing would be found and that it was the safest place of all. They entered a large room by the aid of the dim light and they found it harder to breathe. They were by now in a state of some consternation, and it was not until the old man opened a wooden slat that they could see they were not so far beneath the earth after all but were looking out on clear countryside; dark and rain-beaten but welcome to see nevertheless.

"It's a secret place," said Mr Heeney, "and not known to many."

Being better able to breathe now, they turned and found themselves looking at a vast array of equipment and pipes; they were quiet as Mr Heeney explained everything. There were vats, stills, buckets, a number of chimneys or flues and such things. Heaps of potatoes were stored in the room. They felt a certain amount of surprise and admiration at the sight of the place, and yet it had a strange emptiness – the things looked as if they hadn't been used for ages and there were piles of dust everywhere including on the potatoes, the latter not looking very healthy. It was all out of operation at the moment, Mr Heeney said, as they were awaiting a spare part. When Fred asked what the spare part was , Mr Heeney hedged his reply and was somewhat evasive, saying that it was just some complicated piece not easily found but it would be obtained soon. It was very dusty in there and they all found themselves sneezing.

"Nick himself it was who started up this place," said the old man; "before all we had was an old-fashioned thing that didn't turn out the good-quality stuff at all. Nick got new ideas from a bunch of visiting Americans in Galway – I believe they were there for the races – and he has kept the methods he learnt from them as a secret ever since and it is known to no one else in the world apart from himself and meself. It is not made like the ordinary poteen at all but in an entirely different way that dese fellas told him and I don't believe they were Americans at all but were passing themselves off as Americans. What they gave us, I believe, is the secret of a healthy and long life, for you would never believe the age of people who drink it and not one person who has partaken of it has ever died yet from old age."

"Are these people of a great age then?," asked Trevor with great interest.

"Old Nick Tullock is the oldest man around. He was on his death-bed and had reached the grand old age of one hundred and thirty years when he was first introduced to Nick's brew. Now he is on his feet and getting younger every day. There are many people over the hundred mark who take it regularly – it is especially beneficial for the older folk, for it changes their white hairs back to the natural colour and makes them feel as young as fifteen years. Three of them have got married lately to girls many years younger than themselves. Old Nick can remember Daniel O'Connell and all that time."

Trevor spoke with great anticipation:

"I'd sure love to see that man and have a word with him."

The factory was undoubtedly a very productive and useful place, but due to its present inactivity it held little more interest for them. After a while, they all began to feel the hunger rise inside them.

"I'm starving," said Patrick in a plaintive voice.

Everyone else felt more or less the same, despite their all having had a 'meal' earlier.

Not even the Heeneys appeared to disagree. They began to make their way back and soon they were trudging down the narrow passageway to the house. It was with the relieved sighs of a returned tropical expedition that they entered Jane's room. They were very surprised to see her bed empty.

Patrick was the first to get the whiff of the cooking food and soon they were all sniffing the air. In a state of happy anticipation they moved towards the kitchen. There, Mrs Heeney and Jane herself were busy bending over the cooking pot – it was evident that Jane was in charge.There were potatoes and boiled eggs and bread already laid out on the table and a frothy stew of green vegetables and something else was cooking away in the pot. It was a sight that gladdened their hearts. The loud, sizzling noise of the cooking food and the warming flames of a roaring turf fire served to increase their anticipation and happiness.

As they tucked in, pausing only to help themselves to sips of the poteen, they were fulsome in their praises of Jane. Fred it was who remarked that at last she seemed to be coming out of her shell. Jane appeared to take it all in her stride and smiled quietly. She did not even seem to mind it too much when later on they were all a bit tipsy and Pat was not being very careful or particular with his choice of words.

They did not leave the next day; in any case the day was nearly over when the first few of them were wakening and beginning to move about. The lads were very much at ease in their new setting. They felt more relaxed in the company of Nick's parents. The ordinary coming and goings of Mr Heeney, his practical attitude to life and his matter-of-fact acceptance of everything made them feel that all was right with the world. The benign, if stark countenance of Mrs Heeney also was a sign and an assurance that the complications of life were no regular visitor here. The circumstances of their worrying flight from the city they put at the back of their minds as they settled themselves down to enjoy an apparently endless supply of good poteen. Archibald, despite everything, was really in his prime, enjoying the adventure of their time at the Heeney's and indulging to the full his insatiable curiosity about the Irish countryside and its way of life.

The subject of the advanced age of Mr Tullock came up again – Mr Heeney mentioned that Tullock hardly ever ate anything – and Trevor again expressed a wish to see him. Jane interested herself in the case of Nick Tullock, and said that she was a little bit shocked to hear what his diet was like. It sounded as if his living conditions were very bad. A man like that should not be left living on his own and she thought a visit to him would be only an act of Christian duty.

"He lives just two miles from here, in an old shack on a hill," said Mr Heeney.

It was more the fact that they had little else to do, as well as a desire for some fresh air, that made them all set off for Nick Tullock's that evening. A few more drinks of poteen cured their heads and they went out the backdoor into the night, leaving behind only Mrs Heeney who said that she would be content to sit in the corner with a dram. Everybody gave out a warm 'goodbye' as they left, but she did not reply. Hereyes were fixed on her beloved poteen and her spirit was already entering a secret world that was known to no other but herself.

Mr Tullock lived in an old hut unprotected by any of the conveniences of modern society. Trevor said as they entered that he felt they were going back into a different age. Heeney could remember no one ever having lived with Mr Tullock and a member of the government welfare department was the only person who called in on him occasionally to see if he was all right. Mr Tullock at first did not see them in the dark kitchen – he did not appear to be aware of their presence. He was sitting in a wooden chair with his head in his hands, bent down staring at the glow of the turf fire. He did not look like a man of a hundred and forty or so, but more of a younger person of around sixty years. He was trim and had good haunches. His hair was a silver colour and his eyes, when he turned them towards the visitors, were smoke-fire red.

He greeted them with a nod and he gave an extra nod to Mr Heeney. He spoke quietly to them as they stood there in respectful positions.

"I remember," he said, "Daniel O'Connell and all his doings. I was a young lad at the time. I suppose I was around ten, maybe more or maybe less, and we went to a meeting of the man and all the local people. He was a good speaker and he treated us as equals. He had his own little chair. He saw me in the crowd and pointed at me. 'You', he said, 'come up here now'. I stood there like an idiot in my breeches staring back at him, not knowing what to do. He eventually cadgodled me up there and I stood beside him with his hand on my head. We looked out on the crowd and I remember thinking that their faces looked white and almost dead as they stared back.

They were all attentive, heeding his words. 'Listen here,' he said, 'this is Ireland's future I have here. This young man will live to see a free Ireland, a prosperous Ireland and an Ireland fit for a happy, ambitious youth. You who are hopeless, downtrodden and hungry-look at this lad. He will see better days.'

They cheered loudly and I felt great. He gave me a lump of toffee. Well, here I am now, a long time later. I have seen it all, the going of the landlord was of my time, and I can say that the land that O'Connell foresaw has not yet come. It is a downright disgrace, if I may say so, and the scandalous way the politicians have treated this country is terrible. They would let me starve, I who was a wise man in their grandfather's time, and they try to buy my peace with three pounds a week and visits from a party man who is constantly trying to get me to go to his political rallies and to speak his praise. There is no end to the things I could tell and they know this. Three pounds a week I ask you, in this day and age. Well, I will get my own back on them yet – just you wait and see."

They felt warm in their hearts towards this old man and a feeling of the most heart-felt sympathy for his plight. Trevor was the one who spoke to him once his sorry yet glorious tale had been delivered;

"The poteen is a good drink to keep you going then," he said in a cheerful voice that was full of expectation for an answer.

"Ah yes, the poteen is one good thing about Ireland. The quality of our Galway poteen cannot be improved upon. It is the one thing I would not pass a day without having a sup of. Now tell me what it is that brings you to this part of the country."

He was informed by Mr Heeney that his son and they were a bit overworked at their important jobs in the city at the moment and that they had left for the good of their mental health. There was no better part of the country for recuperative purposes than Galway.

"So you are all fed up to the teeth with Dublin and the government? I admire ye for that and it is a pity that every young lad and lassie in that place does not take the initiative and get out of the damned place. More luck to ye," said Mr Tullock heartily.

"We are going on to explore new places once we leave here," said Trevor.

"I suppose I would not mind going to where you are going either, providing that there are no taxes to pay," Mr Tullock said in a half-joking voice.

"There will be no taxes to pay where we are going," Trevor said lightly; "you can rest assured on that. We are going as far away as possible from the government."

Jane spoke, the warmth of admiration and charity in her eyes:

"Are there any hints you can give us on how to keep out of trouble and to live the good life generally?"

The old man frowned and he bent his face down and he did not speak. It was as if Jane's question, or presence, had somehow caused turmoil in him. When he had lifted his head again, he did not look at them and there was a scowl over his face and it displayed a good deal of enmity. He shook his head slowly as he began speaking, and his words were addressed more to himself than his visitors.

"I was not such a good boy in my youth; nor indeed was I in my manhood. I must admit I was involved in my share of nonsense and skullduggery. In the early days I was even sentenced to be shot by the 'brotherhood' as a suspected informer. There was great money to be had in those days if you were on good terms with the police. I made quite a packet from it – it was a way of life with young men of good sense. I played them all at their game, for I never really gave away any useful information. I would never have given up a fellow-countryman."

He stopped speaking and tears started to flow out of his eyes. He rapidly turned his head to look away in the direction of the fire.

Tullock's revelations were now a cause of silence and some embarrassment in them. Trevor alone still seemed to be enthralled by the man who, having now taken a sip of strong poteen, was midway between a drunken slumber and a deep sleep. For the others, a good deal of the shine had been lost off his image. It was Jane who had the final few words with him, trying to comfort him and saying that in such a long life he must have gained ample merits from doing many works of charity, numerous opportunities for which must have come his way. She tried to make him more comfortable, sitting him up in his chair and seeing that his poteen glass was put ready at hand beside him. Then they all went out quietly from the house.

It was three weeks before they set off, dressed in scatty rags and taking along with them the three goats and a buggy and mare which had been the property of Mr Tullock. It was Fred's idea that they dress up thus – then they would not attract attention as they set out over the land. Meanwhile Trevor had vanished, leaving behind a brief note saying he was gone to fetch the paintings and he would pass on a few words to their families and that he hoped to meet up with them again, perhaps in Galway city. Before he left, they had all faced the sad task of burying Nick's mum.

When they returned from Mr Tullock's they found the old woman dead in her easy chair. A sorrowful Nick had insisted on taking charge of her, lifting and carrying the remains into the bedroom. They were all very surprised to see tears in Nick's eyes. He laid her on the bed and covered her with a sheet. Such was his grief that nobody disturbed him and not even his father appeared as sorrowful. He left his son alone in the death-room and accepted it all with a matter-of-fact air. If the truth be known, the rest of them enjoyed the waking of the next couple of days – and old Mr Heeney was no exception to this. The funeral was to the local cemetery and the mourners made a brisk and cheery sight as they trooped along behind the coffin. There were about twenty people there in all – the whole neighbourhood had showed up, Mr Heeney said proudly – and Nick alone of all of them was inconsolable in his grief. It was noticed that he had stopped drinking poteen or any strong drink at all. At the graveside a pitiful ceremony ensued. They had some trouble getting the coffin into the ground, and this was due partly to their slightly inebriated state as well as being tired from the long walk and the steep climb uphill. All of their faces were grim and drawn by the time the remains were being securely laid in the correct position, and they took the occasion of the priest's prayer as a most welcome opportunity to grab their breaths and recover themselves. As the prayers were being said, they looked with expressionless faces on the coffin lying patiently below. The grim reality of death lay there, staring them in the face. It was an affront to all their hopes and dreams. The cold, visiting wind of death blew amongst them, giving them a chill and an uncomfortable feeling of unease.

"We will all end up like this one day," said Patrick morosely; "that is the one sure thing we know as we stand here."

He had expressed a thought that was in all their minds at that moment.

"Like ruined churches and monasteries we will be one day, our time of glory long past, our spirits departed, our graves the only testament to our existence," said Trevor sadly.

There was more talk of ruins and waste and broken hope. The priest and Jane were the only ones at the graveside who appeared to be praying. A general air of gloom hung over the assembly. At the end of it all they went back down the hill having felt changed by the experience.

When it seemed that they were settling in for a very prolonged stay, they all had a sudden shock in the way Mr

Heeney himself hastened their going. The most charitable way to describe the antics of the man would be to say that he had what looked like a fit, or a sudden turn in the head. This might be understandable, considering his recent bereavement. He went at them one morning in an outburst of rage and abuse. He called them rogues and idlers and worse besides. He said that he could not see how any of them could have a scrap of education, especially considering that they did not know how to appreciate a man's hospitality. His rage even extended to his son, Nick, who was also suddenly in his bad books. They were all told to get out – he hoped the law would catch up with them soon. They hastily fled from the little cabin, their last sight of Mr Heeney being of the irate man chasing after them, pitchfork in hand. They were glad to leave the home of this unpredictable man, and indeed were relieved in the end that no greater harm had befallen them in their going.

It was a scheme that worked very well, the lot of them pretending to be tinkers. Fred remarked that it was a foolproof disguise, as all they had to do was look scruffy and people would keep their distance. He wondered if Trevor, if he ever showed up, would be able to recognise them.

"But I think we have seen the last of the blackguard," he went on; "and if anyone comes looking for us, it will be the guards."

"Set on us no doubt by Archibald," said Dan O'Toole.

"Give him a chance. Perhaps his heart is in the right place," said Patrick.

Dan spoke angrily.

"That is what you think. He only wants your paintings for himself. He thinks that they may be worth something one day. That is all. He would go over your dead body to get them."

"You will have to wake up to the ways of the world, Pat," said Fred; "before you are made a complete fool of. Doesn't he own the paintings himself now? Didn't you give them all to him? Are you an eejit or what? He has gone back to collect the paintings and he will flog them off to some millionaire."

"His great scheme to get us to some marvellous new place is a right cod too. The fella doesn't know his way around the country at all and I don't think he has ever been beyond Dublin before. Sure you could see he couldn't wait to get back there," said Dan.

"We were right fools to let him loose, much less to listen to his advice. He must think we are right amadans," Fred commented.

He added, changing the subject;

"if we keep on our present track and stay clear of the big towns we will be all right. This thing will blow over after a while."

The cartload of travellers, followed by three goats tied to a length of rope at the back of the cart, wound its way along the country road. Whenever they saw a sign pointing to a major town, they went along the opposite road. The goats were an annoyance, and they began to regret having taken them.

"It was Trevor's idea in the first place," Dan reminded them.

"Yes, we were led astray by him," said Fred.

They were very hungry and there was worry over where they were going to eat. Fred said there was no need for concern – it may as well come out now – Dan had a pile of cash which he got in his room where it had been left by Roche. It was ill-gotten gains no doubt from one of the Corkman's many schemes. Dan had felt he could rightly take it, considering everything that Roche had stolen from him and he was making no bones about it.

Everybody felt that matters were now right in hand, and when eventually they came up to a tiny, crossroad's shop,

Dunne asked O'Toole for some cash, with which he duly went in to get provisions. The bread and tinned foods were stored in the back with the poteen and Fred said heartily that there would also be plenty of fresh chickens by the roadside.

"The disguise is working anyway – the bitch of a woman in the shop couldn't wait to be rid of me," he laughed.

They journeyed about twenty miles that day, some of it being by a circuitous route. They were very tired in the evening. At a quiet spot in a little-used lane they came to a halt. Two tents were made at the side of the cart, using old sacks, and Nick Heeney took the mare away to tether her at a ditch. Dan – with surprising facility – lit a fire; he had it flaming in no time. Bread and tinned beans were produced, and use was made of the pots and tin-opener and other utensils which they possessed (they had obtained these also at Nick Tullock's). They recovered their better spirits around the camp fire, and there was the usual consuming of poteen which, better than any fire, kept the chill from them.

"I wonder," said Patrick, "what is going on in Andy Bell's tonight? I'll bet they are glad to be rid of us."

They all thought briefly of the world they had left behind; it seemed quite some time ago now since they were there. The excitement of their first evening out under the stars brought a heightened 'camaraderie' to the party and they were more liable to laugh and be good humoured about things. None of them had too clear a picture of where they were going or of how they would get out of their predicament, but Ireland was a bigger country than many people realised and they would surely find a place that was at least safe from the police.

As they ate and chatted by the glow of the campfire, they saw Nick Heeney showing Dan something in the shadows and the nearest thing to a smile was on Nick's face.

"What is that, Nick?," asked Fred; "what have you got there?"

Dan took the object, which was a bottle with a type of coiled glass tube inside, and held it slightly aloft.

"Nick has taken this from his dad's factory. It was made in America and the best kind of poteen is made with it. He is glad to have got it from his dad and we might be able to use it ourselves to make poteen later."

They were all cheered up immensely now and Nick, who was rapidly overcoming the sadness of his mum's demise and who was now drinking poteen again, sang them another of his songs. It was a new one this time, a song they had never heard before, and for once nobody commented on his singing, one way or another.

Jane was the first to retire, and gradually the others became sleepy and crept into the second tent or under the cart. As a quiet, dead atmosphere settled over the camp, the outlines of their tents became invisible in the dark, vague land. As the night wore on, the three goats which were tied nearby looked hungrily around, seeing before them the old sacks as perhaps the tastiest morsels in that place.

There was a scampering sound in a ditch close by and the silence of the long hours was broken by the stark, shrill cry of a vixen.

Chapter Ten

In the morning there were curses and loud words when they found that the goats had eaten much of their tents away. Naturally Archibald got the blame for this too as the culprits, the goats, had been his choice. Dan pointed out that it was natural for such animals to have a nibble of whatever material was near at hand. He said it would have been better to have given them something to eat.

"How can anything grow in this desert?," asked an irate Fred. They all turned and looked at the land around them, bare and unpromising in the morning light.

"If Trevor was here I imagine he'd be seeing luscious fruit trees growing everywhere and exotic crops all over the place," said Fred;

"he is a good man for imagining things and I suppose he would be suggesting that we all start digging and planting right away."

"With himself sitting on the sidelines watching it all," said a rather bitter Patrick.

They were heating a pot of water over a fire for some tea and the boiling of eggs. They were not short of utensils, as Nick Tullock seemed to have just about everything in his house, and they were becoming quite adept at managing out in the open.

"I wonder if that Trevor fella really is a kind of genius?," Patrick said quietly.

"No he isn't," answered Fred;

"he's a man from the university who has many advanced ideas he gets from books, none of which he or anybody else has ever tried to put into practice."

Dan spoke in a hollow, slow voice, pointing at the land around them.

"In Bailedecoinin this land would be a rich gold-field. The land in my area is so rocky and fruitless that it makes strong men cry in front of their beasts. They would be glad for a portion of this."

"Is that so?," said Fred thoughtfully.

They all looked again at the land around; each one wondered quietly as they contemplated the seemingly hopeless soil. It was a brown, indifferent land, quite similar to most of that which they had already travelled through. It was an 'arizona' of water and peat, scraggy stones and rushes. Wild birds such as curlews could be seen occasionally rising from the useless swamp and their loud, mournful cry was like the farewell of sad, departing spirits. The morning calm emitted a grey-bluish light which gave a 'moving' appearance to the land, and it looked as if the whole earth was slowly moving towards them and then rippling away from them. It was the kind of region that could swallow you up, a feeling that no doubt gave rise to many ancient fears and myths. It was no wonder that succeeding generations of Irish had left this place for safer and drier lands. It would indeed be a prophet who could find any hope in this land.

The surprising thing now was that there was indeed hope beginning to rise in their hearts as they stood there. In that uninhabited, barren land perhaps there were opportunities. As they took the three goats and the mare around to search for sustenance, they began to feel almost like pioneers. There was great interest when Patrick shouted from a distance that he had found a spot with some grass and fresh weeds.

* * *

There were not many who mourned the disappearance of the collection of drinkers from the capital. There were surprisingly few there who were distressed in any way. Not even their own loved ones it seemed were much concerned about them. Andy Bell was the least concerned of all of them, even though for him it meant the loss of a good few pounds due to unpaid bills. He was actually glad to see the back of them and he would even have paid extra money to see them go. They were rogues as far as he was concerned – he had never been more surprised by a bunch of apparently genuine customers. Fred Dunne was the biggest surprise of all. He was a real con artist and he had done a good job of fooling everybody; their many privileges of free drinks had usually been arranged by him. He was the perfect chancer, a sneaky character whose type usually originates in the country and then migrates to the city, attracted like a moth is to a bright light. There he soon finds his forte in the pubs and gossip houses and with people of easy mark. Andy had seen quite a few of these in his time and he had never thought that Fred, a member of the Garda at that, would turn out to be one. He had indeed the highest opinion of the man until that day when he had seen the poteen in the corner.

Andy was still a worried person. Members of the Morals Vigilante Committee had called in to ask why he had allowed people of such dubious morals to drink in his pub. They said that there was now a question mark over his license – the well-being of the innocent community was going to be their first concern. Needless to say Andy let them have a complete account of how he had been thoroughly fooled by them, and of how he detested everything they had stood for. It was not his business to listen to his customers' conversations, but he was often disgusted by what he heard coming out of their corner in the evenings.

A few customers came in at that moment and they were more than willing to join in the conversation and give their opinions. All in all they said, they had felt a blemish to be on the place when those characters had been around. They found it hard to believe that such people could be living in the heart of Dublin, which was the cleanest city in the world. They had wished to be rid of the menace but they hadn't known how to achieve this. It wouldn't have been any harm if the police or even themselves had given a good hiding to the rascals. Many times they had felt tempted to do this. The committee thanked them for their advice, commenting at the same time that it hadn't been asked for.

The stern gentlemen then left, announcing as they went out the door that the matter hadn't ended there. A firm salute from one of them, with his hand raised in perpendicular fashion, was the sole signal of farewell. They left behind a wordless, reflective Andy Bell who stood thinking about what it all might mean. Mike Bell appeared from behind the inner door and he gesticulated to his father to come over. Out of earshot of the customers, he sympathised with his father and produced a few words of advice for him.

"You may have lost the license, pop. There is a chance that they'll close the place down and if that happens the name of Bell will never be heard of in this trade again. But don't worry, you still have me to look after things. Indeed if you hand over to me there will be no grounds for closing the pub.

We will be an entirely new management then. It is not all black, dad. It is not all black at all."

Mike talked in a confidant, cheery way, a youth in the full gusto of his manhood. A sense of despair and a distrust of everything in the world arose now in Andy.

★ ★ ★

Mrs Wood, Jane's mother, was delighted at the news that her only daughter had gone off to the country with her friends. In her opinion it was high time that Jane had had a holiday. It was wonderful that she had found new friends. The priest had told her that Jane had always involved herself in charitable work and that the girl could always be trusted in anything that she ever did. She did not need to be told this. All this bad talk that she was hearing about Jane and her friends was typical gossip and she would not let it spoil the news that at last Jane seemed to have found new interests in life. Mrs Wood was most excited of all by the possibility that these new friends had taken Jane off her hands for good. This was something she had been hoping for years. It would be all so fortunate if it were true. Mr Mollusc, who had come from the government and who had been so discourteous and ill-mannered, had indeed assured her that Jane had gone off with these fellows. He had been very curious about her St Vincent de Paul activities and had wanted all the facts about her. All her childhood details were of interest to him and he spent a long time going through her personal possessions.

"I do hope that Jane gets married soon," said Mrs Wood to the elderly, towering man; "perhaps one of her new friends will be a suitable choice."

"My information has it that she is with a number of men," replied a sombre Mollusc as he scrutinised an old photograph of Jane.

"She is a strange girl and I am not surprised that she has gone off like this – it is not the first time. On this occasion though I am more than optimistic and I am sure that at the end of it we will be hearing wedding bells," said Mrs Wood.

"Your daughter is a strange girl indeed, Mrs Wood. I do not know what she is doing associating with such characters. They are all under investigation at the moment and one or two of them are very dangerous individuals who may not be completely sane. Your Jane would be wise to leave them and to put as wide a distance between herself and them as possible," were the words of Mr Mollusc.

Fred Dunne's wife was not put out too much either by the news of her husband'sabsconsion. She was not surprised to hear that he was in the bad books with his employers. The thought that he would not be home in the near future to annoy her and to insist on personal services pleased her immensely. Mollusc made every effort to be a comfort to her in her 'distress'. She found it tedious to be pretending that she felt great wifely concern, but she did sigh and say that it was sad the way things had turned out.

"Hold your whist, girl," said Mollusc, "and don't be bothering yourself over that scalliwag. Sure from what I hear he nor any of them have any morals or decency at all. That kind of man is not worth the trouble."

"I heard the radio saying something about bandits and such-like people and I wondered if Fred had anything to do with them. There was a description of one of them that could have been something like Fred. I wondered if he was out on some kind of undercover work, as he has been wont to do in the past. But then the description did not really fit Fred at all," said Mary.

"They love disguising themselves in all kinds of ways. Sure they are always making up names for themselves. The Wren

Boys, the Hatchet Kids, the Hooded Gang – these and many other titles they have seen fit to attach to themselves. They have grand plans they are always talking about. Their ideas on life and women would shock the wits out of you. We have had to warn the country about them – and new details have come to light about their characters. Did you know that one of Fred's friends was kicked out of the Veterinary College for cruelty to animals? Another one of them is a scientist who used to be well-known for his lurid medical theories. There is also an artist who persistently makes dirty pictures and sells them to children and other innocents in O'Connell Street. These are the kind of people that your husband is associating with, Mrs Dunne," said Mr Mollusc in a voice that was cold and disapproving.

"Between you and me," he went on, "I wouldn't be surprised if they were plotting a spot of further subversive bother and Fred is mixed up in it."

"My Fred is a real eye-opener all right," said Mary incredulously.

"That is putting it mildly," said Mr Mollusc; "you wouldn't have any idea where they might have gone to? Did he ever talk about a place – any special place he went to for holidays or the like?"

"No. The only place he ever went to was the pub," answered Mary with an air of resignation.

"Ah yes, the drink," said Mr Mollusc, giving a long sigh to equal Mary's own; "the drink has been the downfall of many people."

Hilary Argod was loth to let in the stranger who came to her door. She made him show an identity card and the badge of office before she would let him pass the threshold and this annoyed Mollusc a good deal. He then proceeded to tell Hilary of the police suspicions concerning her husband.

"He has been going to Bell's for months and throwing it back with the best of them. He has been seen to sip sherry which he kept in a locker in the university room. The theory that he has been kidnapped we no longer believe to be the full truth. Your husband was the fellow who waved a white handkerchief at us from the window all right. There is a question I have to ask you, Mrs Argod – have you ever heard the name of Trevor Archibald?"

Mollusc's accusations caused tears in Hilary and she refused to believe that Michael had been drinking.

"I am absolutely certain that Michael has never touched a drink in his life. And Trevor Archibald is not anyone known to me," she said in a halting voice between tears.

Her sorrowful state did not bring any softening in the expression or attitude of Mr Mollusc and he proceeded to talk to her in a stern voice:

"I must ask you to come along to an identity parade tomorrow evening at a place called Bell's. It is a spot well-known to your husband and frequented by him very often. You will be able to meet there other people who are in a similar position to yourself."

"Identity parade," cried Hilary fearfully; "an identity parade for whom?"

"We are seeking to identify this man Trevor Archibald," Mollusc answered.

"Do you know where my husband is, Mr Mollusc? It is not like him to go away without telling me," said Hilary in a sad voice.

"We are trying to find out where he is and you yourself may be able to help us further in our quest tomorrow evening," said Mr Mollusc.

* * *

The atmosphere in Bell's bar was quite unlike anything that it had ever been. Inside were a wide range of people who sat in silence listening to the words of Mollusc who stood in the centre of the pub. On a table before him were O'Reilly's paintings, with Archibald's portrait prominent amongst them. Mrs Wood, Mrs Dunne and Mrs Argod were there, Andy and Mick Bell, the Vigilante Committee, two clergy, an expert on art from the university and assorted members of the public were all present. Andy had provided a selection of soft drinks for the occasion as his license, he was informed, had been revoked pending a legal outcome of the matter. Nevertheless it was noted that Mollusc himself was sipping from a whiskey glass – whereas all the others had just lemonade or tea.

"The professor of art here will have no hesitation in telling you of the worthlessness of these drawings. They are, isn't this right professor, the vain imaginings of a puerile or even infantile mind?"

"That is quite correct," answered the 'professor'.

"Speaking as a layman in these matters," went on Mollusc, "it doesn't take much to see that they are amateurish and ugly. I certainly can't find one amongst them that I would consider hanging up as an adornment in my home or office. There is also a danger element in these pictures. We see here images of nude men and women. Nakedness of men and women seems to be the major theme of this lad's work – he obviously has it on the brain. These pictures of grotesque, bullying and generally nasty officials, especially police and clergymen with their hideous faces, are so anti-social as to be downright subversive. Generally, what is good in the land he portrays as evil, and what is really bad and unwanted he shows as the epitome of virtue. This painting which shows the world as a prison – an obvious criminal type has been given the gentle smile of a saint. Everybody else is a prison warder, vicious, cunning types with – professor –".

He signalled to the 'professor' to take over.

"There is no sign of talent in these paintings. They are indulgent attempts at putting paint on canvas. Classicism is unknown to this fellow. Form and perspective would be a mystery to him. His idea of art is to squash paint on a sheet and hope that it comes out as a picture. Here in one of them he has folded the painting over in four sections in order to get a form – have you ever seen anything like it?," said the expert with much contempt in his voice.

Everybody listened in wonder to this lecture. It surprised them to learn about this painter and they were quite astounded to see his works.

Mollusc asked the wife of Michael Argod if she would come up to the table for a moment to identify a particular portrait. Hilary, extremely unhappy at finding herself in the interior of a public house, did not appear anxious to take any part in the proceedings and she did not respond to Mollusc's invitation.

"There is a portrait here of someone who may be familiar to you. He goes by the name of Trevor Archibald," Mr Mollusc said a little impatiently.

Mrs Argod still sat in silence and turned her head to stare at the wall.

"Well then, I will show it to you," said Mollusc and he held the painting up for all to see.

"That's Trevor Archibald," a number of people shouted together and they all looked at and pointed at features on the painting.

"That is one of them all right," said Andy; "he was in here with the rest of them and he drank like a fish. He had a black beard and the fanciest suit you ever saw."

"He was the queerest one of the lot of them," said Mick Bell; "he used to beat his wife and we even think he may have murdered her, isn't that right lads? He was a bit of a posh one too."

"Yes," said one tiny man from the back, "I nearly gave him a clout one night for his language. He was just not a gentleman."

"Are you going to arrest him then?," asked Andy.

"That is all something that will come in its own time. The thing is it will not be Mr Archibald that we will be arresting, but somebody else on our files whose photo bears a good resemblance to that man in the painting. Do you know him now, Mrs Argod?," asked Mollusc with some gloating in his voice.

Hilary had gasped quickly and held her breath when she saw the painting. There was no mistaking that it was her husband she was looking at – despite the beard; that face, eyebrows and above all the arrogant, royal eyes were those of Michael Argod. The whole portrait of him showed an entirely different character than the one she knew. There was little of the scholarly, mild look in the man in this picture; there was a daring and an adventurous quality instead. With his dark beard and firm-set jaw he looked like a wild man. Hearing now the accusations of ribaldry and rough behaviour being made against her husband, Hilary bent her head and expended all her effort on holding back the flood of emotions that welled up inside her. She appeared to be a forlorn figure, not looking up or speaking to anyone else in the room. There were more acccusations of indecent behaviour, criminal deeds and even wife-beating as carried out by Trevor and they looked at her with a mixture of sympathy and curiosity. She did not speak up to defend him; she could not understand that in all the shame and guilt she was beginning to feel some pride in this strange man who also appeared to be her husband.

There was amusement amongst Bell's customers over the matter of the paintings and when Mr Mollusc asked Andy if he would put them in his dustbin there was prolonged laughter. Afterwards, Mrs Wood and Mary Dunne, with their common concern, sympathised with Hilary and comforted her in her trouble. She heard about Fred and Jane and the other people and Hilary was astonished to learn of Michael's unknown associates. She listened in great wonder to these revelations of her husband's secret life.

Fred Dunne and Dan had gone into town and come back with all sorts of equipment and tools. They had spent a great deal of money and even brought bottles of whiskey and brandy back with them. They frequently travelled about during the daytime and they soon acquired fond words of greeting or farewell for people they came across in their travelling. Heavy summer showers gave to all of their faces a weather-beaten appearance – even Jane looked less pale and more lively now. They learned to ignore the cutting of the wind at the times when it became cold and bitter. People and dogs no longer paid all that much attention when they passed. The place where they set up more or less permanent camp was well out from any town and within the shadow of a rather scrappy range of hills. The hollow where their home was soon acquired an inhabited appearance and an air of permanence, and in the less-than-fertile vale, bounded by bog and lake, they tried growing a few vegetables in the soggy earth. It was Patrick who was the keen gardener and he had insisted that they invest in some chickens which they eventually obtained from an old lady. The acquiring of a pig was the next thing on the horizon, although Fred harped on the need not to become overburdened with livestock. It was suspected that one of the goats was pregnant as well, a result of one of the visits of the wild, shaggy rams that they often found disturbing the animals at night. By now they were feeling the need for a second pony and cart and one clear, bright morning Fred set off to see about getting these.

Dan and Nick Heeney too went out that day. They set off into the bog to look at the snares they had set for catching rabbits. They left the camp at one o'clock in the afternoon, with small sacks slung over their shoulders and a heartening bottle of poteen each in their pockets. Patrick and Jane saw them off – glad to be rid of them for a while as they could both now busy themselves with the gardening to which Miss Wood had also become a new and keen recruit. It was a fact that Dan and Nick were not very interested in planting, preferring to sit around all day watching and not being very helpful to those who had found something more useful to do with their time.

It was a sun-lit afternoon as the duo trudged through the moorhen pastures following the trails of wild creatures well-known to them from the huntings of their youth. In reality, these two lads were pastoralists at heart, whereas the methods of cultivation were, in their minds, the prerogative of a weaker, more self-indulgent civilisation. It was a long time since either of them had hunted and the opportunity they now had for this gave real delight to them both. They didn't talk or communicate much as they went along, except to pause to take an occasional sip or to comment on marks on the trail which might be significant. Slight showers of rain now and then went across the sky and a light breeze, warmed by a brisky, bright sun, freshened their faces. They walked over the treacherous bog with agility and ease, avoiding the dangerous pools and keeping to hard ground as much as possible. Their first snares were empty and as they headed for more which were set a long way into the hills, the evening sky began to dip casting a brown, colourful shine on everything. There came a slackness in the lads as they hunched over as they walked. Nick suggested that they leave it for another day, but Dan insisted that they press on. There was no telling what might be in the snares ahead, he said. A less-than-willing Heeney walked behind him.

It turned to dusk and they still trudged ahead. The next snare they came across was empty too, and they were very disappointed. Still Dan insisted on going on and Heeney just shrugged his shoulders and complied. A white summer moon appeared over the bog to give an extra brilliance to them as they re-set the snares in new spots. Dan seemed to exult in the moon-lit night, his eyes taking in avidly the bog-shadows and listening in silence to the water-sounds and the croaking frogs.

It was an exuberant Dan and a tired Heeney that faced the long trek back. Dan seemed loth to come home even now and he walked at a very slow pace, causing more frustration to Nick Heeney. By this time all of the poteen was finished and Nick at least was feeling the chill in the air.

"It's getting cold, Dan," he said adamantly.

Dan did not reply and Nick saw that he was in a preoccupied mood. The moon came right up to glow down like an ever-enlarging disc of white heat. All at once Dan stopped and stood stiffly in his tracks. He looked up at the sky and a sigh seemed to leave his frame. He saw a dim, white glow light up the brambles and bushes and everything around; a white, trembling light which grew stronger and lit up the inside of his mind. O'Toole's face seemed to be in the grip of a vision – pale and trembling. He looked at the moon and became transfixed by its huge, liberating fire. A type of peace overcame him and he stood there rigidly and without movement.

Nick's patience at last gave out and he nudged and pulled at the Wicklowman in order to persuade him to continue the journey home. There was a wild look now on both their faces and an argument ensued between them. There were blows struck by both men and Nick was felled with a knock to the head. Heeney did not even see Dan pull out the gun; all he knew was the blinding hot force of a bullet going into his head, and then the dissembling of unconsciousness.

Dan, still in a rage, did not even ascertain if the Galwayman was still alive before he dragged his body away – he pulled Nick to a nearby boghole and bound him with snare-wire to a heavy boulder. Then he pushed the weighted body into the pool and watched it quietly sink. Gradually he became calmer and as he watched the final signs of Nick disappear from view, a semblance of normality returned to his breathing and composure.

Fred was very proud of the new pony he had bought at a little village some miles distant. He secured the filly to a post and spent much of the evening grooming her and boasting about what a good judge of horses he was. They scanned the darkness for any sign of the returning lads.

"They've been gone a long time now," said Jane.

"Those two know this type of countryside like the back of their hands," Fred said.

"O'Toole fears the Pooka like anything; perhaps it got them," joked Patrick.

Eventually they retired to their camp beds. The moon struck Dunne as having an extra bright shine that night.

In the morning they found Dan sitting morosely on the ditch at the other side of the camp. He was alone and he spoke indistinctly when Fred greeted him.

"Is Nick gone somewhere then?," asked Fred quietly.

Dan continued to stare at the ground, his eyes glazed and distant, his coat and general appearance damp and in a worse condition than even the wild bog nearby.

"He is dead," he muttered eventually.

Jane and Pat edged closer to try to comprehend the talk. Fred signalled to them to be quiet.

"Tell me what happened, Dan," said Fred gently.

"I put him in a boghole; he was dead already. I think he must have died suddenly, for one minute he was there alive and the next minute he was dead," said Dan slowly.

Fred said nothing and clenched his teeth as he collected his emotions.

"Let me see the gun, Dan," he said when he had recovered his ability to speak.

O'Toole handed the gun over quietly and then went back to staring at the ground, his head hunched between his shoulders.

"A bullet has been fired from this gun all right. Are you listening to me, Dan? There has been a terrible event. I will hold on to the gun for a while. If you feel an attack coming on again, tell me. Will you Dan? Will you tell me if you feel like going killing again?"

There was desperation and urgency in Dunne's voice. Dan made no answer but continued in his state of depression. Fred held his own emotions in check as he watched Dan's face cloud over with despair and a grievous expression of sorrow was in the Wicklowman's eyes. Concerned, he helped Dan to get to one of the tents as Patrick and Jane watched from a distance. When Fred re-emerged from the tent he went over to them.

"I have a sad announcement to make," he said grimly.

He told them about the event out on the bog. They were extremely shocked to hear this information and cries and moans escaped their lips.

"How did it happen, Fred?," asked Patrick.

"Is it the truth?," Jane asked in a hoarse voice.

Fred had some difficulty in quietening and calming them and he explained to them about Dan's emotional state. The fellow was very upset by it all. He and Nick may have had a ferocious argument while they were out and Nick's death was probably the result of a fight between them. Poor Dan was still not himself.

It was a most subdued group that retired to their respective tasks for the rest of the day. They could not believe that Nick had been killed. They hoped that it was Dan's imagination and that Heeney would show up at any moment. They shut it from their minds that Dan could have killed his best friend. They kept a watchful and fearful eye on the tent but Dan did not reappear for the rest of the day and he did not come out for food or drink that night.

Trevor put his car, which he had picked up at its secret hiding spot, in the open car park at the Police Headquarters, considering this a clever ploy as it was where nobody would think of looking. He then went on a nocturnal visit to his wife, Hilary, carefully taking off his disguise which he had retrieved earlier. He had mislaid his door key and he had to drop pebbles gently against her bedroom window in order to awaken her. Her face eventually appeared at the window. Down below she saw her husband, Michael Argod, causing her to cry out sharply and then to feel something like a great emotional release, not to mention immense, self-righteous anger.

"I have a great thing to tell you," he said when she let him in, halting her first, stammered words in mid-flight; "something that will make you proud of me. A vision of mine has come true. I have seen it – the future."

"They have said the most terrible things about you," said Hilary, "I have not known what to believe. Why have you come home like this, suddenly, in the middle of the night? I had come to believe that you had deserted me."

Michael put his arm on her shoulder and this made Hilary uneasy as such displays of affection were not in the character of the man she once knew.

"Do not pay any attention to the lies people spread about me. When you are on to a good thing there is no end to the jealousy that is aroused in some people. They go to the most unbelievable lengths to concoct the tallest tales imaginable."

"I have seen your portrait and disguise. I have heard the name you have been using and all about the wild drinking of your cronies. I know that there is a girl involved who, from what her mother was saying, is a very loose type indeed. We are now the laughing stock of the community. In the public places and at the university they laugh about us and defame you name," said Hilary.

"Let them laugh and talk," said Michael, "I will achieve greater things. I respect and admire my comrades and am thankful that they are not run-of-the-mill members of society."

"This is not the way to reach the top, Michael. Give up all these foolish ideas and take your rightful place in the proper circles here," Hilary pleaded.

"I have to return to my friends," said Michael, "they depend on me for many things. They will be interested to learn that their fame has increased in the city and that the works of O'Reilly have become widely known. Do you have any idea where those paintings are now?"

"After Mr Mollusc had finished with them at the pub called Bell's they were put in the dustbin," said Hilary.

"That man is a right bastard. One day he will go just too far," said Michael angrily.

"Is it true then that you have been drinking?," asked Hilary in a soft voice.

"No. A drop of that stuff has never passed my lips," Michael lied.

"You do disguise yourself, change your name and dress up at times?," she enquired.

"It is necessitated by the activities that I am involved in," he told her in a firm voice.

"I will have to go home to the north," said Hilary weakly, "I cannot live down here any more."

She suddenly felt ill and Michael had to help her to the bedroom where he gently made her lie back on the bed.

"Perhaps if you did go back up to the north for a while it would be for the best. Your relatives will look after you and give you all the care you need now that your time is approaching," he said.

It was not certain if Hilary heard him for her eyes were closed and her arm was drawn limply across her brow. She was pale in the dim light of the room and Michael felt guilty as he stood up to leave. He had disturbed a tired and burdened woman at an unearthly hour; and it was he who had put her in her condition in the first place. It was all his own fault, he thought to himself.

He went downstairs, sat on a chair in the kitchen and wondered what he would have to eat. He felt himself to be a changed man. For instance in the past nothing less than a full-fledged, wife- produced meal would have satisfied him – now he would be quite happy with just a crust of bread. He sat with one hand holding his chin, thinking things over. In no time at all he and the others would reach 'home', a healthy and remote part of the country out of the reach of officialdom. There the few inhabitants would be improvable, open and mild. His child, when it had reached maturity, would be proud of him and would have no difficulty in forgiving him for abandoning his family. Michael sat back, the palm of his hand holding his dreaming chin and he smiled to himself. He would get the paintings first thing in the morning and when he returned with them he would be a hero – they would trust him now! He took the small bottle of poteen out of his pocket, uncapped it and drank a few sips. After a few more sips he determined to sneak out of the house before dawn, so that his sleeping spouse would not be disturbed.

At the mahogany desk in his palatial office Policeman Mollusc was sitting with his feet up reading a racing returns magazine and ruminating on the sheer crookedness of some of the racing crowd. The tricks they get up to – a bitter memory came to him of a time in Wexford when a Three Card Trick gang had pulled a fast one and he had lost the shirt off his back plus the annual funds of the policemen's Benevolent Activities. He had tried to pull rank on them, to no avail, and showed them the pistol that was in his pocket, again with no success. If it had not been for his car-driver on that day – a young policeman by the name of Dunne – he would have been in serious trouble with his fellow-guards. Quick thinking Fred had assured everybody that he had seen a robbery done by the same men, that their cause was as good as lost in court, especially with a policeman like Mollusc as a witness. This, as well as some strong-arm stuff from the same Fred, had won the day. Fred had also been very useful later in sorting out some blackmail business with the same people when that came up. The trouble however was that Mr Dunne had never let him forget all this in later years, always insisting that he deserved the easiest jobs in the service.

"If there's one thing I hate, it's people who change their colours to suit the wind," he said bitterly to himself.

A man came in complaining loudly about the two cyclists on the road outside whom he had knocked down; it could have been a fatality and 'serve them right'. He went to a corner desk and then asked Mr Mollusc why he had such a dark look on his face.

"I was just thinking of something in the past that went wrong," he replied.

The second policeman was Mr Mollusc's likely successor and he was privy to all the great man's inner thoughts – or at least to some of them.

"Our man is doing a good job," said Mollusc; "did you see this report that has just come in?"

He pointed to a note that lay on his desk.

Mollusc's knack was in making people feel small, by pretending that they could possibly have information that was known only to him. They could then receive this information or knowledge gratuitously and second-hand from him.

"How did that get here?," asked the other man, whose name was Inspector Murray.

"A dicky bird dropped it in," said Mollusc happily.

"Oh," said Mr Murray, acknowledging again to himself that he too must expect to have to put up with Mollusc's barbs now and then.

"It came to me via the parish priest of a small area in Galway and it is extremely confidential as to its contents. The news from our man is that things are fine. They are going all the way to hang themselves with that length of rope we have given them. Even the tinkers are ashamed to be seen with them or near them! It is terrible to think that Mother Ireland can produce these people," said Mollusc.

"They have shown us their true colours,!" said Inspector Murray.

"One thing is sure – they have done a real service to this country. People will cop on that there are no end of chancers willing to cod them and lead them astray through the supposed gardens of delight with their queer talk and their exotic tonics. Their empty promises of an infinitely better substitute for ordinary everyday living were a real danger in the innocent ears of the common citizenry. Nevertheless, we were quick enough to pull them up before their idleness and waywardness got a chance to put in roots and spread like a common or garden weed. Now they can continue to sink as low as they like. We'll let them roll about in the gutter so that everybody can see them," Mollusc intoned with disgust.

"He's a good Christian to be doing what he's doing," the other loudly enthused.

"I'll let you into a little secret," said Mollusc; "the way we get our information is very easy. Our man just writes a little note saying where they are and what they are doing and leaves it in a very unobnoxious place along the route they happen to be travelling. It doesn't take long to find these notes."

"The clergy are pleased too, I hear," said Mr Murray.

"The ones that count are – one particular curate said that they were just poor misguided eejits and we ought to leave them alone – the naivety of some people! They are glad that they are gone from Dublin and were very worried by one report. They are still investigating it. It is said that a vote was held in the pub one night on whether the Church should be abolished," said Mollusc slowly shaking his head.

Mr Murray clicked his tongue to show his own concern; eventually he positioned himself to leave the room. He was held back by the wide, friendly palm of his superior.

"Have a drink before you go man. Sure you're always rushing about after one thing or another. Refresh your mind once in a while – it will do you good," Mollusc said in a most friendly fashion.

"Well I do have a lot of things to be doing, but I suppose a little drink wouldn't hurt," said Murray.

Mr Mollusc, whose first name was Seamus, had by now got both feet up on his desk and was sitting holding the back of his head with his hands. He gestured to his confidant to sit down on a chair and he pulled open his drinks' drawer and set up two glasses of a white-water drink.

"It's good stuff," said the Superintendent.

After only one sip Mollusc was cheerfully happy and with his next comment he introduced an air of lightheartedness which, for that place, was almost recklessness and sheer abandon.

"You know, Murray, in my long life not one person has ever addressed me by my Christian name. Oh, it is well-known what it is, by everyone, but not even my wife when she was alive ever called me Seamus. When she was dying I was tempted to lower the barriers, but I decided that it would be unwise in the end. The country was in a bit of a state at the time. Murray. . . to you from now on I am Seamus," he said in a pleased voice, raising his glass in a salute.

Murray was surprised and pleased.

They both raised their glasses in mutual toasts and drank in the significance of their newly-enlarged intimacy, in what was almost a kind of celebratory ceremony. Then they settled down to a second filling.

Chapter Eleven

There was a lack of bonhomie and a decided air of low spirits in the camp, brought on by a general feeling of depression. There was not the same lightheartedness among the group. O'Toole did not speak to anyone and he kept himself to himself, while Fred and the rest went about their different activities in rather sullen moods. Nick Heeney had not, by some miracle, shown up and they accepted the fact that it was not likely that he would be coming back.

Fred was missing his wife more than he had done; he was feeling more lonely now. There was Nick who was gone; and no Trevor Archibald with whom he could have a conversation. Patrick and Jane were, it seemed, more and more preoccupied with their gardening. Indeed the job of pulling weeds and planting cabbages and lettuces appeared to have become a kind of ritual with them. Fred himself looked after the two horses, and turned in more on himself as the days went by.

One day he went over to Dan's tent and said that he would like a little word with him.

"I am a bit concerned about those two," he said, alluding to Pat and Jane;

"what with their intensive gardening and what, I am wondering if we will be starting up a farm soon. I didn't know that they were farming types anyway."

He spoke angrily, a touch of irony in his voice.

"What?," said Dan, "I have been minding my own business."

"Are you still worrying about Nick? Sure hasn't he gone away and left us without a trace; nobody need ever know about that accident out on the bog," Fred said in a friendly manner.

"It wasn't an accident, Fred," said Dan grimly; "I am cursed."

"You should not have such a bad opinion of yourself – it is the cause of a good many of your troubles. You are better than that O'Reilly," said Fred adamantly.

"I was cursed the day I left Bailedecoinin," said Dan in a low voice.

"Bailedecoinin. I have heard you talk about that place. What is it like?," asked Fred with curiosity.

"Bailedecoinin is a poor enough place, but for jollity and life it puts this district to shame. I did not think that such a terrible area could exist in all of Ireland," said Dan bitterly.

"Bailedecoinin sounds like not a bad spot at all, then. Did you leave it because you were fed up? I suppose you were hopeful for a better future in the world?," inquired Fred with interest.

"I was a fool ever to set foot in the outside world – I only wish I was back in Bailedecoinin now. I think it is coming to the time when I will return there," Dan said quietly.

He looked up from the floor and gazed around him.

"Were you saying something about Pat?," he asked.

"Do you see any sense at all in their working out in that field? Don't you see that it is the cosiness that brings them together? They are no two innocent song-birds that go out in the day just to work the land. I do be thinking that there are other things they do get up to," said Fred vehemently.

Dan did not reply. He showed hardly any interest in Fred's words.

"She is your girl, O'Toole. He has no right to her. That lad has no right to her," he shouted in a very angry voice.

"I am glad that she is not hounding me now. That is all," said Dan.

Dunne looked at O'Toole. He wondered if the man was natural at all; what Jane had once found of interest in him Fred just could not imagine.

"Have you felt any way queerly of late?," he asked Dan in a quieter voice.

"I do see red fire in front of my eyes and there is thunder in my ears now and then, but that is all," Dan replied.

"You don't feel murderous or anything like that?," Fred asked.

"No, I just feel bored and fed up most of the time," was the reply.

"I'll see you in a little while then," said Fred, rising from his squatting position.

"Can you drop me in a slice of bread and a bit of lettuce?," asked Dan in a very mannerly tone.

"I'll see what I can do," Fred said back with a smile.

Fred returned again later, under the pretext of bringing the food, and once more began to indulge in a general tirade against Pat and Jane and to moan about the camp situation generally. Nothing pleased him and he did not give Dan much chance to eat the bit of food he had just received. It was O'Toole's first bite for days. Fred had taken control of the money and the stocks of the company and was proving a very miserly quartermaster indeed. Dan was half-starved and Fred seemed to think that his good advice and well-worked-out opinions were all that the lad needed. He continued to moan and he did not let Dan have any peace. O'Toole's patience finally gave out.

"Will you shut up and get out," he shouted at Fred; "I am sick and tired of your gab."

This was one thing about Dan that had always annoyed Fred; that he never seemed to be affected in any way by anything that he (Fred) ever said. O'Toole was one of those ignoramuses who could not care less about anything, it seemed, and he showed no respect for any man or thing.

"What?," said Fred.

"You are just a loud braggart. And I'd like to know what you have been spending all the money on? You go out and come back with all sorts of stuff that I never get to see. I am starving half the time and then I can smell beef cooking somewhere," said Dan contemptuously.

Fred's face grew larger with anger but he thought twice about any further argument; he turned around and stormed out of the tent.

There was an open dispute the following day between Fred and Pat. It was over the question of the goats and the horses. Fred was extremely possessive of the two ponies, considering them as part of his personal fiefdom, and he had taken a negative attitude to the goats and other animals, which he seemed to consider as inferior beings. When he discovered that the goats had eaten the horses' priceless grain down to nothing and had soiled all over their enclosure not once, but for the third time, he approached Pat over the matter. There were heated words between the two, with Fred having the advantage by far in invective. A red-faced and hot Patrick went off alone down the lane to sulk.

By this time Fred had acquired the reputation for being a bit of a stinker and he was left even more to himself. Each day brought a new weariness to the relationships and soon there followed another incident between Pat and Fred. Fred had discovered a page of writing in a hole in a concrete pillar of a farm gate just down the lane. It was Pat's diary, part of a series of accounts of daily events, love notes to Jane and romantic, imaginative wanderings. These the lad was leaving all over the place, like some eccentric, love-struck artist. Fred was beside himself with fury as he showed a page to Dan.

"Did you ever see such stuff? The blasted idiot is dropping them everywhere. Anyone can pick them up. All our names are in there – if the guards or Mollusc get their hands on this stuff it will be a lovely account of each and every one of us. He talks about you and Nick in there. Any old farmer or passer-by walking down that lane could pick one up. Artist how are you. . .," said Fred in a rage.

There was another showdown and this time Fred slapped Patrick across the face. A red-eyed O'Reilly ranted and shouted that he would pulverize Dunne. The next morning Pat announced that he was leaving; he would go to Galway city and sleep out rough. He had had enough of Fred, who continued to bait him with snide comments and even to make covert threats. Jane came out to say, in a deliberately calm voice, that she thought Patrick was being a bit hasty in his decision to leave; there was no place for him to go to and he should stay. A sad-faced though proud O'Reilly haughtily put his few possessions in a bag and slung it over his back. His jaw was firmly set and his manner was determined and purposeful. Fred sat back and watched it all with enjoyment while Dan appeared at the entrance of his tent to observe the event from a distance.

* * *

When Pat had left, Fred looked at Jane and wondered if she would be lonely now. He had no means of discovering her feelings as she ignored him totally, obviously blaming him for Patrick's rash and sudden flight. Dan O'Toole, not speaking much to anyone either, had started wandering around the camp at odd hours of the day and night; both Fred and Jane heard him on more than one occasion talking quietly to himself.

* * *

When Fred and Dan discovered that there was no more of Heeney's poteen left, it suddenly came to Fred that Nick's secret was with him at the bottom of the pool. There was an unavoidable conference between the two and when Fred went on his next shopping expedition to the town, he brought with him a useful and practical suggestion from Dan. It was then that he returned with a special spirit which, when mixed with ordinary poteen which was readily available in those parts, made quite a good substitute for Heeney's brew. A certain peace returned to their hearts and Fred found that he was more happy than he had been for a long time. He did not concern himself now with Jane and what the girl might be getting up to. As for Jane herself, she gave herself more to reflection now and neglected the vegetable plot to a great extent. Dunne's peace of mind was soon to be disturbed by the visit of a guard. The officer of the law came in the mid-morning to enquire who it was who resided in the camp and when they would be moving along. He also complained about the dirt which he said they were piling up about the place. It was Fred who met this gentleman, and afterwards he had great difficulty in describing the visit to O'Toole.

"He came up to me from the back," Fred said when he had got his clear remembrance back again; "and I was barely able to make out his face. It was shining and his eyes were as wide apart as the moon from the sun. His whole head was like a vast ocean, stretching westwards and eastwards with great waves of red skin moving about endlessly between. I couldn't catch his eyes that sailed like ships and his voice was thunder that sounded loud but did not make any sense. After a while I think I caught his attention and he said that he wasn't very pleased. I got worried as hell for I thought it might be Mollusc behind it all, trying to catch us on the hop. But as sure as anything I've never seen anything like this guard – from the looks of him I don't think he could have been one of Mollusc's men. He was as fat as a tree and he wasn't able to walk. He took every word I gave him as a priceless gem and he became very pleased when I told him all our wrong names. I thought he might start snooping around the tents but he didn't. Then he did go over to the ditch where you were sleeping, Dan, but it was only after I had to help him over. He smiled and never said anything about it. I suppose he just could see that we were a peaceful lot, which I assured him of anyway. The next thing is, though, he says that he will be back again soon and that there was some checking up to do. I thought when he had gone that I should have told him of my position in the Force and put him in his place, but it was too late once he was gone. I just wonder what he is up to," said Fred worriedly.

They both thought that the best thing to do right then was to have another drink of their new 'special'. They were quickly able to forget their worries about the visit of the guard and after a time they were past caring about anything, the guards, Mollusc or even the physical discomforts around them.

Jane came out of her self-imposed retreat the next day, and she found both of them sprawled out and sleeping deeply. Quietly, she took away their dirty clothes to be washed in the stream and tidied up generally about the place. She prepared some food on a newly-lit fire and then awaited their coming to.

* * *

In the course of a long, tiring journey to Galway city Patrick was able to recompose himself and recover some of his equanimity. The ogre-figure of Fred and his insults receded temporarily in his mind, and he noticed the wild flowers and nature-life of the fields, as well as the swim-brushes of the changing colours of the sky. He opened his lips wide and smiled at the air and his eyes moved in a short dance of delight. He felt a glow in his heart and a new feeling of freedom came to him. He was glad to get away from Dunne. When he thought about it, he was even glad to get away from Jane; he was no longer under a strain and did not feel the strange, frustrating urges that he always suffered in her presence. Galway might be a good place to stay; he had heard lots about it and he believed that the people were not so rough there. It would be nice to be among friendly people for a change. Mrs Eileen McNulty of Bohorborevin felt sorry for him in his requesting of a cup of tea, and she helped him on his way with a night's sleep and lashings of soup. He thought as he walked up the lane from her home, that she must have been a very holy woman, as when he had surmised more or less to himself that a drop of poteen would have been lovely, she had immediately produced a bottle of the liquid for free, with the request that he hand in a second bottle to her friend in Galway town later on. She was only too anxious to give away free bottles of poteen and she seemed bent on ensuring that everybody else in the world have a good and happy life with her poteen while she herself was happy only to supply it. Pat felt very content as he set out with four bottles of poteen in his bag and he waved back in acknowledgment of the woman's hearty farewell. If however Patrick had been back in the cottage a little later, he would have been shocked to see the antics of the same woman, who now set about with cursings and strange spells purifying her abode of her recent guest and carrying out strange rituals of exorcism in her kitchen and throughout the house.

Farmers' sheds were his shelter on the three days' hike to the western capital. He approached the outskirts of the town in the late evening, with a gang of clouds frowning on the horizon – still at first, but which suddenly began advancing rapidly and menacingly towards him. A lonely, somewhat lost feeling was in his own heart. The grey, subdued buildings of the town were like a reproach to him in his low mood; it was more of a cemetery than a town, with headstones of dwellings rather than the gay metropolis he had been expecting. He had visualised a bright, glamourous place full of dancing and singing native folk who were replete with the absurdities of life and oblivious to the realities of the world. Instead he found as he went up the first street a sleepy, dead atmosphere with no colour or signs of any art whatsoever.

It was certainly not the Galway of world-fame he had often heard about and he had to check a few times by both the reading of signs and the speaking to persons whether it was Galway at all that he was in. The answers he received confirmed the glum news in his heart. Devoid of spirit or strength to go and seek a more comfortable home for the night, he sought out a hollow in a little field by the railway line, not more than a few yards from the Galway water so famed in song and story. There were rocks there too aplenty, and a careful resorting of these made for him a wind-shelter. As he lay on the field which was like a mother to him, the sky and clouds closed in over him and darkness came like a victor; the victor of disillusionment over his earlier hopes and dreams. In his sleep he breathed thinly, and the poteen was a weak ally against his nightmares. At half-past two in the morning he was roughly awoken and kicked out of the shelter by a young tinker fellow who had come to take possession of the field. With loud shouts he berated Patrick, who also received a number of sores, cuts and bruises from him.

When morning came it had a cloud-sunny appearance and a half-shine was on the faces of the newly-appeared inhabitants. Patrick walked his way with them and past them, and headed in the direction of what was most likely to be the centre of town. No hands grasped to greet the shoddy, tattered visitor as he plied his way along; nor were any eager elbows bent to help or guide him along the route. The cough and splutter of cars hurt his ears and every now and then he glanced aside at a window or shop's-glass to see himself treading slowly and hesitantly by. His bag was a heavy load and he felt tempted to discard it at each corner. At nine o'clock an approach was made by Pat to a man standing not more than three feet from the door of a public house. This man was not everything that he appeared to be; in fact he used to be a prosperous Galway merchant who was lately drinking away his family fortune that he had built up over many years. The two main reasons for this changing of his ways were, firstly, the nagging behaviour and unscrupulosity of his wife who taunted him with the certainty that she would outlive him and, secondly, the fact that he had estimated that his life would not last longer than two more years, it being unknown as to how he had worked this out. It was this man who gave Patrick one pound for all of his poteen. This pound then obtained for Pat one full meal in a city-centre cafe, with a substantial amount of change left over. After his meal, his new strength enabled him to stroll around a bit more and to see some of the city sights; he liked the little man's statue in the square the best. That night he made another shelter under the railway bridge by the water and contemplated later as he lay sadly at rest, on how Galway's estuary could be so full of romantic memories and visions for people around the world, and yet be so lonely, barren and useless a place to him.

The next day, hungry and dispirited, he came across a very surprising sight further out from the city centre, along the bay where visitors and tourists are apt to congregate.

He saw a group of people gathered around a tent near the seaside and on top of this construction was a sign in bold letters. He had to read the words on the sign three times before their meaning clarified itself to him; even then he stood there in incomprehension.

UNIQUE PAINTINGS BY UNKNOWN ARTIST
SEE THEM FOR 3/6
LAST STOP BEFORE AMERICA

Patrick read the sign again and stared at the name at the end of the poster:

EXHIBITED BY TREVOR ARCHIBALD, Prof., F.R.A.A.

That same gentleman now appeared at the tent entrance, with his beard and all the old trappings on, and with a broad smile on his face. His eyes became quizzical when he saw Pat standing there; but an even broader smile and a loud greeting soon replaced the surprise and Trevor was being his old familiar, friendly self again. He took Patrick to one side as he organised the entry of some ten people into the tent to see the show. Trevor was jovial with his customers and showed them obeisance in every way, but he was obviously highly organised too.

"Your paintings are a great success here," said Trevor quietly when everybody else had gone in;

"come in for free and have a look."

It was a royal exhibition of Pat's works, with intense, detailed descriptions of each painting attached. Archibald also had a sign up to the effect that all the works of art were for sale. There was one poster with a written account of 'the rumoured artist's life', with the emphasis on the sensational and exciting aspects to the neglect of the more mundane features of his life, and with an elaborate attempt at creating out of a rather ordinary story the saga of a great artist, an eccentric magician, a genius who was almost a madman. Pat was surprised to read at the end that this artist was now believed dead, having, with his faithful disciples as witnesses, jumped off the highest cliff on the west coast as a protest against the country's neglect of all art in general and his own art in particular.

Pat was amazed and baffled, astonished and perplexed by all of this.

The people were looking in admiration at the display of paintings and Trevor turned aside from Patrick momentarily to give an impromptu talk on the worth and importance of the art they were now seeing. The satisfied group of art lovers and curiosity-seekers then left the tent.

"I have been offered a large sum of money for the portrait of me," said Trevor enthusiastically;

"£35,000 no less."

"£35,000!," gasped Patrick.

"I couldn't find you boys," Trevor told him, "but now you'll all be glad when I get that money from the American and we can share it out together. I am seeing him tomorrow."

Trevor then told him about events back in Dublin and of how he had rescued the paintings from imminent destruction. He had been hoping and waiting since then and knew he would soon meet up with them again. He was glad to hear that the lot of them were still free of entanglement with the guards and was concerned to hear about Nick having gone missing. He thought that the crafty old lad was up to some game or other and would turn up again in time. Trevor was bright and ringing with confidence, and he gaily showed Patrick around the tent and described how and why he had arranged the paintings in their particular order. Patrick, for his part, was taken aback by it all and did not know whether to accept what Archibald said or to show extreme discretion and caution as would most surely have been advised by Dunne and O'Toole. But the sound of the £35,000 was good in his ears.

To his disappointment, Archibald now turned slightly cold in his manner and suddenly put on the aspect of a preoccupied, harried businessman. He said that he would have to be about his affairs and would be glad to see Patrick again the next day when they could make arrangements for them all to get together – Dunne and co., etc. . . Patrick told him of his impecunious position at that moment and Trevor, a little impatiently, 'lent' him two shillings. The next time, Archibald said, it would be five hundred pounds he would be getting and that would be for starters.

"Goodbye," he said as he showed Pat to the entrance; "don't hang around too close to the tent in case that American comes back and he sees you in your raggy clothes and wonders what you are doing here."

"Goodbye," said O'Reilly hesitantly, "I'll be seeing you tomorrow."

Patrick was drenched in rain that night as he lay asleep under the railway bridge; there was no escape for him from the eastward-blowing gales and their accompanying sister, the rain. When he awoke the following morning he found that he was almost floating in a pool of water, while at the other end the sea had arisen to lap at his toes.

"What a terrible place it is," he thought as he shook the water off himself.

He set out, cold and miserable, for the beach. When he arrived there, he was shocked to find not a sight of the tent or of Trevor. He scanned the seaside in every direction but there was no evidence of the previous day's exhibition. Moody and suspicious, he set off on a long walk across the beach, ruminating on what he felt to be his own innocence as well as the depravity and treachery of the world. He looked with increasing anger on all the people who were coming out to enjoy themselves in the sporting sunlight.

At the counter in Greeley's pub Dunne sat moodily over a pint of dark porter. He was the only customer in the place and the fat lady who was the publican's wife did not talk at all to her customer, whom she felt was on the shady and untrustworthy side. Fred sipped his drink and sighed when he thought on the business that had been the chief reason for his coming to Galway. Dan O'Toole was proving increasingly difficult to manage back at the camp; he had been somewhat stormily-erratic in his moods and Fred had decided that if Dan was to be stopped from harming either himself or others, he would have to be contained. The means for doing this would be presented in the shape of a pair of good handcuffs, he had decided, and it was these that he had come to Galway for. The trouble was they were an extremely hard item to find.

Fred sipped another portion from his glass and shook his head as he thought of the prospects. He hoped that everything would be all right back at the camp; he had left a concerned and unhesitating Jane to look after Dan, who was in a state of unconsciousness when he left. As he sat there moping, a dirty-faced and rough-looking boy came into the bar, a pile of newspapers under his arm.

"Give me a copy of that," said Dunne softly, hoping to find something in the advertisements and handing out sixpence for a copy of 'The Galway Evening Socialist Rambler'.

"Do ye want yer change sir?," inquired the boy in thick, Galway tones.

"That's a good question coming from a brat like yourself," snapped Fred angrily, and he made a lunge in the direction of the boy, slapping him across the face.

The youth handed him back the change of one penny , sullen and silent; but when the same lad had reached the safety of the door he swore and cursed at Fred.

Dunne shook his head again, reflecting harshly on the poor behaviour that was prevalent in the country.

Before he turned to the advertisements his eye was caught by the big, glaring headline:

STRANGER IN TOWN CAUSES BEACH RIOT

skinny lad beaten up by local boyos

From what he now read in the paper, he came to the immediate conclusion that the skinny stranger in question could only be Patrick O'Reilly. A certain young man had gone walking down the beach and approached a group of local youths who 'were about their legitimate business' in that area. This interloper from other parts had brought upon himself the wrath of the local lads who, enraged at the sight of such a tattered and badly-dressed stranger in their midst, had set about 'cleaning up' the beach by giving the fellow a good hiding and then sending him on his way. The stranger, in resisting the rightful wrath of the community, had made things worse for himself by his insults and provocation and he now lay in the Regional Hospital in a critical condition. It was believed that the Last Rites had been imparted.

Fred rushed out of the pub and asked the first person he saw for directions to the hospital. When he arrived at the white-faced institution, he was refused admittance at first. He had to indulge in quite a good deal of persuasion before he could gain entrance and enter the ward. Patrick lay on his bed with his eyes closed. A curtain had been pulled around the bed, to give peace and quiet to the injured artist.

"Don't waken him," the nurse said softly as she left Fred sitting sadly at his 'son's' bedside.

As soon as they were alone, Fred spoke to Patrick:

"Wake up, wake up," he cried, shaking him.

Patrick opened his eyes almost at once and stared bleakly at Fred. There was a look of complete hopelessness about him, as well as the absence of the joy of living and, almost, the abandonment of reason itself. He had been gravely marked all over his exterior and it was apparent that his spirit, in addition to some of his limbs, had been broken. Fred showed shock and sympathy. In a broken voice, Patrick told him of the attack that had been made on his person, of his hard time in the town and of the strange circumstances of Trevor's appearance. Fred was enraged to hear of Trevor and of his possession of the paintings. After a while, Patrick relapsed into what was senseless talk, incoherent words and almost a babbling. Fred decided then that it was best to leave him. He said Goodbye but O'Reilly did not even acknowledge his departure.

Fred returned to the camp after a scouring of Galway in a fruitless search for Trevor. He found Jane still caring in a dedicated fashion for Dan, who had now more or less returned to a state of semi-consciousness. Fred had a fit of jealousy again, and wondered how it was that a person like O'Toole could be a subject for sympathy from anyone, let alone an eligible young woman like Jane.

"It's highly unlikely," he thought to himself, "that she sees any worth in him. He is a charity case."

He announced the reported sighting of Trevor in Galway and he gave an account of Patrick's condition. Tears came in Jane's eyes and O'Toole looked up to inquire how it had all happened. Dan lost control of his temper when he heard the full story of Patrick in Galway and he started shouting and jumping around. He said that he would kill Archibald the next time he saw him. So turbulent was his temper that Jane became afraid and Fred thought Dan might kill somebody right there and then. Dunne quickly and smoothly produced the pair of handcuffs that he had eventually managed to obtain in Galway, and he snapped them on Dan's wrists as he was pretending to show them to the Wicklowman. An astounded O'Toole was wordless for a while and Fred informed him that he himself would take care of Trevor. He would be going back into Galway and in the meantime he – Dan – would be looked after by Jane, as he was not really well. It was also for his own good that he ought to stay in the camp, as if the police got their hands on him they would be wanting to know about Nick, as well as other things. Both Jane and Fred eventually persuaded Dan that for his own good and the control of his turbulent moods he should submit to being bound hand and foot until Fred's return. He would have plenty of drink beside him.

"When I get back after I have put Mr Archibald in his place, we will take you home to Bailedecoinin," said Fred with a smile. Dan nodded his head slowly in agreement and sipped gladly from a newly-filled liquor bottle. Both Fred and Dan now noticed that Jane had ceased from remarking on the drinking; she offered no comment on the liquor or on Dan's drinking of it.

Fred put on the new straw hat he had recently bought in Galway as well as his new brown suit. He fixed his bow tie properly and examined himself thoroughly before he prepared to set off. He looked very much a man of the world and his pockets were stuffed with money notes as he stepped in front of Jane's tent in order to take his leave. It was the week of the Galway Races, of world renown, and Fred thought it was a likely place for Trevor to show up, as well as being a good venue for an afternoon's entertainment and possible money-making exercise. He took his leave of Jane, hoping that she was impressed by his appearance and he commended her again for her good work. He gave a wave to Dan and set out for Galway (he hoped to cadge a lift) in a purposeful, if light, mood.

The crowds at the Races were large and boisterous and Fred could not believe his luck when he spied an individual the very image of Trevor Archibald, or Michael Argod, in the middle of a crowd at the edge of the racetrack. He spotted him just after the second race, on which Fred had regained the money he had lost in the first. He moved closer and saw that it was Trevor, though there was no tent and he had just a shabby suitcase at his side. He was speaking to a large crowd of people that was gathered around him. Fred listened to Trevor's voice, which was noticeably high-pitched and shaky. The elusive professor was speaking very loudly, haranguing his listeners with spurious claims of his own elevated achievements and status, and in particular making specific references to his own royalty and blue blood. Fred saw a bulge in his pocket that had the shape of a whiskey bottle and he noticed an unusual unkemptness about Trevor. Archibald was being highly critical of the ordinary people of the country and was, Fred thought, being generally offensive in his remarks about policemen, politicians, clergy and most of humanity itself. Fred felt for the pistol in his pocket and he made a step in the direction of Archibald, anger rising inside of him.

Then the loud laughter of the crowd made him stop. It was evident that no one there paid the same, critical respect to Archibald as Dunne did and even he himself now smiled when he saw the anger and frustration on Trevor's face at the sound of the laughter. He saw that Trevor's words were greeted with mockery and contempt; that he was a source of amusement to them; and many moved on to the next entertainment after a short spell of listening to Archibald. Fred laughed now too at some of the things Archibald was saying. After a while he went over and gently removed Trevor from his 'rostrum', quietly warning him to come away without giving any trouble. The crowd were not too concerned about his departure. Trevor did not complain and he walked off with Fred's firm grip on his arm.

Fred saw the paintings in the suitcase and smiled knowingly. He asked Trevor what had become of his car and was told that a dealer had paid £200 for it in Galway; Trevor showed him the notes which were in his inside pocket. They both set out for the camp, a smug smile on Dunne's face. Archibald was exceedingly nervous at the prospect of the treatment he would receive when he returned to the 'fold'. Fred told him that Dan was ready to give him a good trashing, and even worse. Patrick's sorry condition would be held to be Trevor's responsibility, and Archibald was forced to admit that he had been trying to 'con' people in the city over the paintings and with his brazen talk. He said that with a bit more luck he might have made a lot of money, while the name of Patrick O'Reilly would have become known throughout the land. Fred was increasingly vindictive towards Archibald as they approached the camp and he became downright nasty to him at the end.

There was a shock for Trevor and indeed for Fred in the camp on their return. A woman had turned up in a red, new car and enquired as to the whereabouts of one Michael Argod, her husband. Hilary was waiting for them as they came up the lane and a pale look went over Trevor's face. He could not believe his eyes and he took the whiskey bottle from his pocket and gave it to Fred before they had got close.

"There you are, you no-good trickster," said Hilary in a steady, vehement voice, staring at her husband with anger in her eyes, "you thought I wouldn't find you. I have been hearing all about your antics here and in Dublin. I think it is disgraceful the way you have been telling lies and misleading people. I will never let you out of my sight again – you cannot be trusted for one moment, you rogue. And don't tell me any more of your lies about the drink – I know that you have been indulging in it, for I have been talking to people. I never suspected that that was behind it all the time, but I was blind and silly not to."

Fred, Dan who was sitting up on a stool, and Jane were silent as Hilary talked – she was not at all the person they had imagined her to be and they were astounded at her pluck in coming there to get Archibald. Trevor was quiet too and he cowered in front of her and did not try to defend himself. Hilary gave them all a critical look and for a moment they felt the shame of being accomplices in Trevor's disgrace and downfall. Fred Dunne however felt a bit peeved at having himself considered to be in the same mould as Archibald and he now took steps towards righting any misleading impression of himself that Hilary might have got. He gestured to her to come to one side and told her confidentially that Trevor, her husband Michael, had been a target for fun and mockery in Galway and that perhaps he might not be all that well at the moment. He, Dunne, had gone to get him and was trying to keep an eye on him. Hilary replied that with all the drinking it would not be surprising if he were unwell and it was no excuse. He would have a lot of answering to do when he returned home.

"I will be in trouble with the guards if I go back to Dublin," said Trevor morosely.

"That will be your own fault, won't it?," replied Hilary sarcastically; "in any case, I have had a word with Superintendent Mollusc and he says he is not in the least bit interested in you."

"Oh," said Trevor with obvious surprise and disappointment; "he isn't, is he not?"

"Not in the least. Now you get your possessions and come along. I am sure your friends will understand your having to leave like this."

Before he left, Trevor, sullen and with a look of defeat, gave £100 of his money to Fred and he handed over all the paintings to him. He did not say a word as Hilary led him to the car and put him in the passenger seat. As they watched the couple drive off, the others saw a look of relief appear on Archibald's face and a kind of smile that might have been one of self-abasement or even of self-parody. Dan swore loudly at Trevor but Archibald did not bother to look back or wave goodbye.

They stood looking at the car as it moved off down the lane and take the winding road into the distance. Fred was annoyed and felt a little cheated, as he had the suspicion that Trevor had still somehow managed to make fools of them. This annoyance and feeling of having been conned increased the feeling of shame caused by Hilary's words. Dan too, despite his mood of anger and outrage, felt a little ashamed himself and the two of them did not look at one another or speak together or to Jane for some time afterwards.

Chapter Twelve

"There is no doubt that either Mollusc or his guards will be here in no time. We must head for somewhere far away from here. We must travel across the country again," said Fred to Jane later.

"What about Dan?," asked Jane; "he is no condition to travel and I fear his health is entering into a very detrimental state."

Dan indeed was not very well and he was coughing a lot and was scarcely able to walk. They both felt that his earlier poor condition had returned, but this time there were signs that the illness was more serious and advanced.

"We will have to leave anyway," said Fred; "if we stay here he will die too and it may be that he might see his days out in a better place. Perhaps we will reachBailedecoinin, where he will be in his own home and among his own people."

They cleared up their belongings and gathered all the goats and pigs into one batch.

"We will put the pigs into the cart and let the goats travel behind us and sell them all in the first town we come to. The chickens I will kill now and they will be food to us for a few days. Our other pony can also travel behind us," said Fred.

Dan was very weak and Jane had to get Fred's help to put him in the cart. He was exceedingly low now; going through his heart was the doctor's assurance of an early demise and he cursed that quack for his apparent connivance with death. Still, it would be up to God or the devil in the end.

They left the camp at three o'clock on that same afternoon. It was a most cumbersome departure, and Fred said what a pity it was they hadn't got the volkswagen or Trevor's car, as that would have been so much more convenient.

"We must get rid of these animals as soon as possible. They are a nuisance and a disgrace and they do not bring such a great return. I am thinking about starting up a little industry with our money instead. Once we get to a suitable establishment, I have many ideas for using our considerable wealth. The animals will make a profit too, and Pat's paintings may be worth something as well. I suspect that Dan, despite what he says, knows a thing or two about Heeney's poteen-making methods and I might be able to persuade him to help me set up a factory. You and I will never have to worry about money in the future, Jane. I will see to it that you are never short of anything. It is just as well that Archibald and Patrick are gone, for they are very unreliable characters," Fred said, talking more or less to himself as they went along, for Jane was at the back keeping a strict eye on Dan O'Toole.

The ragged collection of people and animals and utensils clattered down the sloping lane and headed for the open road. Fred tightly held the reins, and thought through the dust and grime that in future he would make sure he travelled in proper comfort; perhaps he would get a very expensive Mercedes car at the least.

He lit a cigar, of the rare and not cheap kind he had taken to smoking lately, puffed it between his teeth as they journeyed along and then started to dream of many things; of rich and fabulous cities, goblets of wine and luxurious easy-chairs, of a happy, fulfilled and pleasurable life.

It was as the result of a dream that Dan O'Toole had, as well as his conscious talk, that they turned and headed eastwards in the direction of Wicklow. Dan had woken up shouting and it took them a long time and all of their effort to calm him. He had heard the voice of his father calling him in his sleep, he said, and the old, bedraggled face appeared shouting at him and telling him to get back home as soon as possible. The aged patriarch was very angry and berated Dan for going away in the first place and for delaying so long in returning home. The grey, tottering figure was loud and long in its denunciations of Dan and as much as Dan tried to reason and talk over things, no attention was paid to his words by the apparition and it went on with its tirade. At long last the denunciations ceased and now Dan saw a resigned look appear in the eyes and the sad, despairing face began to shake its head. The figure moved away, giving Dan a disapproving and disappointed look as it went.

Another figure appeared out of the mist and this time it was that of a man dripping wet and with hair covered in water-weeds. It had a gaunt shape and made straight for Dan, a terrible look of vengeance in its eyes. Dan thought that for sure he would be destroyed by this ghost, and it was his scream that brought the others to his side. When he was calm and had recovered himself again, he said that the last apparition had been of Nick Heeney himself, who was as clear as daylight and as alive as any of them there.

"He was very angry with me," said Dan, and his voice showed his obvious distress.

A drink of liquor helped Dan to recover from his dream and he was encouraged to lie back and rest. He was a much more nervous person now than the Dan O'Toole they knew, and they did their best to make him feel relaxed. Fred even handed him the pistol once more, laying it on his lap and jokingly telling him that it would be a protection against any further evil omens. He knew it would give Dan confidence; he also felt that O'Toole would not be a danger to them any longer. Jane encouraged him also, and it was noteworthy that Dan did not object to her presence now but indeed seemed to welcome it, saying nothing when she gave him advice and in no way showing any impatience or a desire for her to go.

They came to Moat market the following day, having discovered from a passing donkey-trader that a sale was to take place there. Fred said that it was a risk to enter the town as they were, but it was an opportunity for them to sell the useless cargo and make a few bob as well. The three of them worked hard to get the goats and pigs to the market square, where the hundreds of other beasts of every description stood around making a lot of noise and, along with their owners, causing the place to be the scene of anarchy and general disarray. By midday Fred had obtained £50 for the pony he was selling and £50 for the rest of the animals together, but it was obtained only after hard bargaining.

It was evident that Jane wished to leave at once, and Dan was barely able to hold himself up on the street corner, but Fred insisted that he had to take a drink with his business partners in the pub and said that he would not be long. Jane and Dan waited outside and the next thing is they heard a great noise inside and Fred appeared at the door arguing and then fist-throwing with a number of individuals who looked very angry with him. The upshot of this fuss was that Fred was knocked to the ground and Jane quickly ran to his side.

Dunne was semi-conscious, having taken a blow on the chin and his face was also marked and bleeding from small cuts. She helped him to his feet where he recovered his bearing after a while. It was a haggard Jane who led the two men out of town and to the side-lane where the pony and cart were installed. The strain of caring for Dan and the hectic life of recent months were showing on Miss Wood and her face seemed to be permanently hardened now, but she still retained the air of a dedicated, innocent spirit.

"It wasn't the boys I sold them to at all," said Fred later; "but some other fellas who said that they knew me. I'll be damned if I recognised even one of them. They were drunk, I imagine."

"They could tell that Fred was a guard I'll bet," Dan muttered to Jane.

It was one week later that they reached West Wicklow and soon they were rambling through the lanes and gaps and passes of that deep and hidden countryside. There were no signposts to Bailedecoinin and no person they asked had ever heard of it. At long last they came across a man who did know of the townland of Bailedecoinin.The grey-coated and grey-capped individual was digging a hole at the side of the road. He was in his seventies and he was a true Gaelic speaker.

"It is, mind you, extremely hard to get to and the people left up there – they are wild. If you go round that mountain in front of you till ye comes to the ruined mansion in the wood, you will find a narrow trackway that goes to the south. Follow it and you will come to The Gap of the Wild Hares. Go through that Gap and there you are," he said in a friendly way.

The mention of The Gap of the Wild Hares struck a note of recognition in Dan.

They found the derelict house in the wood after a day's travelling and soon they were trotting through the Gap with

Dan wide awake now and looking around at everything. They came into the moorland – surrounded hamlet as dusk was falling. There was not a soul in sight and a quietness hung over the entire place. To their surprise, no youngster or adult, old woman or child came out to witness their arrival and there was not even the barking of a single dog. Dan directed them to a little cottage at the edge of the settlement and they came to a halt in front of its shuttered window and door. On alighting from the cart, a happy Dan was helped by Fred and Jane to walk to the entrance of the house. O'Toole pushed it and the door opened of its own accord. The three of them walked in calling 'hellos'. The darkness was lit up by a candle light coming through the open bedroom door and in there they found old Mr O'Toole, bandaged from head to foot and grievously ill. He knew Dan, saying his name many times over. He had been alone in the house and that suggested to them all and to Dan that Mrs O'Toole was no longer in this world.

His father raised a bandaged hand and Dan moved closer to him, bending down at the side of the crude, wooden bedstead and trying to get a glimpse of his father through all the bandages. He expected it had been Mrs Sheerin who had done the medical job, as she was the chief midwife, nurse and doctor-surgeon in that region. He thought to himself that she could have made him a bit less uncomfortable.

His father spoke in a croaking voice, his breath barely wheezing through:

"Your ma is gone and I am soon to go. I saw you in my dreams and where you went and all that you got up to. The land and farm is your's now, boy. Look after the chickens as they will miss me. I am sorry all the other critters are dead."

"These are my friends here, pop," said Dan with half-hearted enthusiasm; but his father either did not hear or did not listen.

"I will not be long after you," Dan said, in a quiet though calm voice, but there was no response from Mr O'Toole and they all moved closer to see if he was breathing. He was – barely.

They settled into the house, and had as food the eggs that were in abundance about the place as well as the wild-grown vegetables in the fields behind. A wild hog was slaughtered. To Fred's surprise, no neighbour called in to welcome them or to enquire as to the condition of Mr O'Toole Senior. Whenever Fred glanced down the lane in the direction of the village, he saw only a bare place with not a single person in sight. Late in the evenings and in the early mornings he thought he sometimes heard a voice or a shout, as of one in search of livestock or about the business of the land. Once he thought he saw the moving form of a shawl-clad woman slipping round a corner at the furthest end of the village.

A death-watch was kept by them all for one week after which Mr O'Toole suddenly expired with a shout of glee.

Dan could not make it to the funeral, and it was left to Fred and Jane to do the burial, without the assistance of a priest as the one who had been sent for did not come. Jane thought it would be all right as he would come later and bless the grave. There was one other person present at the funeral – an old man who turned out to be Mr O'Toole's brother; that is, Dan's uncle. He looked sadly down into the hole dug by Fred, in which lay the shroud-covered remains, and said eventually some words, presumably in Gaelic, words that Fred and Jane did not understand.

Back home, Dan did not seem too saddened by his dad's demise; there was an air of resignation about the lad, and he lay back on what had been his parent's bed, saying that everything was for the best.

"Dan will need some looking-after now, as his coughing has reached a serious stage," said Jane to Fred that evening after they had returned from the funeral; "he is in his bed and I don't think he will be getting up for a while."

"I see," said Fred, as he sat at the kitchen table munching a baked potato left over from the previous evening.

"I will need to look after him day and night, and I think that for his sake and your's too, as the disease is infectious, you should go to live in the outhouse. It would be the best place, and in any case I am a single lady and the people around here would be scandalised if you continued to live here," said Jane in a strong voice.

"I see," said Fred, keeping his private thoughts to himself.

"Oh it would be the best arrangement, Mr Dunne. I am sure you are a gentleman, as you have never given any cause for anyone to think otherwise," Jane said in a congenial tone.

So it was that Fred went to live in the outhouse, where he carried out a frugal existence. Dan was lovingly looked after by Jane, and when Fred did eventually meet some folk from the village, they all commented on the love and devotion of Miss Wood for young Danny O'Toole. Rewards were mounting up in heaven, they said. Fred was peeved by the whole affair, considering it to be a travesty of justice that he should have to live in an outhouse, and commenting to one or two people that it was a wonder such a derelict and hopeless village could at the same time have a people with such a Puritan morality. Fred met with the occasional person in the village pub. He discovered this building one day when he took a walk through Bailedecoinin. It was a low cottage with an extremely large window and a small door. The window was blurred, so that he could not see inside, and he wondered what the place could be. At the same time the concoction of spirits that he and Dan had made up had now almost run out and Fred was wondering where he might get supplies of the local poteen that Dan had often spoken about. He thought that this building must be some kind of shop and pushed open the door. Inside was a counter, with stools around it. A few empty bottles were distributed along the shelves and Fred thought he could detect the sweet smell of stout.

He sat on a barstool and waited for someone to come in or out. After forty five minutes a man appeared from the back room; it was another old man and bespectacled in this case, Mr O'Byrne, the Bailedecoinin publican. A dreg of poteen and a pint of dark, home-brewed stout was produced for him and finding Mr O'Byrne a not very communicative person, Fred went to sit at the table near the window. He noticed he was barely able to see what was outside of the window because of the blur. It was still a better place to be than his outhouse and he soon took to spending every day and much of the evening at this same table.

Later he found his food, which Jane had provided, being put on a plate and left at his outhouse door. Jane hardly ever spoke to him now and he did not have any contact with Dan beyond having the odd bottle of poteen passed in to him 'courtesy of O'Toole'. A feeling of hurt festered in Fred and he resented more and more his exclusion from the O'Toole household as well as still being extremely envious of the attention Dan was receiving from Jane. Somehow he doubted the 'death sentence' that was supposed to be Dan's. It was unfair that a person like himself should have such little importance in the opinion of others. He had only to compare his own achievements in the world with those of Dan to see that there was a vast difference; yet no one paid any attention to him. He sometimes told this tale of woe to the shepherds from the hills above who occasionally called in for a drink and a sit-down. These wild men did not talk much either to Fred or among themselves. Instead, they spent their hours in O'Byrne's more or less staring at Fred, who seemed to be a subject of interest to them. Fred complained rather loudly to himself about Trevor Archibald. A terrible coward and traitor, he called him, to a disinterested Mr O'Byrne.

"I wouldn't mind his company here at the moment though, for at least he could talk, that man. He was always one to disappear at the moment when he might become useful. I have never come across a more worthless turncoat. That man is a townee and an untruthful scoundrel. He ran back to his wife, you know. There he was trying to make some money dishonestly with some faked paintings and pretending to be the greatest person ever to trod the turf of Ireland. And what does he do – he goes back to the easy life, the benefits of a steady job and easy living," said Fred haughtily.

One day he brought Patrick O'Reilly's paintings into the pub, with them bundled under his arm. It was clear that Fred was quite drunk. He showed them to Mr O'Byrne and to two shepherds who were present, but they showed no interest in the works of art.

"All right," shouted Fred fiercely, "I will show Archibald and the lot of you. . . . I will destroy them here and now."

He set alight the paintings and they went up in blue flames, for he had already put poteen over them. Mr O'Byrne and the other men were greatly alarmed at this act of arson in the pub, but it was too late to stop the fire and at the heel of the hunt it was just two buckets of water that saved the floor and fixtures from serious damage. They did not say a word to Fred, for fear perhaps of antagonising him and encouraging him on to greater outrages.

Fred's spiteful attitude increased rather than diminished, and the burning of the paintings did not seem to assuage his anger, especially since nobody in the village was in the least bit bothered by their demise. Soon after this incident, in the pub where he now was even more carefully watched, Fred spent many hours composing a letter. He wrote it at the window table and, in his new mood of suspicious hostility, he hunched over himself to make sure that the publican or anybody else did not get a glimpse of his transcriptions.

The letter was addressed to Mr Mollusc at his official headquarters in Dublin. Fred wrote an account of how he had come to be in Bailedecoinin and included a description of the route to the remote village. He apologised for his previous behaviour and said that he thought he was ready to return now to his post and to take his punishment as well. He was asking for his job back, in fact. Never before did he appreciate, as he did now, that solid job he had once held. Give him the chance to have it back, and he would be a better servant by a hundredfold. Bailedecoinin, he wrote as he looked out at the dim and quiet street, is a dead place and soul-destroying for anybody with an active body and mind.

". . . it is a terrible place and it seems like ages since I've been sitting at this window trying to see any sign of life through the grey glass. I sometimes wonder if I am dead. I have got some good ones to tell you about Archibald, O'Reilly, O'Toole and that Miss Wood. . .".

He went on to say that he missed his wife Mary dearly, and enquired of Mr Mollusc whether he had had the opportunity to visit her. He knew that Mary would only confirm his good character. By the time he had finished the letter it was getting dark. He took an envelope from his pocket and put the letter into it. Then he wrote his ex-superior's name and address out and put a fourpenny stamp he had on the envelope. As there was no Post Office in Bailedecoinin, he would have to send the letter by the only route that was available to anybody in the townland wishing to make contact with the outside world – that of the van which came at irregular intervals for bartering purposes. So the letter was handed to Mr O'Byrne who acted in the capacity of unofficial Postmaster (as well as other things) for the townland. Going home that night Fred felt that some of the burden was gone off his mind.

The first known murder ever in Bailedecoinin took place the following day. In the morning, Fred went to his usual window seat and sat down. Despite his writing the hopeful letter, it was still evident that his self-esteem was going downwards rather than holding steady or improving. His face was unshaven and he was dishevelled. He folded his arms and stewed over a pint of stout. Great was his wonder when he saw Dan, or someone who looked like Dan, coming down the street. Fred was suddenly overjoyed at the prospect of a chat with the Wicklowman, no matter what he thought of his relationship with Jane. The door of the pub was roughly opened and sure enough it was Dan who stood there glaring at Fred. Dunne saw that O'Toole had the pistol in his hand.

"You rotten liar. You bloody spy. I am going to shoot you now," shouted Dan O'Toole.

"What is up with you?," asked an incredulous Fred, staring down at the gun at the same time.

Nobody could, or would, say how it happened but somehow the letter which Fred had written came into the possession of Dan O'Toole as early as that morning.

"This is what's up with me," said Dan, waving the letter in his other hand; "you give away everything and then invite the police in here. It is you who are the spy and were spying on us all along. Mr Archibald and the others are innocent! I should have known that a policeman would never change his ways."

O'Toole waved the letter again in Fred's face.

"Well, I am sick of the lot of you," Dunne said aggressively; "I am sick of Archibald, O'Reilly, Heeney, Miss Wood and you too, O'Toole. I don't see why I should have to put up with these threats and these insults. How dare you threaten me!"

Dan raised the gun as though to fire at Dunne, but he was overtaken by a sudden fit of coughing and the weakness that plagued him. Fred took the opportunity to grab the gun and, before the wide-open eyes and shocked expression of Mr O'Byrne, he shot Dan O'Toole at point-blank range. Poor Dan fell down on the floor and, after a few short groans, expired completely.

Fred dashed out of O'Byrne's and locked himself up inside his outhouse, not re-appearing until one week later. When he came out, nobody spoke to him, or interfered with him, or even mentioned the killing of Dan to him. O'Toole must have been buried by now, he reasoned, though there had been no sign of the funeral through the cracks in the outhouse. There was no sign at all of Miss Wood and the food that was still left at his door was becoming very scanty and irregular in its appearances now, he noticed. Fred went back to sit at his window table and he found Mr O'Byrne to be courteous and helpful where before he had been at best, indifferent.

A few days following this, while sitting in the pub, he saw a car pull up outside in the street. A door slammed loudly and a large figure appeared. This figure was so bulky that the bottom half alone filled the whole doorway of the pub, shutting out whatever light had been able to get in. It was Superintendent Mollusc, who now came in (with some difficulty) and cordially greeted Mr O'Byrne. Mollusc's face was grim and yet there was a glint of satisfaction and of inquisitiveness in his eyes as he looked at Fred Dunne sitting at the window table.

* * *

When Garda Mullowney came to see Fred there was some relief as well as immense curiosity in the village. It was the first time that anybody could remember that a policeman had come on a visit. The garda sat down beside Fred in the pub and before he had even opened his mouth, Fred was confessing a multitude of crimes to him. He admitted first of all that he had shot Dan O'Toole, but that was a matter of self-defence. Mr O'Byrne was a witness to that. There were certain criminal tendencies in O'Toole and he suspected that Dan had realised that he (Fred) knew about certain things and so had tried to silence him. O'Toole definitely committed two murders and there were other serious crimes which could probably be laid at his hands. There was serious arson committed in Dublin, the burning of certain important public buildings would be known to Garda Mullowney. Illicit liquor smuggling had gone on. O'Toole had been egged on by Archibald and others, people who themselves were responsible for many crimes, subversion and fraud.

Archibald, he said, also had an ambivalent relationship with his wife and Fred doubted if the lady was at all safe in his hands. Another one was Nick Heeney – killed by O'Toole. Heeney had been a vicious thug, fond of the strong-arm stuff. He knew all of their crimes, thieving, blackmarket dealing and murder – he could chronicle all of it. True, he himself had to go along with the misdoings, at least for part of the way; this was so that he could retain their confidence. He would also honestly confess to a few crimes of his own, but these were gravely overshadowed by those of all the others. A young slattern by the name of Jane Wood, again acting under false pretences, was a temptation to society and the cause of many vices. She was living there in O'Toole's house right now.

Garda Mullowney had a word with Mr O'Byrne later. O'Byrne said that Mr Dunne was in a highly excitable state. He explained that Fred of late had shown a deterioration in his state of mind. It was terrible the effects prolonged unemployment had on a man. Fred was almost a recluse and his only relief ever seemed to be in talking to himself. Of late, everybody had been worried as his fits of eccentricity had become exacerbated and there had even been one or two instances of violent acts. He had taken to shouting and abusing people in general and only yesterday a friend of his had walked into the pub and Fred had attacked him. If it had not been for his inebriated state, he might have hurt that man. Another incident that had caused concern was when Fred made a bonfire of some papers in the pub, for no apparent reason, beyond saying that even though they were very valuable he needed to keep warm. This was symptomatic of the fantasy world he was living in – the self-engendered importance of a man with little else in the world. Fred imagined many things about himself, that he had done this, that or the other in the world. They were wondering if there was a case for having Fred put away.

Garda Mullowney thought that there was not a case for confinement, and certainly nothing that might necessitate him having to take Dunne away to the station; not unless there was someone that is, who had a specific charge to make against him.

Garda Mullowney left after his chats with Fred and Mr O'Byrne, and nary a bit of information did anyone get as to the reason for the garda's visit. They could only muse. It brought to the fore again an old rumour concerning Fred Dunne. There was a claim that he had been to the outside world; that he had in fact married a wife there. Nobody believed this; but there was indeed a period when Fred was younger during which he was absent from the village. It was assumed that this dreamer of a man had gone to the upper hills, there to live on wild hares and birds; to an exile and hermit's existence which was in fact the only alternative for an unemployed young man in Bailedecoinin. This exile was often considered as being good for a person, and he was allowed to get on with his life there without undue interference. Others claimed that Fred had never left Bailedecoinin at all.

Now what made them think about the possibility that Fred had indeed been to the outside world and had married was the piece of paper Garda Mullowney was seen showing Fred and then what happened afterwards at the outhouse. He had produced this piece of paper in O'Byrne's for Fred to look at and then was seen to lecture Dunne in a stiff and formal manner. Both of them then marched to the outhouse and Fred walked inside in front of the garda. Some minutes later Garda Mullowney reappeared at the outhouse door with a bag in his hand. When Fred's face reappeared also, it was evidently angry. There and then, in front of Dunne, Mullowney opened the bag and counted out a sum of money. Apparently satisfied, he put the money back into the bag, with a nod of his head. He waved, a little feebly, at Fred, who did not respond, and then walked away. Fred, still angry, went back inside hastily and closed the door with a bang. It was believed now by many that this money could have been maintenance money for a wife owed by Fred; and going back over the years it would have amounted to quite a considerable sum.

Fred's brusquerie with Bailedecoinin increased after this and his temper became worse. There was an increase in complaints, as Fred could scarcely pass anyone without making a derogatory comment or insulting the person in some way. Everybody became fed up with him. The limit was reached when, a few months after Garda Mullowney's visit, Mrs MacCrechan complained and said that Dunne was coming around her cottage at night and peering in the window. It was known that for long Fred had had a fancy for Mrs Joan MacCrechan, a 'well-off' Bailedecoinin lady who had been thrice married (all her husbands dying), and who had sometimes provided Fred with food or otherwise seen to his welfare, though from a distance. Fred would assure her that he had drank with all her husbands.

It was agreed that something would have to be done.

A word was said by the publican (generally considered to be the most powerful man in the townland); a contact was made and Fred was taken away, shaggy and unwilling, by the shepherds to the upper hills.

With his departure, Bailedecoinin returned to its original and customary peace and calm.

* * *

When Superintendent Mollusc had come into O'Byrne's Fred's hopes had risen and he had been greatly pleased. He had hoped to gain Mollusc's approval with his account of his friends' activities and his own repentance; instead he found Mollusc interested only in the matter of his wife, Mary, and the question of her maintenance. When Fred had offered to accompany the Superintendent out of Bailedecoinin and back to Dublin, he had been rebuffed and was told that Mary and everybody else thought that Bailedecoinin was the best place for him. Nobody had the slightest wish to see him in Dublin or anywhere else. It was a clever and diabolical scheme of Mollusc's, Fred said bitterly to himself as he climbed the hilly slopes in the company of the bearded men, to keep him in Bailedecoinin and prevent any disclosures about the Superintendent's corrupt past.

Fred was peeved by the attitude of the village. The sight of the hated slopes, the bearded men and goats brought back to him the memory of the last time he had gone up a mountain top, when he had gone to fetch O'Reilly with Trevor Archibald. How happy and joyful that day seemed to him now, even though he hated heights; how he wished he had the company of O'Toole, Archibald, O'Reilly and Heeney now, for at least he possessed more in common with them than with these silent shepherds. His ex-friends were also better conversationalists. The cold, white mists swirling past them made him shiver and he looked down over the deep valleys below. He was going where he didn't want to be, but perhaps there was a chance that these unsociable men might have some really sharp poteen or mountain brew up there, he thought as he continued the climb up the steep, windy hill.

THE END